AF570284

The
Peace Escalation

rLilywater

Original in Swedish with Title
EN DRÖMMARES MARMOARER
Cover based on oil painting by the author

Förlag: BoD - Books on Demand, Stockholm, Sverige
Tryck: BoD - Books on Demand, Norderstedt, Tyskland
ISBN: 978-91-8057-803-5

To Raymond

PART I

Pure Phantasy

Preamble

I. Karin Werdhem

The children who played in the gravel and rubble of the ruins could not be older than four or five years. They were maybe half a dozen or a few more in number, hard to tell exactly, because they played hide-and-seek and many did not appear in the open. There were both boys in shorts and girls in floral and checkered dresses, but otherwise they were simply children, s-he creatures, neither she nor he and without a pronounced conscious gender. This condition would not last long, so that boys and girls would soon be segregated, despite the fact that they would jointly start in co-educational school. Boys would despise girls and not touch them and not under any circumstances interfere with them. They would sit in their benches only boys with boys and girls with girls, never together. This state of affairs would last for at least another seven years, when the desire for the opposite sex would re-emerge.

So far, however, the lust was already in full swing, when five-year-old Calle frantically tried

That day Karin's mom Anna had stayed at home, because she had felt unwell with menstrual pain that stretched over her stomach. On a normal day, Anna would otherwise have been long hours away from home. She was part of a group of "ruin mommies" who had the task of collecting and cleaning up what was left of the bombed-out buildings. Apart from the cleansing, the main task of the ruin mommies was to knock off excess mortar from the bricks they could find. The focus was on bricks that were intact and suitable for recycling in future masonry. These were stacked in pyramid-like piles, ready for transport.

The young ruin mommy Anna Werdhem had received Karin as a farewell gift from the visiting, but now returning home, soldier ensign Malcolm McShloermatt. McShloermatt had been fascinated by Anna's long blonde hair and long straight legs. Due to the hardships during the final phase of the war, the lack of food had helped to give Anna an extraordinarily slim fashion model's figure. Compared to the mostly severely overweight women in his homeland, Anna resembled a bony cloth hanger. In civilian life, McSchloermatt was a tailor to the profession, with his own modelling agency, and he liked the way clothes hung loosely on human cloth hangers. Anna, on the other hand, had been fascinated by Malcolm's seemingly inexhaustible access to chocolate and cigarettes. In return she had let him do with her whatever he desired. No wonder, she was later heralded with an anglish annunciation.

It was summer and the ruin would have been perceived as an idyllic place, close to the pastorale and as created for a *Schäferstündchen.* McSchloermatt did not waste any time to go into theorising reasoning, but immediately went into practical attack with his handsome sabre in the highest blow. And so it became a little Karin of this friendly battle, a Karin who grew up without her father, who had returned to his rural parental home outside Albuquerque, New Mexico. During his absence, his tailoring business including his model agency, had been foreclosed on by state authorities due to unpaid taxes, and Malcolm had to relocate, moving in with mom and dad.

There he sat, Karin's father, wearing rattlesnake boots, under a slack Confederate flag, this sardonic banner of slavery, and gave Karin's mother no deeper thoughts. In fact, he did not think of her at all, but fantasised about the neighbour's daughter Elvira and her broad buttocks. The two were engaged and the wedding date was set. However, the marriage had already been pre-consummated, when Elvira had been humped by the war hero. For the first time the very day of ensign McSchloermatt's homecoming.

Anna Werdhem would later marry a man named Herman Sczermonski. Mr. Sczermonski, however, was not a gentleman, but a scrap collector with rough hands. As it turned out, he was a brutal abomination. He would force Karin to call him "father" and then violate her, when she was only a delicate six-year-old. When Karin first began to understand what Mr. Sczermonski's game of AlfaPick was all about, she swore to herself that one day she would kill him. Thankful for her soul, she never had to keep her promise, because Mr. Sczermonski unexpectedly perished when he tried to seize a rusty three hundred kilo bomb and this one finally burst. This iron monster had been lying on the bottom of the ruin for years, without anyone worrying about it. Mr. Sczermonski's rough hands and lacerated member sat glued to the concrete wall, which had once belonged to a bathroom and given Karin and Calle some secluded privacy.

Some time later, Karin started smiling again, a little shy at first, but then more and more confident. Anna deleted the other half of her last name, the one that came after Werdhem and the hyphen, and promised her daughter and herself never to marry a scrap dealer again.

II. Carl Crassasius

The other of the two little love-making children, Carl "Calle" Crassasius, lived across the street. Calle was never allowed to play with Karin again and she was never seen again among the ruins. In Calle's memory, the contours of Karin's so slender body eventually faded away and she became some kind of colourless cloud being. On this side of the street there were fewer piles of rubble, because the house had been almost spared by the air raids. Only one half was blown away. In the remaining part there were still habitable apartments on three floors and Calle lived in the one at the top. There was no elevator in the house and the steep stairs were difficult for his grand parents.

Unlike little Karin, Calle had not been born with a rusty iron spoon in his mouth. His mother, Mrs. Letitia Crassasius-Levin, had told him that his family was of noble descent. The Crassasiuses were considered quite wealthy, as they could afford to pay rent for their accommodation. The mother claimed that Calle's father, Hubertus Crassasius, was in direct descent related to Marcus Licinius Crassus. Crassus was also commonly known as Rome's uncrowned Croesus. This Croesus, however, had not been Roman and lived several hundred years before Crassus. Crassus, in turn, lived - and died - several decades before the birth of Christ. And therefore, Calles mother Letitia argued, the Crassasius family could not be associated with the Christian church and, consequently, would as such not to need to pay any church tax. Letitia, whose family came from the east, had a pronounced thrifty orientation.

As it turned out, however, Crassus had not left even a single *as* to his late descendants. Consequently, with the facts in hand, the claim of the family's prosperity must seem unfounded. But, in accordance with his supposedly glorious past, Hubertus had adopted a Latin motto, UT DESINT VIRES TAMEN EST LAUDANDA VOLUPTAS, which in poetic words means *even if the potency was lacking, one ought to praise the lust.* This quote was a bit extravagant for the rather colourless music curator at the city conservatory. Hubertus had been ambitious at first, but playing the first violin had been denied him. Since then, he had increasingly withdrawn and avoided contact with his colleagues. After all, they only belonged to the *plebs.* His wife Letitia naturally agreed.

Calle had never adopted his parents' arrogant and demeaning attitude. His intimate association with ruin-Karin could have been seen as proof of this. But he had simply been horny and then, as a five-year-old, he had no clear ideological view of anything. However, he unknowingly carried within him a perceived philanthropy about the equal value of human beings, just as he felt this love for animals. He loved petting horses, cows and sheep and had also buried a dead sparrow once. On the grave he had placed some of the ruin's flowers, mostly dandelions, and a small cross made of sticks and strings.

In elementary school, Calle had been a really little wild thing. He lacked respect for the teachers, was cheeky and could not stand any reprimands. During the breaks in the yard, he whipped up the older boys in the senior year courses. These had smacked at his classmates or had mocked them. But this only applied to boys, he had no relations with the girls. And then it was obvious that girls were not beaten. It was cowardly. As cowardly as continuing to hit someone who had given in or kicking someone lying on the ground.

Even though Calle's wild nature had little in common with Hubertus' timid nature, he had inherited his father's love of music. Calle literally lived for the music. He loved listening to contemporary avant-garde artists. He himself abused tenderly his guitar and hammered ecstatically on his home-made drums. Later in life, when he was about twenty years old, the highlight of his life had been the day he played with Amon Düül during "Essen 69". Essen 69, however, had nothing to do with food, even though the word *essen* means *eat* in German. The 69 also had nothing to do with sex. Unimaginative imagination could turn Essen

69 into lobster and champagne with fresh strawberries served on an undressed beautiful couple, lying head to toe, each with their own delicacy in their mouths.

It basically started with a three-day out of house concert in August 1969 near Woodstock, USA, outside of New York. The hip hippie life during the festival attracted a lot of attention from the American tabloid press, as it came completely free of charge over pictures of naked women's breasts. Paper sales skyrocketed. More naked women's breasts would later be shown in a several-hour cinema film. Woodstock's unparalleled fame as the world's best breast festival was thus a fact.

But just a couple of months later, another three-day musical delicacy was arranged completely independently of the Woodstock Festival. In Essen, a town in the German Ruhr area, the offered artistic presence was colossal with performers such as Deep Purple, Fleetwood Mac and Pink Floyd to name just a few. Other cult bands included East of Eden, Free, Nice, Spooky Tooth, Steamhammer, Tangerine Dream and many, many more.

As for example a, back then, completely unknown gang from England. Their international debut was an indescribable success. When Yes started playing, people got up from their camps of blankets and pillows and stood up, danced, roared and clapped their hands. On stage stood a graceful figure in a long black caftan. Everyone wanted to see the girlish angel with the long black hair and who sang so sweetly. *I see you* got the neck hair to stand up and people got really wild. That night Yes was born and would live a long time. Everyone wanted to buy their record, but at the festival their first album was handed out for free! Their live version of *end of the night* was their final. That song made Essen's Gruga Hall rock like an eighth magnitude earthquake on the well-known, but equally misunderstood, Richter scale.

But for Calle, the greatest experience was Amon Düül. Not because the music was of any remarkably elevated quality, but because of the enormous sense of freedom and human community that their performance art entailed. It turned into an outstanding jam, where people from the audience stepped up on stage and sang and danced. It was all dreamy and Calle was like in a trance, went up to the happy-go-lucky party, found an abandoned drum set in the back of the stage podium and started playing. Whether it was good or bad or in-between we should leave unsaid, but he felt enchanted like another Ginger Baker and bathed in an indescribable rush of happiness.

Then he awoke disappointed, when the alarm clock rang in a new day, filled with new, never-ending obligations.

III. The Pariscope

Karin and Calle were reunited in adulthood. This happened completely randomly and they did not know about each other. They met at the Pariscope, a place that made an effort to provide elements of Frenchness with details such as signs that said Bistro, Pernod, Steak Parisien, Escargots, Grenouilles and the like, as well as various price indications. Drinks and snacks cost different on different days of the week. On Monday to Wednesday it cost more than on Friday, Saturday and Sunday. The reason was that, compared to the weekend, there were fewer guests during the first days of the week. The owner of this "frenchised" establishment wanted to keep the cash flow lively and constant at all times. On Thursdays it was closed and then of course it cost nothing at all.

The Pariscope was built like a submarine, long and narrow. When the guests arrived, typically after one o'clock at night, it quickly became very, very crowded, which was completely according to plan. The enormous congestion meant that people were rubbing against each other. Boys against girls, girls against boys, boys against boys and girls against girls. The degree of rubbing was determined by personal taste and sexual orientation. Every now and then a masculine hand could find its way to Calle's stern, a circumstance he, however, sharply disliked. But for the most part, a friendly reprimand was enough to remain spared from repeated rubbing and patting attempts.

On the black-painted walls shone in intense self-luminous coloured shapes and figures that let you think of Joan Miró. Large projections of oil drops in various colors between two glass plates changed shape continuously. On the dance floor in the submarine's bow, the music thundered and the stroboscopic flickering of the white dazzling light made the dancers appear in magical slow motion.

The deep bass tones were felt throughout the body and the vibrations in the stomach gave the dancers a rush of happiness on the verge of pain. The jungle drums of Iron Butterfly's *In A Gadda Da Vida* reinforced this dreamlike experience. The poor grades at school, the stressful labours of the workplace, the eternally gnawing worries of money, and the stinging pain of a broken heart were far, far away, totally absent from this blissful moment.

Calle queued at the bar, when his gaze fixed on a wonderful creature with long curly hair and large round eyes a few meters away. The wonderful creature had noticed Calle's unhidden stare. A wonderful smile came in response, while the wonderful creature tried to mate up to him. "Hi, my name is Sofia. When you stop staring at my breasts, you can tell me what your name is. Then we can have a pilsner together. What do you say?"

Calle did not intend to stop staring at her lovely breasts. Not right now. His answer had to wait. Then he mumbled “Calle to my friends. Enchanté, beautiful lady”. Finally he tore his eyes from the garnish, looked up and added “A pilsner would not be bad. Not bad at all. My treat.” Sofia’s answer came swirling fast like a bumerang “okay, the next one is on me.”

A light, almost imperceptible, rubbing made Calle’s trousers tighten at the front. He responded to this somewhat frivolous approach on Sofia’s part by moving a little sideways, so that she could make contact with his tense thighs. She laughed in his ear “Your little rogue” and kissed him on the neck.

That’s how they met, Calle and Sofia. At the Pariscope. A submarine, where you ate snails and frog legs, but where you definitely did not listen to sobbing songs in French.

Together with the clear dazzling colors, the underground music amplified previously unexperienced boundaries by the brown Moroccan, the red Afghan or the black Nepalese, whose black color stemmed mainly from the richly mixed-in opium.

With or without Moroccans, Afghans or Nepalese, this evening at the Pariscope became full of magic.

Some days, or rather some nights, various live performances were offered and at one point, there was this guy who sat on a bar stool with his guitar and played something that at some stage came to be called *Space Oddity.*

IV. Unconcealment

After four romantic months, the Sofia-Calle couple decided to consolidate the covenant of love by moving together. After searching for a while, they found a small cozy apartment, the price of which was within the framework of their joint finances. When signing the contract, it was revealed that they had been dating each other in a complete *incognito*. Karin called herself Sofia, because she associated the name Karin with gloomy memories, which she sought to bury in the deepest corners of the amygdala.

Once they had established their personalities and calmed down a bit after the revelation that caused considerable confusion, they hovered on a grass cloud back to their childhood and their shared ruin memories. They both remembered very well their awkward first attempts to get to know each other's genitals together. And how these early attempts had been nullified by Sofia's, that is, Karin's mother.

Sofia told Calle that she had never met her father, but hid her cruel experiences with the disgusting Herman Sczermonski. The school had been mostly dull and her awake intellect had lacked stimulation. The same was true of the male acquaintances she had half-heartedly maintained over the years. Until she met Calle, this her very first boyfriend. The curiosity on all sides of life, which the school and the men had managed to kill, was revived. Above all, she had become less shy, indeed, even unashamed and cocky.

For Calle, life had taken a completely different turn. As his parents had put it, Calle "has to become something proper, a doctor or a lawyer or something like that." They therefore sent him to a school that was extremely reputable and had a formal high educational potential, at least on paper. The school's motto was also very much a saying in Latin, Non Scholae Sed Vitae Discimus, which emphasised the humanistic character of the school, but was as uninspiring and boring as Caesar's De Bello Gallico. Had you taken a degree at that school, all the doors would be wide open for you. It was a school of the old school, where each graduating class came to form the society's upper class.

Calle had inherited his father's love and devotion to music. Thus, he devoted more time to his band than to schoolwork. The band was called *dikemen* and mainly engaged in copying the works of other music groups. The repertoire contained very little material of its own and consisted mostly of other people's pieces of music. The instrumentation of the *dikemen* was the usual setting. A doo-wop chorus was also part of the band. This consisted of two slender girls who, however, were in fact transvestites in a very feminine design. Under the imaginative and colourful costumes hid the attributes of the masculine genus. In tight-fitting swimsuits, they could therefore seem comical. The two had given the group its name, but despite this they were no lesbians. As a small anecdote, one could mention that they called each other *slut*.

Calle's professional music career was very short. After numerous brave attempts to find a serious producer for their virtual demo files *Homo Dikeman* and just as numerous refusals, he finally gave up. A beaten man. Empty of will to live. Until the day he met Sofia. Like her, he had regained the spark. The two gave up the bohemian lifestyle and now devoted themselves to university studies. Sofia studied nutritional physiology and Calle cell biology. They lived on student loans, a special kind of loan provided by the state, as well as odd jobs to supplement their insufficient cash.

V. A Child's Golden Section

One of these days, during a joint lunch, the couple had had an initially interesting, then increasingly lively, discussion, which had finally derailed and they had ended up in a quarrel with each other. Afterwards, there was a certain mood in their home. But as a once-hippie-always-hippie as they were, they would, in a bonobo way, settle the threatening conflict with sexual activity. With unbridled carnal desire, he took her from behind this sunny afternoon. Sofia stood on all fours on the edge of the bed, while Calle's balls rhythmically struck her most sensitive place, the clitoral area, which gave her even greater arousal, lust, ecstasy. To the melancholy tones of Fanz Schubert's Eighth Symphony, Calle fired a well-aimed shot straight up at her right fallopian tube. Although this destination detail is completely irrelevant in this context, it is a fact that Sofia became pregnant in less than fifteen seconds.

They experienced the following months of pregnancy in devotional anticipation, mixed with terrible anxiety concerning the child's physical and mental condition. Finally, the time of childbirth had come and the delivery went entirely normally, with endless, strenuous torments and unbearable pain for the mother.

The newborn baby was extremely slenderly elongated, eighty centimeters long, but at three thousand two hundred and fifty eight grams, the weight remained relatively close to normal limits. It is by no means uncommon for the head of the newborn to have a distinct elongated shape. That is why no one attached any importance to this in Sofia's birth, but due to the long body, an extra midwife needed to be called in who could help support the baby's soft back row. The risk was obvious that this, after the passage through the birth canal, could otherwise be broken off.

According to the latest findings, the newborn baby should not have its umbilical cord cut immediately, but would have to wait for three minutes before the procedure was performed. This is to provide the baby with a proper flushing of the mother's blood to prevent all kinds of immune deficiency diseases.

During these three minutes, there was ample opportunity for everyone present to use the time to explore the child's external proportions. These did not seem to closely follow the norm for the golden ratio. Apart from the remarkable body length, however, everything seemed to be as it should be, ten fingers, that is, five on each hand, and also ten toes, on two feet. On the other hand, when the sex of this remarkable child was to be decided, it could not be agreed whether it was a girl or a boy. In fact, the child's gender was, at first, rather indeterminate. It seemed to hang a little boy's penis out of a little girl's vulva. Possibly it was an enlarged clitoris that had made its way outside the intended, but closed, inner area.

When the parents were to decide shortly afterwards what the child's name would be, it was decided that, due to the indefinite gender position, names such as Hermes or Aphrodite would for the time being be declared inappropriate and had to be excluded.

Sofia and Calle thus decided on the prefix Eli as their working name. Once the exact gender of the child had been established, the rest could be taken. That is, the suffix, either -sa for a girl, i.e. *Elisa*, or -as for a boy, i.e. *Elias*. If it was neither, that is, something in between, it would probably be *Hirudinea*. S-he was affectionately called Hiri by hir parents. However, this nickname should not be confused with the name of the language spoken by the Motu people of Papua New Guinea. These two are completely different phenomena.

Letitia Crassasius-Levin, who came from the east, was as her maiden name suggests of Jewish descent. Since only one half of her was Jewish and she had not been particularly versed in the Mosaic faith, she had later also neglected the traditional commandments of her own family. She had never taken her son Carl to the slaughterhouse. But in recent times she had become proud of her people's many thousands of years of history and believed that her children's family would now preserve and carry on the beautiful traditions. She therefore told Carl and Sofia that she would like to see an honest and traditional circumcision of the male part of Hiri. The child's parents did not believe their ears, were utterly terrified and upset by this quote: *insane proposal* and told Letitia that such a thing would be completely out of the question and would never happen.

But Letitia, in her newfound religious zeal, had abducted her grandchild behind hirs parents' backs and handed hir over to a scalpel master named Nathan Guldblom. This Guldblom was in some circles known for performing genital mutilation in a very exquisite and artistic way. The fact that the children at the time of the circumcision used to cry heartbreakingly and scream loud and pitifully was not much cared for. As a result, Hiri did not currently have to pull down the foreskin, but the glans was still proudly and pompously exposed between her outer labia. That these would not meet the same fate was due to the fact that the child's parents had given Letitia a restraining order and that they no longer left Hiri out of sight for a second.

VI. The Triple Helix

After fifteen years of Hiri's gender ambiguity, the official name, as it is written in a person's passport, finally became Hirudinea Crassasius-Werdhem. In the small box on the passport application, where you would write an F or an M, hir mother Sofia put an mf. It can be added that another ambiguity was that the baby's body length had hardly changed since birth. By and large, these were still the same values, that is, eighty centimeters plus or minus one and a half centimeters, depending on whether the hair was freshly washed or not.

The weight had not risen significantly either. The head possibly become even more elongated. But Hiri's macrocephaly was not artificially conditioned, as in the case of the Monbuttu people in the center of the most central black Africa. There, the skulls of the newborns were tied together to achieve the long-head effect.

Hiri was, of course, an extremely interesting study object for the life sciences. The sequencing of hir genome revealed that the nucleotides were five in number, consisting of the usual amino acids A, C, G and T. And a viral U. These five were put together in a triple helix, in a very different mixture of so-called DNA and RNA. This triple helix was now called DRNA, pronounced Dirna. The germ cells were also peculiar, the chromosomes were neither XX nor XY, but XYZ.

The discovery of DRNA was sensational and self-evident in the Nobel class. The remarkable thing about the prize was that it was awarded in the subject of medicine, as if one had discovered, and successfully fought, a notorious or previously unknown disease.

Hiri's physique was above average healthy, so there could be no question of any disease. In addition, s-he was super-gifted intellectually. However, the committee in charge never even considered for a second to award the prize to young Hiri, but chose an obscure biochemist from Minnesota. He was a male and had family ties in the Royal Swedish Academy of Sciences.

The other two laureates, one from China and the other from India, were also male and both were active at the Institute for Humanoid Race Evolution in British Birmingham. All Nobel laureates had long since blown out more than eighty candles on their birthday cake and were still alive when their names were announced in early October, entitling them to receive the award from the monarch in December of the same year. In Sweden's proud and beautiful capital.

The Chinoindian duo had early on suspected that Hiris' gene mutation would involve fundamental changes in human survival. Among other things, they had predicted that Hiri would develop hir own metabolism that would prove to be significantly more energy efficient than what is commonly the case. For example, Hiri peed only every two months and pooped every four. Of course, it goes without saying that Hiri ate very sporadically. Hiri could often sit motionless for long periods of time, even for several weeks, as if in a kind of dormancy. With the people in hir immediate vicinity, s-he was then also completely non-communicative.

What was generally considered to be the most important conclusion was equally grand, namely that Hiri was aging extremely slowly. Hiri's DRNA telomeres did not wear as fast as the DNA ends of "normal" people. Interest in this remarkable circumstance increased extremely rapidly, especially in the general news media and in the so-called low-iq *reality shows.* Government members around the world reckoned that their time in power could almost legitimately be extended indefinitely, and consequently they also increased research funding to unprecedented levels. This took place on a global scale with the competing scientists in many countries, even in those which usually cared very little about scientific research that was not of an explosive nature.

Knowledge of most research results was reserved for a very small group of people with special qualifications. The non-secret material was published in the newly founded journal *The Triplehelix Cognitive News Letters*. This publication was extremely reputable and the researchers considered it very nice to appear in it with their names. To emphasize the sensational news value of the articles, the number of pages was limited, but also because people did not have to read so much. You had so much else to do.

This lack of space could mean that the content was not sufficiently reliable or less trustworthy. Several of the often many co-authors of the articles could be interviewed on TV, a coveted employment in paid working hours that could lead to a notoriety at national, even international, level. This narcissistic playground attracted more and more dreamers of wealth and celebrity. Fewer dreamed of the progress of science for the best of mankind.

The information that did leak to the media included Hiris' diet. The interest in the same was based on many people's vanity to acquire or maintain a slim figure. Perhaps to be expected, mostly middle-aged women were among the slimming enthusiasts. However, they expressed concerns about the essentially non-existent breasts of Hiri. To the extent that Hiri's flat front could be attributed to the lean diet, the women felt maneuvered in an information vacuum. In them a seed of concern was planted, namely, that one might expect a considerable bust loss. This would clearly be an unwanted side effect. So far, however, this fear has not been substantiated by reliable data. The scientific community was silent.

In dollyish Scotland, on the other hand, people were not on the lazy side. There they were in the process of sowing new seeds, as they had done so successfully before. The purpose of the experimental work was to produce copies of Hiri through cloning. There were also far-reaching plans to persuade Hiri to reproduce parthenogenetically.

Hiri had so far responded with indetermination. But Hiri also realized that the purpose and benefit of having access to an entire population of hiris is, of course, the opportunities that open up for long-distance travel through space.

Although the technology has been mastered since long, cloning of humans has so far not been allowed due to ethical reasons. In any case, no cases of cloned individuals were known. However, the conspiracy theorists believed that there was tangible evidence in the form of tons of cytoplasmic material in the waste bins in many laboratories around the world.

Who could resist the temptation?

VII. Ad Medinam

Sofia and Calle mostly tenderly called their child Hiri-darling, Hiri-love, Sweety, Little Beauty and the like. On the few occasions when they felt that the child had done something stupid, they used the old name Eli. In short, Eli. Only Eli meant trouble. But for the most part, the calls were loving. And Hiri reciprocated her parents' warmth, s-he loved them dearly and deeply.

One sunny late afternoon, Calle watched as Hiri with poised lifted arms danced gracefully in wavy movements. Hiri had gone to one of her favorite places, a tiny glade in a tiny forest grove a few hundred meters behind her parents' home. Hiris' shadow was almost ten meters long and gave the dance a magical dimension. It was summer vacation and Hiri was carefree and happy. Before the holiday, after only four months of study, s-he had mastered Finnish as the seventh foreign language. S-he hummed a Finnish version of the Swedish Midsummer song *Little Frogs* with her own, slightly free, translation that read

lyhyet jalat, pitkät jalat, häntä poispäin
suuret silmät, pienet korvat, mansikka-pensasaidat

which was something like

short legs, long legs, tail away
big eyes, small ears, heck of clay

and so on.

When Hiri became aware of another person's presence, s-he stopped dancing and looked around. Hiri saw that it was hir father and wondered in surprise, "What are *you* doing here?"

Calle: "I came to talk to you, my darling. Thought to hear from you, what you think where we would go on vacation this year. Do you have any idea?"

Hiri: "I do not know, if you think it's a good idea, but I would really like to go to Tamanrasset at some stage."

Calle: "Where did you say you wanted to go?"

Hiri: "To Tamanrasset. In Algeria. In the middle of the Sahara desert. To the Ahoggar Mountains."

Calle: "Yeah, you. To Tamanrasset. I'm going to talk to mom. Oh, how far is it there, by the way? Ah, it was nothing."

Calle set out to find his wife Sofia. He already knew beforehand what she would answer, but still thought it would be polite to ask her about her opinion on the matter. Both she and Calle tried to fulfill all of Hiri's wishes, that is, to the extent that these were reasonable and practically possible. They were worried about the risk that Hiri would not live that long, because they had learned that dwarves seem to have reduced lifetimes. In any case, they were completely unaware of what was causing Hiri to stop growing. If it was a question of some kind of illness, then there was a significant risk that this was in its terminal phase and Mr. Dead could knock on the door any day.

"I had hoped that the cutie had said Saint Barth or Bora-Bora or something like that, but Tummyrasslat? Have never heard of it and do not even know where this place is located", Sofia sighed. Calle replied laconically "*this place* is actually as big as Bath, dear". But both parents had already made up their minds and immediately started planning the trip. Visas were obtained and flights to Gibraltar in southern Spain were booked. From there it takes only half an hour by car to the ferry terminal in Algeciras.

The short crossing from Algeciras to Ceuta went smoothly and without significant incidents. It only takes an hour by boat to jump from Europe to Africa. In summer, the waters of the Strait of Gibraltar are usually calm, especially on the Mediterranean side. There was plenty of time to enjoy the Moroccan national drink, a glass of sweet hot tea with fresh mint leaves. The Crassasius-Werdhems soaked up sun and tea and were cherished by the warm breeze. They sat in the bow on a simple wooden bench and did not attract any special attention.

In Gibraltar, Carl had ordered a rental car that

was off-road. It also had a winch on the front bumper. Now Calle was busy studying a wrapped Michelin map of North Africa. It was red and was called “Carte a 1/4 000 000 - 1 cm pour 40 km, **AFRIQUE** NORD ET OUEST”. He pondered which route would be best to take. That is, least dangerous. Through the Sahara, the world’s largest desert, without access to water, without a drop of the elixir of life, but full of scorpions and other vermin.

Sofia had a crossword puzzle in her lap and chewed on a pencil. She mumbled “refractive inability, vertical eleven letters” and Hiri’s quick response came back like a boomerang at supersonic speed: “astigmatism”.

“By God, you are *so* smart!”

“Come on, Mom! It’s not that hard. I had that in the anatomy course.”

“I know, but you answered so quickly.”

Sofia looked pensively and her big wide open eyes rested questioningly on this strange child of hers. She loved her child so desperately, that sometimes it even hurt inside. With her new haircut, Hiri looked like a cute little girl, in t-shirt and jeans. And with painted lips. Hiri did not paint her nails, “you should be able to see that they are clean”.

Hiri most of all wanted to get to Tamanrasset as quickly as possible. Hir physiognomy therefore assumed an annoyed look, when hir father Calle declared that they would first go to Fez. Calle wanted to cash in on the city's medina, which now houses the domestic market with all sorts of oriental seductions. There they were to buy their own *shalaba*, a kind of kaftan with a hood. According to Calle, this item of clothing would be the "absolutely best in the heat and cold of the desert".

Later he would perform an experiment. He wanted to measure what the temperature actually was. It had been rumored that at night it could even be frost. People's experience of such cold could possibly be due to the large temperature differences between day and night. When it could be over forty degrees in the middle of the day, twenty degrees at night would probably be experienced as quite cool, he reasoned. To find out what actually applies, he had bought a special outdoor thermometer. This was a conventional mercury device, but graded between minus fifty up to plus fifty degrees Celsius. In general, outdoor temperatures are measured in a shadow. In the Sahara stone desert, however, there was no such thing, and consequently Calle placed his thermometer just straight out on the ground, in the scorching sunshine. After a short while, the thermometer exploded and Calle later noted in his travel diary "noon sun, only lower limit of fifty degrees; the thermometer is broken, can not measure at night". Ergo, the mystery remains.

Hiri pointed out that Fez was clearly in the opposite direction and going there was clearly a detour. In addition, tourists were warned in the travel guide that one should enter the kasba only in groups and then only with the help of local guides. Since the kasba seemed to lack sensible urban planning, tourists would easily get lost and be exposed to unwelcome inconveniences. As for foreigners, assaults, robberies, and even murders were often reported.

Neither Sofia nor Calle embraced Hiri's intimidation propaganda. The democratic family voting resulted in two to one in favour of Fez and its kasba. Sofia in particular proved to be extremely keen to visit the kasba. She had heard about the fantastic leather goods marketed there and she wanted to buy a pair of saddlebags for her motorcycle. They would be "so much cheaper than what you got for a pair of just leather items at home".

Inside the kasba, there was a throng of stalls, goods and people. But it was very helpful that the neighborhoods were divided according to their product range. Here, all beautiful vessels and art in copper were provided and there, was shop after shop with carpets, then gold jewelery and silver work, and so on. Calle made his way to the shalaba department and after a while of searching, they finally stood in an alley with lots of colorful Moroccan clothes. Calle's eyes fell on a white shalaba that hung in a clothes hanger under a striped canopy. When he curiously fingered it, the store owner appeared in the dark doorway. "Ah, nise peepel! Wont nise peepel by nise shalaba?" The store owner turned his attention to Carl, who kindly replied "We would like three of those, one for our child, one for my wife and one for me. Are the sizes available?" The shopkeeper who, as it would later turn out, was called Altair answered politely but resolutely "Jes, Jes, Jes! Misjiu nise. Ay shou." He disappeared into the black hole and returned shortly afterwards with three garments. "1400 Dirham for woan nise shalaba" he proclaimed, "Woan fourr la petite, woan fourr Madame ent woan fourr joo, Sire".

Two children, a girl and a little boy, appeared in the doorway and looked curiously at their father and the strangers. The girl could be five, the boy maybe three years old. He and Hiri were about the same size. The children had been attracted by the large number of Dirham that their father had shouted out loud, clearly and distinctly, so that the competitors around could also hear this.

Sofia tilted her head slightly and said "But Carl,

one thousand four hundred dromedaries for one nightgown! Isn't that too expensive?" "Darling, it's not dromedaries, but Dirham. Their money is called that. Like Drachma in Greece but in Morocco." Carl was able to get Sofia even more confused, but Hiri came to the rescue, "Dad, I think he wants us to bargain. Fourteen hundred of their money! It's ridiculous!" Carl collected himself and then turned to Altair, as it would soon turn out that this was his name: "My good nice man! I think that we need to discuss the price a little further. Don't you think that fourteen hundred a piece is a little hefty?" Altair waved his arms and exclamated "Ah. Jes, Jes, Jes! We can go inside and have some tea." Carl thought "His English has suddenly improved. We'll see how it goes" and then they all went through the dark doorway into the room behind. It was a little cooler there with a fan spinning in the ceiling. On the floor there were large pillows around a large round copper table. There were also a couple of short-legged chairs with camel fur on, or maybe it was sheep skin.

A small woman with her face hidden behind a piece of cloth came in with a tray. She placed drinking glasses, a sugar bowl and a copper-colored teapot on the round table. Then she disappeared. The children were still standing. Their father nodded at them with a wide smile. "These are my children. The name of my girl is Aisha and my boy is

Ahmad" he declared proudly. "Your daughter and my boy are of the same age, yes?"

Then he poured the tea and invited his guests with a courtly gesture to help themselves with the sugar. "Welcome to my humble home. I am Altair. I hope the tea will be to your liking." "Oops," thought Hiri, "that was unexpected," referring to Altair's English. Carl said "That was very kind of you, Altair. I can see that you have quite a lot of foreign customers. What do you say to 800 Dirham for all three shalabas? 300 for the big ones and 200 for the small one." Carl went out hard. Altair's response was not long in coming: "Oh, Mister Nice! Do you want my children to die of starvation? I could give you my best offer of 1300 for each of the shalabas." And so the bidding started. It would take many glasses of tea and take more than two hours, before finally agreeing on 1400 Dirham for all the long shirts. It was still an overprice, at least Altair's children did not have to starve.

Carl was a little annoyed. He had wanted to continue negotiations with Altair to bring the price down to a more acceptable level, but Sofia pressed for them to continue to the kasba's leather sales. It was late in the afternoon and soon it would be dark outside. And then she did not want them to remain in the kasba. But to her despair, they found neither the leather goods outlets nor the way out of the kasba. They wandered around, went in circles and then came to a small square. Sofia looked up and remembered that she had seen the ladder leaning against the wall, on which a two-meter-high vanilla orchid had been tied, and the freshly painted sign with the letters

TropischegewürzbedienungsabteilungsLeiter

It hung above one of the shops and she had seen it several hours earlier, at the very beginning, when they had just arrived at the kasba. Apparently, the kasba was frequently visited by tourists belonging to the Germanic language family. The place was also very correctly marked on the guidebook's map and the three were finally able to find their way out. Sofia was disappointed that she had not got hold of the saddlebags. Well, at least they had the caftans as protection against the expected scorching Saharan late summer sun.

VIII. Intermezzo

Hiri's grandmother Letitia considered herself superior to others. In particular, she looked down on the other tenants who lived in the house of the Crassasius-Levins domicile. The nature of her arrogance led unsought thoughts to of what happened a few years ago in America. There, they had a real fogey as president. This very strange figure, lying and insidious as he was, had gone to the polls with the motto "Make America Great Again". Letitia liked the spirit of the campaign slogan, but wondered in her quiet mind if it would be possible to use it in Europe too. For example, "Make Germany Great Again". What would the country's neighbors say about that?

Letitia's roots were in the east, in that country which was once very very large. Once upon a time, Vikings sailed there, but for a long time the population was settled, mostly farmers, and to whom their rustic food meant a lot. The recipes of the unpretentious hearty kitchen had been inherited for generations and Sofia had learned from her mother, just as Letitia had learned from her, and Hiri wanted to learn from Sofia.

The dishes often reflected the geographical origins and the time, when the aristocracy did not wash and spoke French. Hiri, for hir part, had in this tradition found hir beloved dish that was called *Boulettes de Viande Mont Royal, Pommes de Terre à la Vapeur, Sauce aux Câpres.* This was a very simple dish that was also loved by Prussian kings, especially the one named Freddy the Old. Freddy or Fritz, who could barely speak German, preferred French as the recipe suggests. When dining with his friend, who called himself Voltaire, that Frenchman, however, would wrinkle his nose. But, please, enjoy - below is the recipe.

King's Mountain Meatballs in Capers Sauce

3 - 4 servings

broth:

1 l water
1 1/2 meat stock cubes
1 1/2 dl dry white wine
1 bay leaf
1/2 small yellow onion
5 black peppercorns

meatballs:

400 g minced meat
1/2 small yellow onion
1-2 slices white bread
1 dl cream
3 anchovies
1 egg
1 teaspoon thyme

sauce:

1 1/2 tablespoons wheat flour
25 g margarine
4 dl strained broth
1 egg yolk
1/2 dl crème fraiche
grated lemon peel + the juice of 1/2 lemon
150 g capers

1 dl cream over the bread, edges cut. Mix the ingredients in the minced meat, form meatballs. Peel and finely chop the onion, fry blanc in a little shortening. Bring to the boil; the meatballs are simmered for 12 - 15 min. Fry shortening + flour in a saucepan, dilute with the cooking broth, a little at a time, simmer the sauce for about 10 minutes. Season with salt and pepper. Stir out the egg yolk with crème fraiche. Take the sauce off the heat, whisk down the mixture. Taste with lemon + capers. Add the meatballs and pour over the sauce. Serve with steamed potatoes, sprinkle with finely chopped parsley.

Serve with the rest of the wine. A good wine at an affordable price is Pouilly-Fumé (Sauvignon Blanc), slightly more expensive would be Pouilly-Fuissé (Chardonnay); alternatively a cold beer (Schultheiss Pilsener from the capital of Prussia) or water (Perrier from Voltaire's country).
But, a good Chablis (Chardonnay) is never wrong, of course. The wine that is drunk should be the same as that in the sauce.

IX. Ad Desertum

At the next day's breakfast in the "hotel's dining room", a shaky outdoor table with a pair of rickety wicker chairs outside the hostel, Sofia whined to repeat her desire to return to the kasba. Carl wondered if she knew exactly where they had saddlebags for motorcycles. Sofia replied that she thought that in places where they had leather stuff there would probably also be saddlebags in leather. To both Carl and Hiri, this answer seemed unconvincing and, given the vagueness of Sofia's plan, they proposed a new family vote. Sofia had no chance. They packed the car and left Fez heading for the border with Algeria.

Near a larger community, Oujda, they stopped for lunch. The restaurant was a simple shack with a couple of tables under an airy roof. Sofia expressed her dissatisfaction with the hygiene facilities. The menu consisted of a blackboard on the wall behind a kind of bar counter and on which only one dish was stated with up to a dozen price indications. The name of the dish was written with a piece of white chalk by hand, in Arabic, which was therefore hard to understand. The prices were also written in Arabic, but these were of course easier to decipher.

Due to some communication difficulties with the owner of the establishment, they never really found out what was being served for lunch. But even the most expensive option was so cheap that they decided on this. The restaurant owner took out three tin plates and scooped up three hearty portions of couscous. Then he lifted the lid of a large pot and put pieces of meat and vegetables, as well as soup, on top of the couscous mountain. The three guests ate with a healthy appetite, the dish was really good.

After the meal, they tried to find out what the other dishes contained. They pointed to the first row on the blackboard and looked questioningly at the chef. He again lifted the lid of the large pot and pointed to the contents. Carl then pointed in surprise at the bottom line and it was obvious that he was wondering what the difference was. Besides the price, of course. The chef looked like he was having an Aha experience. Then he opened his almost toothless mouth, said something in Moroccan and presented a giant smile. Pointing and laughing, he explained that the price variations were determined by the accessories for the soup. The cheapest variant consisted of soup only. Then came soup plus couscous. Then soup plus vegetables. Then soup plus couscous plus vegetables. Then soup plus meat. And so on. His guests seemed to understand and they parted in a friendly consensus.

The journey over the Atlas Mountains was full of endless beauty. Alternately barren mustard yellow and slate gray-blackish mountains and untouched, wild green nature. They barely met a soul on the bumpy, rock-hard road. It took two days to get to In Salah, where the potholed, but paved, Algerian Autobahn ended. Then you had to choose which route you would take that was hopefully least harmful to your vehicle. Sharp stones sticking out of the tightly packed soil could easily puncture the tires of the car. The corrugated roads that were like giant washboards would vibrate so much that any vehicle would finally break into pieces.

On an endless plateau under a relentless sun, the Crassasius-Werdhems plodded along the desert floor of sharp stones. Not even the slightest hint of shadow could be expected. The chlorinated water which they carried in plastic containers had a disgusting taste and its temperature was above forty degrees Celsius. Even though they had wrapped the cans in wet towels to keep them cool, the desired effect had long since gone to its grave. This was the real, irreconcilable Sahara. It had no resemblance to the postcard-beautiful soft-rolling dunes that travel guides advertise. Nor were there any of the oases depicted in storybooks. This was not paradise. This was hell.

Hiri, Sofia and Calle had their mouths, ears and noses full of the fine desert dust. Coarser grains of sand squeaked between their teeth. They had covered their faces with cloth and pulled their hoods as far down as they could over their heads, but these measures were of only minimal benefit. Their white shalabas helped withstand the heat, but their thirst remained unquenched. The water was on the verge of becoming undrinkable even though they tried to flavour it with fresh lime juice. They had no choice but to swallow the nasty fluid for they needed it to replace what they had sweated out. And this perspiration was neither seen nor felt. It evaporated immediately into the hyper dry air. It left no trace and it did not smell either.

On the horizon loomed images of gorgeous cool water features. "But it's probably just a *Fata Morgana*", Hiri thought. But mirages do not usually grow in size as you approach them. But that was what seemed to happen to this particular one. Gradually, a lovely oasis appeared, with date palms and lime trees. And cold, clear water.

X. Soft Dune Oasis

For the sake of rarity in this part of the Sahara, the oasis was surrounded by high rolling dunes of fine-grained sand. These beautiful formations resembled lying nudities with the sharpness in the contour of pointed breasts. To reach the oasis, one had to cross these mountains of fine-grained gravel. “Fortune favors the bold”, Sofia thought, as she took charge and steered straight towards the sand barrier. It went well in the beginning, they managed a good piece of the dune. They went halfway up and then it was a stop. “Not much favor here”, Sofia thought. The car’s wheels had spun, lost their grip and finally dug deeper and deeper into the sand.

“Get off for everyone!” Calle sounded like a busy stationmaster at the terminus of a choo choo train. “Now it’s going to be digging, digging, digging,” he shouted as he began unloading shovels, one of the spare tires and the two sand ladders ontop of the car’s roof. Then he started digging a pit in front of the vehicle and encouraged Hiri and Sofia to do the same thing, that is, to help dig. In the relentless heat, doing this was very strenuous, and it did not take long before they were completely exhausted. The sand kept falling from the edge over and over again and it seemed to take an eternity to get done with this miserable Sisyphus chore. Finally, they had dug a hole that was just over a meter wide and one and a half meters deep. They stuffed the car tire into the hole and anchored the winch wire and carabiner to it. Then they filled the pit again. They poorly cleared the car's rear tires and placed the sand ladders in front of them. Sofia sat behind the wheel and the winch slowly began to pull the car out of the sand. After the cable had been disconnected, Sofia drove the car carefully up to the crest of the dune. Then it was just a matter of digging again to take care of the spare wheel.

The weary travellers decided to stay in the oasis until the next day. They felt dirty and most of all wanted to be able to wash themselves. Fortunately, there was a bathhouse in the village. In large yellow letters, it said *Bain de Soleil* on the wall. Hiri entered the house, where a long corridor ended in a large blue hall with a tiled pool. In and around the pool there were about a dozen people. All were women. And all were scattered naked. The pubic hair was plentiful and black in everyone. However, the shape and size of the breasts varied considerably, everything from hanging gourds and coarse pumpkins to god-shaped busts like ancient marble sculptures. Hiri perceived all this in less than a millisecond and noticed that the bathing women's happy chatter stopped abruptly, when they saw Hiri, wondering who the little figure might be. The women decided that it was a little girl and returned to their conversations and laughter. That figure was harmless. Hiri spun around on hir heel and returned to hir parents and explained the situation. Carl was absolutely forbidden to go there. If he was discovered, it could be a beheading. They would need to find another waterhole.

They tried to ask where to take a bath, but people did not seem to understand or did not want to understand what it was, they were looking for. Perhaps their incomprehensible faces were due to Carl's sloppy French "Meeseieu seevouplay. Bang." Or did the asked persons think that Carl's simian dance was ridiculous, when he tried to describe with gestures that he wanted to wash. The three wandered around and ran around in circles. Finally, they came across a young man of maybe sixteen years who led them forward, not far from the *Bain de Soleil*. Actually on the same street, but on the other side. When Carl was to thank with some money, the boy firmly said that he did not want any tips. This was very unexpected. Normally, many people wanted a little *bakhshish*, whether they deserved it or not.

There was no sign that distinguished the unassuming clay house. In front of the entrance there was a curtain of plastic strings in different colors. They entered a room with a few beds in it. There was no one there and they continued to an adjoining square room that was empty except a couple of oil barrels filled with water. A modest light was let in through the shutter windows under the ceiling.

A man in his forties appeared out of nowhere and gestured to them that the price for using his spa facility was eight dirhams per person. This did not include soap, shampoo or towel. But Hiri, Sofia and Carl carried these paraphernalia with them in their backpacks. Since the place was completely empty of people, they undressed completely. They enjoyed and laughed with delight as they poured the warm water over their heads. The water had been stored in an old oil barrel and warmed to a comfortable room temperature in the hot room. It felt wonderfully cleansing to soap up and rinse off again and again.

What they had not expected was that suddenly new bathers would appear. Or rather, more peeping Toms. All belonged to the masculine part of the population and were relatively young. Among them was the boy who had led them to the laundry. "Yeah, it was like this, he made his money," said Hiri, facing hir father. Two of the young men entered the laundry room and began to wash themselves. They wore sunkissed short veils, intended to hide the private parts. However, they were not shy enough to stop staring at Sofia. They stared alternately at her breasts and below her belly. They had stopped looking at Hiri because they thought s-he was a guy. Although Hiri looked very young, s-he had black pubic hair and a small snout protruded from the bush, which apparently made hir uninteresting. In any case, nobody, from the very beginning, cared about Carl. Hiri and Sofia ended their washing orgy facing the wall, so that the staring ones were allowed to look only at their well-shaped buttocks.

When they had dried off and put on their clothes, they were kindly pushed by the owner into the room with the beds, for a nice post-spa rest. They each lay on their divan and enjoyed this pleasant quiet moment.

After a few minutes, they were joined by the two domestic bathers. These pulled the blankets over themselves and it did not take long before the Crassasius-Werdhem family realized that the two were jerking off. Sofia burst out laughing: “They washed themselves with their clothes on, they were so embarrassed! And now they lie here and wag right in front of our eyes!” The two young men seemed completely unmoved and continued with what they were doing. “You must take the custom wherever you go! MASTURBARE NECESSE EST”, Hiri shouted delighted.

It had become evening and darkness had settled over the oasis like a velvet blanket. The silence had also spread, this absolute silence. No sounds were to be heard from either people or animals. When you held your breath and stood still, the only thing you could hear was your own blood circulation whistling inside your eardrums. Otherwise it was totally silent. And black. In addition to the thousands and thousands of stars that could be grasped with just your hands, they seemed so close. The moon had not yet appeared.

They had found a small cozy place to spend the night. It reminded them in a way of the Christmas fairy tale stable in Bethlehem, though a little more luxurious. They had bunks to lie on instead of straw on the ground. And the sheep waited kindly outside. In the light of the kerosene lamp, they were reading. Sofia about leather bags and leather works in the travel guide and Hiri about the pictorial decoration of the Ahoggar caves in an article in the *Amateur Archaeologist.* Calle sat outside the stable studying the starry sky and tried to read the constellations he knew, but gave up after a while. These confusing myriads of dots of light were just too many and erased all recognisable patterns.

The next morning, Hiri got hir way and they got up very early. The moon was up now and lay on its side like a cradle. The sun had not yet climbed above the horizon, when they set off towards Tamanrasset. They did not arrive until much later, after sunset, after the long journey on the bumpy road. They stopped outside the city and camped outdoors.

The sky had turned lead gray to carbon black and there was lightning and thunder from the north. A storm was fast approaching. Calle, Hiri and Sofia became aware that they were the only objects that protruded more than ten centimeters on the absolutely flat plateau they were on. They hurried to roll up their sleeping bags and got back in the car. Immediately after the car door slammed shut, lightning struck their vehicle. It probably jumped a meter into the air, but the family remained unharmed. A violent downpour thundered down on the car's roof. It was the first time in fifteen years it rained in Tamanrasset.

They woke up the next day in a fairytale landscape. As far as the eye could see, countless different colored flowers had transformed the barren landscape into a flourishing paradise. This was a miracle.

It was the water's own power of life and no one

needed to walk on it to prove its grandeur. The seeds of the plants had lain in the dry ground, waiting for this rare moment. Only once in fifteen years!

Then the desert flowering was over in just a couple of days.

The seeds of the next generation had already been sewn. Then the Sahara was the same again. Rocky gray and trembling dry.

XI. Towards the Petroglyphs

In Tamanrasset, they bought supplies and provisions for the upcoming excursion to the Ahoggar massif. In particular, they stocked up with fresh water. After the night's heavy rain, the city's water reservoir was full. Fresh fruit such as figs, dates, lemons and oranges were also found on the market. In a grocery store, *L'épicerie de Soleil*, they supplied themselves with basic goods such as pasta, rice and beans as well as chocolate. Then they handed in their shalabas to a local laundry. The color of the garments had gone from white to beige to gray to dirty red and might need a proper scrubbing.

They sat outside the grocery store and drank sweet sweet hot minted tea and watched the life of the people in the square. One incident struck them with surprise. In the middle of the square there was a crowd of women of different ages. They squalled, squealed, shouted and laughed so loud that it could be heard all over the area. It was fun to watch, but at one point Hiri saw how an older, corpulent madame in long, buttoned-up, black clothes unexpectedly parted her legs. Just a little. Hiri told hir parents what s-he had just seen: below the woman was a puddle. The woman regained her previous leg position and continued to chatter completely unaffected. The point was that the woman had stood upright and peed. Earlier, they had seen several men at the bus station squatting and peeing straight out. Here in Tamanrasset, men sat down and women stood up, when they urinated. Adding that all this happened in the open and in broad daylight made the Crassasius-Werdhems think that this was quite remarkable.

Inside the grocery store *L'épicerie de Soleil* Calle tried in his terribly bad French to get some information about the area's cave paintings and how to get there. Indeed, it was the cave paintings they had come here for. The shopkeeper somehow magically made Calle realize that his brother and cousin worked as professional, legitimate tour guides and that he could contact them to find out if they were available. The store owner's brother and cousin showed up shortly afterwards - as if they had been waiting and listening just around the corner behind the store - and Calle shone up. The two men, perhaps in their thirties, had a trustworthy, honest look. Like the shop owner, they belonged to the Tuareg people and were therefore mostly masked behind blue cotton cloth in front of their faces. But when they saw the foreigners, they took off their veils and revealed their tanned faces. Their eyes were blue and on their heads they wore blue turban-like wrappings.

Tuareg women, on the other hand, usually do not hide their faces behind veils. On the contrary, they like to show off with henna paintings and silver earrings and jewellery. Their hair with braided silver strands is also fully visible. But their costumes were like the men's, blue. No wonder the Tuaregs were also commonly called the Blue Berbers.

The Blue Berbers have their very own language

with a myriad of different dialects. These depend on which tribe you belong to. For Calle, it was virtually impossible to memorize the guides' long complicated names, let alone how they would be pronounced. He could not just call them A and B and decided that one, he with the scar over his right eye, would be named Ali and the other one Beli. Pointing at them he indicated "You Ali, and you Beli, okay?" The two seemed to understand and nodded.

Calle agreed with Ali and Beli that they would meet next week about a hundred kilometers away, at a crater in the Ahoggar Mountains. There they would set up their base camp and from there they would continue on foot. The most well-preserved and best-known rock paintings are in Tassili, several hundred kilometers away, towards Libya. Twenty thousand year old animal images can be viewed there.

Hiri was well acquainted with the archeological treasures of Tassili, but s-he wanted to visit the completely newly discovered and completely unknown works of art that were found somewhere in the middle of the wild mountains of the Ahoggar massif. Hiri asked the guide couple if they knew about the cave paintings in Ahoggar. The men replied in Tuareg French that they probably knew what Hiri was referring to and that they had an idea of where they were. They glanced at the family's sandals on their bare feet and remarked that they would need to get more sturdy footwear, as there was a lot of miserable terrain in front of them. Hiri reassured them that the family was well prepared:

s-he had made sure of that.

The preparations also included making sure that there was fuel in the petrol cans, oil in the oil pan and water in the radiator. The rim of the wheel that had been buried had taken a turn and needed to be straightened. The mechanics at the gas station were extremely skilled and did a very good job. They also pointed out that the ignition should be adjusted, which Calle said they were welcome to do so. They worked for several days with the car, but the final cost of all the work was less than what they had given for the family's shalabas. Their rental car now felt better than ever before.

XII. Carvings in Stone

On the way to the agreed meeting place, the Crassasius-Werdhems met a small nomadic family consisting of seven members, two men and two women plus three children. The two youngest could be five six, the oldest maybe twelve years old. The men rode on single-humped camels, while the women and children trotted beside them. “Real gentlemen! These pompous men sit comfortably and ride on their dromedaries, while letting their ladies and children use shanks’s pony!” Hiri exclamated contemptuously.

When they reached the edge of the crater at lunchtime, Ali and Beli were already there. They were about to bake bread in the hot sand. They had wrapped a flattened lump of dough into a piece of linen cloth and dug it all down. After only half an hour or so it was ready, freshly baked bread, steaming hot and tasty. Absolutely wonderful! Of course, hot tea was served. Beli took out a piece of a sugar top and broke it into smaller pieces. The tea became very sweet as usual.

After lunch, the two blue men withdrew and lay in the shade under a rock shelf. Calle, Hiri and Sofia set up the tent and made themselves at home. In the late afternoon they went down to the crater bottom and wandered around. There was not much variety and not much to see. The crater landscape was very monotonous, flat and rocky. They returned to their camp and it was an early “Good Night!”

Hiri had a strange dream. S-he hovered high in the

atmosphere, where the sky had a yellowish shimmer. Far below, a giant continent spread out, also very gray-yellow, surrounded by a large black sea. Somehow a large map book appeared that was put overlaying on top of the continent and the sea. On the map were Thetys and Gondwana. North of Gondwana was a land called Laurasia. Although no one lived there, so it could be called anything. Or nothing at all. Things were not really called anything at the time it went. In the middle of the magnetic map, a cross marked the “treasure”, something inside Gondwana. The map changed appearance again, this time by superimposing paleogeomagnetic data. Then everything became diffuse, dissolved in a gray porridge and Hiri fell into a deep black sleep.

In the morning, Hiri told hir parents that s-he had had a very strange dream, but that s-he did not remember what it was about. Just that it had been something important. S-he had a very definite feeling about it, it was just like that. Calle and Sofia nodded understandingly, but shrugged inexplicably. As scientists, they did not attach much importance to dream interpretation.

Just over a year ago, Hiri had started to bleed, but it did not turn out to be regular menstruation. That is, the bleeding did not occur at monthly intervals, but it would take years between them and it would now be time for her second annstruation. Maybe as soon as within two weeks. Hiri then most of all wanted to be back to some kind of civilisation, with access to water and hygienic facilities. So, it was a bit of a hurry to find the cave paintings. The two guides did a solid job and led them to a significant number of caves. And exposed rock walls. Many actually had signs of human activity, including drawings of animals and of humans on the walls. But these were generally not very old, usually with very well-preserved colors, and might even be of contemporary date.

On the fourth day, however, they seemed to have found the pot of gold at the end of the rainbow. Ali had taken them to a bare mountain with very steep sides. They had to use ropes and harnesses to reach the opening of a rock chamber. This cave was quite large, about ten times fifteen meters, and high in the ceiling, maybe five, six meters. The walls consisted of granite or gneiss and had blasted black shiny glassy material. On the ground lay vases of the black material. These appeared to be processed. Probably with granite tools. Hiri was convinced that the cave had been used by humans in prehistoric times. Several thousand years ago, this black obsidian was extremely coveted and used by the arms industry of the time for the manufacture of arrow- and spearheads. The sites were few and were closely guarded. Obsidian was a highly valued commodity.

Hiri and hir parents were very excited by this discovery. They danced and shouted and hugged the two Tuaregs, who were terrified. Being hugged by women in a public setting, apparently did not belong to their normal behavioral patterns.

Carl believed that the remains on the workshop's floor could well be twenty thousand years old and that one should immediately contact the *National Geographic* society to arrange archaeological expertise. Carl also told Ali and Beli that the two would get a hefty bonus. Fantastic job! Very well done! The two smiled broadly.

This evening it was difficult to calm down. The company sat near the cave entrance around a fire and drank tea and laughed. Ali and Beli communicated with hands and feet and actually seemed to be able to make themselves understood. Finally, they all fell asleep with a smile on their faces.

The next day, they examined the cave in more detail, especially the walls, to find any traces of its original users. Very rightly, they found faint paint residue on one of the walls. Possibly one could discern faded figurative images of both animals and human-like beings. What a catch! Great cheers erupted and everyone was talking at once.

It was too dark in the cave to photograph the faint paintings. They had no headlights with them up here and Sofia therefore sat with a watercolor pad in her lap and drew with a pencil what she saw on the wall in front of her. Calle tried to be helpful and pointed to parties she had missed. It became tiring for the eyes and they needed to take a break. Hiri sat leaning against the opposite wall, staring incessantly at a special place. S-he had guessed something there, but was not entirely sure that s-he did not merely see a phantasy.

As the sun made its way into the cave, Hiri suddenly solidified and called hir parents "Mom, Dad! Look over there! There is something there! Something really nice and very elegant." Hiri had discovered faint shadows through which carvings in the rock had been revealed against the smooth stone surface. These were three figures who seemed to dance in wave-like movements with outstretched arms. This figurative display was slightly beside the murals and the figures were much smaller than the other motifs. The stone these small graceful figures were carved in also looked different. The stone was a hexagon with its six sides perfectly cut, like nurseries in a beehive.

Calle marked the location of the cave on his Sahara map. His attempt to download more accurate coordinates from satellites failed. There was no signal. Ali and Beli were busy hiding the traces of their stay. They used their camel's saddlecloth to sweep it over the dusty ground, so that their foot prints were erased. It was best that no one found the place, before they themselves had returned. The Crassasius-Werdhem family was very determined on that point. This was their find!

The following year, *National Geographic* sent a lavish expedition to the Crassasius-Werdhem Cave. There were experts from the most diverse fields, each performing advanced experiments. Geologists determined that the rock had been formed fairly early in Earth's history and was nearly two billion years old. Paleoanthropologists suggested that the three figures on the smooth stone slab could belong to an extinct human species. The art historians and restaurateurs found that the carvings were made with extremely careful, very straight edges. At high magnification, the crystallographers found that all three carvings had a constant depth of three micrometers. Their conclusion was that the carvings were made by machine and consequently not of historical value. Forensics found no traces of hair or any other DNA material. The materials scientists performed various experiments and discovered that the smooth surface of the carved stone resisted all attempts to determine its degree of hardness. Glass-hard obsidian immediately crumbled and there was no trace of scratching on the surface. The researchers worked their way up the hardness scale and finally they would scratch the wall with a diamond tool. They did not make even the slightest scratch. That part of the wall was harder than diamond, the hardest substance that could be found in nature.

Now the astonishment of the materials scientists had turned to sweaty excitement. Using nitric acid, they dissolved some of the stone and send the sample to a lab in Japan. The color of the material changed between gray and black and the discoverers Crassasius-Werdhem had named it grartstone. The Japanese alchemists, by means of mass spectroscopy, made the astonishing discovery that the grartstone consisted essentially of rhenium diboride! In contrast to diamond, rhenium diboride is not found in nature, but is a ceramic material that is produced synthetically in modern laboratories.

This Japanese result was extremely astonishing. The experiments were repeated in different forms and independently of each other in laboratories around the world and they all came to the same conclusion. The material was unambiguously identified as rhenium diboride, ReB_2, of very high purity, i.e. “really hard stuff”.

One of the researchers, named Frida Barrenius and a resident of Bofors Bruk, expressed herself in a TV interview a little carelessly “this is a conundrum - not of this world”. Area 51 conspiracy supporters spread wildfire across the globe and cheered “What is it we have said for years? !”

XIII. Ecce Homo Humilis

In both Scotland and China, intensive work was unfolding to mass produce new individuals of Hiri. They were transported to a solitary farm outside Phoenix, Arizona, and there were now just over two thousand of them. They lived in specially built lengths and most of the time they devoted themselves to sitting still in deep, sunken meditation. Those who were active and awake studied a variety of subjects, ranging from modern and Bach-influenced music history to Tibetan sand mandala and late medieval Zen calligraphy. All were familiar with the lemmata and theorems of contemporary mathematics. The laws of physics in non-Euclidean space times had become peanuts for most of them.

For the public and curious reporters, the facility was a forbidden area. From the outside, the living quarters looked like ordinary horse stables, but the by Marines guarded interior hid a state-of-the-art laboratory landscape. The barns were filled with large transparent plastic tents in which the new hiris were located. They all shared a common problem. Equipped with an almost non-existent immune system, they were extremely susceptible to infections. The growth *ex vitro*, instead of in a womb, had deprived them of the mother's vital and necessary immune system through the umbilical cord. The slightest cold could eradicate the entire hiri colony.

Hiri hirself lived with hir parents. Thanks to hir growth in Sofia's uterus s-he had no major problems with infectious diseases, no more than anyone else in any case. Being allowed to live at home was one of the conditions for Hiri to agree to be cloned. But s-he visited regularly hir new relatives. Hiri and hir offspring felt a very strong sense of belonging. Together they developed a collective consciousness, where all became a single individual. This was an overwhelming feeling. The Phoenix complex's computers, the latest in Artificial Intelligence, the so-called AI machines, however, had no emotions. But the speed of the machines, albeit with limited precision, in harmony with the hiri collective's creativity and problem-solving ability, had led to breathtaking results. The combination AI-hiri was phenomenal. In all sectors of society, new solutions were found to old problems and improvements to things that were not perfect.

One of the predicted fears of the AI-domesday prophets, namely that the machines would develop awareness and aggressive lust for power and exterminate all of humanity, had come to shame. The hiri collective was far superior to the machines and had full control over worldly events. Hirinature did not allow itself to be molded into a Darwino-fascistoid stereotype. The question, however, was whether they, with their devout philosophy of peace, would survive in the long run. After all, there were still those who called themselves homo sapiens sapiens, the superwise man. It was not enough with just one *sapiens*, but these hominids demanded two, a bunch of Socrates squared! Such a colossal presumption was completely foreign to the timid hirinature. They also lacked use for the

Svante law, which was so important to people, which was named after the philosopher Svante Eriksson and which regulated social forms of human interaction.

One circumstance that spoke in favour of the survival of the hiris was their very special genetic material. The triple helix provided access to target beads, a special group of interconnected atoms whose main constituent consists of ribonucleic acid, i.e. RNA. The purpose of these target beads is to roll into the cells of the body and to anchor to the double helix of deoxyribonucleic acid, so that it can thereby convert to a triple helix. Without exaggeration, this can be said to be one of the greatest breakthroughs of evolution. The mutation brought a whole new dimension to human life: a really long life. These target beads conferred on the human cell system a unique hibernation ability that can be derived from simple viral RNA functions.

The intended use of the hiris by the military camp command was obvious.

XIV. Ad Astra vel Non Ad Astra

In many places, one was contemplating long distance space travel. One of the most popular targets was ζ^2 Ret (pronounced *zetatworetikulee*), a star quite similar to the Sun but almost forty light years away. That corresponds to millions of times the Earth's distance from the Sun. Members of the Area 51 club claimed that the Earth had on several occasions been visited by creatures from that star. Last actually not so long ago. And they had got water on their mill with the discovery of the Crassasius-Werdhem cave. However, there was no conclusive evidence for the hypothesis that the grartstone figures were about remains of extraterrestrials.

Likely more serious would be that, if the dating of the grartstone to a billion years is correct, ζ^2 Ret could hardly be the home of these hypothetical creatures. During that time, that star and its planet would have made as many as four whole laps around the centre of the Milky Way, wiggling along its path, bobbing up and down about the Galactic Plane. If relatively close to each other a billion years ago, ζ^2 Ret and the Sun would not be that near to each other today. They would have lost touch already a long time ago.

But the Area 51 club did not want to take on that criticism, disregarding it completely. So, they planned for a departure to ET's home. As bad as it is, ζ^2 Ret rushes away from us and with today's technology, the journey there would take at least two million years, which is why the hiris were needed. Not because they were expected to lie dormant there for millions of years, no, but because they were expected to deliver new ideas about vehicles, engines and fuel as well as logistics, *et cetera*. Even in the best case scenario, the travel time would be hundreds of years. Could hypothetical visitors have managed it? Could this really be reasonable?

A prevailing hypothesis among the ETists was that the grartstone was a remnant of aliens, in the style of the plaques on the Pioneer and Voyager probes. Idiotically enough, and in contrast to the grartstone, there was on these detailed information about where the depicted creatures were in the Milky Way. This, when the probes were sent away from a small speck in the image.

However, the purpose of the grartstone was unclear, but could be something as banal as space graffiti. "We've been here," so to speak, and nothing more. Like tourists in the Canary Islands carving their names, hearts, vaginal symbols and penises in the volcanic lava rock. What might contradict this interpretation was the effort the visitors had put in. The grartstone was seamlessly inserted into the material of the rock, the age of which had been determined to be two thousand million years. It seemed as if the granite had still been liquid, when the grartstone had ended up there. Then it would be another thousand million years before the first plants appeared on Earth. And another several hundred million years before the Earth was inhabited by a rich fauna, in other words, the grartstone people did not know what was going to happen on this unwelcoming planet. Or did they?

Perhaps the message of the grartstone was a notification that would bridge the eons between the existence of different life forms? A cry from the depths of the past "WE HAVE EXISTED !!!", a legacy to perhaps succeeding life forms? Because they disappeared, went extinct? In the beginning, the oxygen level in the Earth's atmosphere had been low and constant for a billion years, but then it had increased tenfold to today's pillar stand. Was the oxygen pure poison for them?

Speculation had not yet been exhausted. Apart from the possible drawings in the cave in the Ahoggar Massif, there was no evidence whatsoever of extraterrestrial visits to either Earth, the Moon or Mars.

Of course, there was also a serious scientific debate. Often the questions were of a purely academic nature and no one really expected any concrete answer. But in some areas, the identified problems seemed serious. For example, the age of the grartstone was considered to be of crucial importance. The age of the material was a fundamental parameter, without which all other discussion about its origin was meaningless, it was said.

One of the known methods for determining the age of a substance is to use radioactive decay of its isotopes. As the name suggests, rhenium diboride consists of rhenium and boron. For all practical purposes, boron has only stable isotopes. For the most common rhenium isotope, ^{187}Re, the half-life is more than three times the age of the universe and the decay product, i.e. ^{187}Os, makes up only a few percent of all osmium, of which there is not much at all to start with. The other rhenium isotopes are either stable or have much shorter half-lives and are thus unsuitable for geological dating. Due to the very low concentrations, this procedure is therefore encumbered with large error bars. The results of the measurements did not indicate an exact age, but it could be stated that the grartstone is definitely older than eight hundred million years. The scientific community dropped its jaw.

The most common way out of the ET dilemma was that "it is a very unusual type of meteorite and someone had found the stone and engraved it with some type of special instrument." No information, let alone more details, were given regarding the nature of the special instrument. Or how the grartstone had ended up in the rock, for that matter.

XV. The Return to Ahoggar

Hiri and hir parents were on their way to "their cave". They had returned to explore the mountain more thoroughly. Perhaps the mountain itself hid secrets and they wanted to look for clues that could lead to the solution of the grartstone mystery. This time they did not take the long overland road through the desert, but came by plane via Paris and Algiers directly to Tamanrasset. The former unassuming desert village, with uncomfortable ancestry from the French occupation and the cruel garrison of the Foreign Legion, had grown into a respectable metropolis in the middle of the Sahara.

On the city map in the guidebook, Calle found a place with a French name that indicated that it was a caravanserai. They took a taxi from the airport to the place, where they expected to see a lot of people in domestic clothes and, above all, lots of camels. There was not a camel, or dromedary for that matter, as far as the eye could see.

The place turned out to represent only the hostel part of a conventional caravanserai and was now intended mostly for rich foreign tourists. When asked why there were no camels there, the owner asserted that he could arrange a camel excursion including everything, with guides, photographing and a picnic basket. The whole thing would take four hours and the price was twenty thousand dinars per person, which was pure robbery. Before anyone in the family had time to get really angry, they thanked for the "generous offer" and said goodbye. The hotel owner probably thought that he might have exaggerated a little too much and shook his head, when he followed them with his eyes.

Calle, Sofia, and Hiri, of course, were still anxious to rent transportation, and they went to the grocery store *L'épicerie de Soleil*, where they had once met Ali and Beli. The store was still there, but had changed owners. The three became a little confused and did not really know what to do. They could not ask for Ali and Beli. No one would know who they were, they were called something completely different, something in Tuareg.

Hiri got an idea and began to draw in the dusty ground two male Tuareg figures, with cloths in front of their faces and wrapped around their heads, pointing to Calle to indicate their physique and height. That solved it all and it was not long before the two Tuaregs stood before them. This time the two men were not as frightened as the time they parted and endured the hugging and cheek kissing with equanimity. They even seemed to like it.

By drawing with their arms in the air how the sun went up and down, the blue friends managed to convey that they would meet the family in less than a week at their overnight quarters. Calle, Hiri and Sofia had their Moroccan caftans with them, freshly washed of course, but needed to buy most of what they would need for their desert trip. The market in Tamanrasset had pretty much everything imaginable on this Earth and they had no difficulty finding what they were looking for. But it took its little time. The negotiation and bargaining felt endless.

Then it finally set off. Ali and Beli had four dromedaries with them, which they borrowed from a relative, for a reasonable penny, of course. The two Tuaregs and Calle each had theirs and Sofia shared her with the little Hiri. In any case, they did not have to walk. The foreigners were unaccustomed to the rocking gait and at first had a hard time staying in the saddle. Once they got used to it, the ride became very sleepy and they had to stay awake so as not to fall off. After several hours of camel rocking, they finally came to what Ali claimed was an oasis to rest for the night. The "oasis" consisted of a single tree. One and only one tree, not large, maybe three meters high with a few branches. The tree was some kind of thorny coniferous tree with small gray-brown leaves. It hardly cast a shadow, not worth mentioning anyway, and stood all alone on the rocky desert earth. A beautiful mountain chain with sharp pointed contours could be seen at the end of the horizon.

The very existence of the tree indicated that there was water nearby. That the place was visited regularly was proved by the amount of human and goat droppings. There was surprisingly little camel poop, in fact, virtually any at all. This was probably because the camel poop was used to make fire for the night. There was not much wood to speak of, not even the smallest chip. After all, it was thankful that the little tree had been left standing.

Despite its barren beauty, it was not a nice camp. But Ali and Beli insisted that they spend the night there. After a short consultation, the three visitors came to the conclusion that it was probably best to trust the two blue experienced desert foxes. They tried to find some fecal-free spots on the ground to roll out their sleeping bags. The next morning they were awakened by a loud scream "there was a scorpion under my pillow !!!" Hiri stood trembling all over hir slender body. The scorpion had probably become just as scared, forgot to sting and hurried off to hide under the nearest rock. Calle comforted his beloved child soothingly. Deep down he was just as shocked and did not want to think about how it could have ended up here in the wilderness. An adult would probably be able to handle a sting from a scorpion, but a small human like Hiri would surely be seriously injured. Or maybe even die. They had no refrigerator and therefore nothing with them against either scorpion sting or serum against snake bites and decided that they would continue to be more careful. They started by shaking out their boots, before putting them on, which would become a habit and a common standing morning routine for the rest of the trip.

Already in the distance they recognised "their mountain". As the party approached the grartstone mountain, they encountered high fences. Signs with flash symbols and the text "100,000 Volt" indicated that the fences were electrified. In large letters, and also

Chinese characters, it was stated that the whole area was contaminated due to high levels of radioactivity and that it was life threatening to stay there. The message "Turn around!" was clear. Calle and the others knew, of course, that all this was one big lie: the Algerian state was trying to shut out unwelcome guests. The archeological site had become an extremely popular destination for ETists, utopians, religious fanatics as well as ordinary tourists.

The state's closure of the grartstone area meant a catastrophic loss of income for the local merchants and their imports for their own part of Ferrari, Mercedes, Lamborghini, Porsche and other desirable goods had largely stopped.

The private airlines lost their customers and the luxury hotels in Tamanrasset had to close, as the guests who were willing to pay their monstrous prices did not show up. The dealers' newly acquired busy hypocrisy returned to its original relaxing tea conversation and the city fell back into its pleasant desert slumber.

Sofia suggested that they should be going to the rear side of the mountain and find out if the cave would be more easily accessible from there. The others did not feel particularly convinced, but had no better idea. They set off, more or less optimistically, and eventually came to the end of the fence.

The back was open! That was unexpected. In addition, the mountain here was less steep and it was possible to climb up without aids.

XVI. Communards of the Caliphate

Climbing is arduous and sweaty. About halfway up to the top there was a ledge where you could rest. Oddly enough, it felt like someone else had already been there before them. Hiri discovered a half-hidden, empty anchovy can whose pink color blended in with the mountain. “No wonder it felt strange,” the little one stated, “so that was the forbidden mountain.” They all looked at each other in surprise and shook their heads. “What is this supposed to mean?” Calle asked, most rhetorically. “This reminds me of the tale of Snow White,” said Hiri, “when the dwarves return to the cottage in the woods. Hope our visitors are just as kind.”

This naive hope, however, was not fulfilled. In front of them, two figures with Chinese-made machine guns suddenly appeared. They stared in amazement at Hiri, this homunculus whose like they had never seen before, and grunted something incomprehensible. The Crassasius-Werdhem family and the two Tuaregs knew no better than to raise their arms. One of the bandits ordered them, pointing with the Chinese-made machine gun, to go down on their knees. It was probably best to obey. At least, for the time being. The men were not Tuaregs and did not hide their faces behind the veil. Instead, they wore unkempt ruffled beards. They also did not wear blue clothes, but were generally dirty.

Calle whispered to his people, even though he did not think the two Chinese-made machine-gun armed figures would understand their language, "we are four and a half against two and their weapons are made in China. They are probably junk and will click. I think we can take them." Hiri did not like that bit of "and a half," but nodded in agreement. S-he was not as convinced about the "click" thing either.

Sofia frowned, parted her legs slightly and stared at the smaller of the two thugs. He licked his lips, got ready to approach her and Sofia got inside her panties, ran her right ring finger up into her vagina, spilled a good portion of secretions and stroked it over the back of his hand. He was not versed in the subject of women and had no experience whatsoever of their intimate forms of intercourse. Sofia smiled and looked up. Right into his eyes. This made him ashamed or confused or whatever it was, but he lost for a fraction of a second the concentration on what he was doing. Sofia had waited for this moment and quickly as lightning connected a strong thigh grip around the man's waist. He stared at her in surprise. At the same time, both Calle and Beli had thrown themselves at the other bandit and overthrown him. Meanwhile, Ali had taken the arms of the man sitting on Sofia behind his back and held them. Hiris' contributing effort was to feverishly search their bags for something they could tie the two attackers with. In the end, she found a pair of Sofia's nylon tights and these had to do the job. To begin with, at least.

Ali pulled a few ropes from his camel saddlebag, like the one that Sofia had wanted to buy, and tied the arms and legs of the two men. He also quickly made loops that he pulled over their heads and anchored the ropes around a large rock. Then all five (here you go, Hiri) friends sat in a circle and discussed the events. And what they would do next. One thing Hiri thought was worth pointing out was that the click hypothesis had never been tested by them in real life. "Well, let's see," Calle said, unsecured one of the machine guns and pulled the trigger. The Chinese-made machinery woke up spitting to life and sprayed life-threatening projectiles all over the ledge. "We made it anyway," Calle looked at the party and grinned broadly.

"What should we do with the prisoners? They are clearly of the supervillainous type of villains and should be handed over to the police", Calle said. An almost tumultuous palaver erupted, where everyone spoke in each other's mouths. "One by one", Sofia finally said loudly, pointing to Beli, that he should start talking.

Beli seemed to understand what Sofia wanted from him and he spoke Tuareg with French fragments inserted, very slowly and articulated. This would not have been much help in itself, but he gestured at the same time as if he were playing a charade. Sofia and her family immediately picked up a few things and thought they understood most of what Beli wanted to say. Throughout the show, Ali sat and nodded eagerly. He agreed with his cousin completely. It was concluded that Beli's plan was probably the only sensible thing they could do. In short, it was that unfortunately they had to cancel the trip to the grartstone cave and that they needed to return to Tamanrasset immediately. To the police station there. And hand over the villains to the local law enforcement. Then they would come back to the mountain. Now that they knew how to get to the archeological site, it would all go much faster and smoother. They would leave the next morning.

The shooting exercise had caused an enormous noise which was amplified by the echo from the surrounding mountains. This had attracted more unwelcome visitors to their camp. A group of young people, armed with long knives and pistols, suddenly appeared in front of the small party that was heating canned food over a fire. They received blows to the body and head and finally lay flat on their stomachs. Beli had a boot heel in his neck and Calle had been beaten bloody by the larger of the two who had previously been their prisoners. He who had tried to rape Sofia gave her such a strong slap that she almost fainted. Ali lay stretched out on the ground. He had been shot with a pistol by what appeared to be the attackers' leader.

Long afterwards, they realized that the two men with the Chinese-made machine guns and their companions belonged to a group of French-born descendants of North Africans, mostly Algerians and Moroccans, who in Paris had formed what they called a "revolutionary cell". By "revolutionary", they meant that they belonged to a fundamentalist Islamist movement, but which was really conservative and old-fashioned.

The word cell could indicate that the movement was relatively small, with few members. They had been trained for a few weeks by Syrian brothers in guerrilla warfare.

Admittedly, they had been few in number at first, but then the movement had spread first over most of France and then over virtually all of Europe. At first, smaller terrorist attacks had been organized within the European Union, where one could travel freely without presenting passports or the like, but recently they also operated in North Africa. Since then, the cell had multiplied and grown avalanche-like due to its "spectacular success" throughout all of the Sahel area.

The name of the revolutionary cell had been replaced by the "Islamist Liberation Front". The public media, especially in the western world, had with their detailed reports endowed the Front with a high status in large parts of the eastern world. Most viewed film clips on international media platforms were video recordings of beheadings.

In addition to car bombs and suicide missions, they now also engaged in the kidnapping of Westerners. For their release, considerable sums in ransom were required. This activity was very lucrative and financed almost the entire operational activity.

The people who were part of the Front's administrative part sat safely and comfortably in various big cities around the world and had their rich livelihood taken care of by the princes of the Middle East. Usually, the lives of these Front leaders did not strictly follow the strict injunctions of Sharia law. Things like alcohol consumption and homosexual prostitution were seen between the fleshy fingers.

As for Calle, Hiri and Sofia, the Islamist Liberation Front sent its demands to the Prime Minister of Australia, a robust woman named NamNam NumNum-Smith, who had a fit of laughter when she read the message. She was half Aboriginal, belonging to the Ngunnawal people, and half Caucasian, with a British felon as her ancestor. She was generally very nice and mostly in a good mood. She loved to laugh. The ILF demanded four million dollars for the lives of Beli, Calle, Hiri and Sofia and the release of Ahmad ibn-Ben el Brutto, a notorious terrorist from Paris who had been arrested in Brussels the year before after a failed assassination attempt on a French agricultural politician.

The Australian Department of Home Affairs had informed NamNam NumNum-Smith that as far as was known there were no Australian citizens in the area. In addition, the official policy was not to pay any state money to kidnappers and terrorists. This rule was not always followed unofficially, a circumstance the Islamist Liberation Front seemed too faithful to. NamNam NumNum-Smith considered it unworthy of an Australian Prime Minister to respond to the rude e-mail, but gave her answer during a press conference in Canberra, which was a short and clearly resounding "NO !!!"

The reporters present had been invited by the Australian Prime Minister to also ask a question at the end of the interview: why on earth did they demand the release by the Australian Government of four people, who are neither Australian citizens nor had ever set foot in Australia?

The Front was not prepared for this. Which of these stupid warriors had made the claim that the three whites were Australian citizens? The misjudgment of the nationality of the hostages gave the kidnappers an element of uncertainty. In sheer frustration, but also to emphasise their cruel determination, they beheaded Beli in a live broadcast on international media.

As if this were not enough of abominations, Calle and Hiri were forced to witness how Sofia was raped several times right in front of their eyes. Hiri was terribly shocked and despairing. S-he cried incessantly for days and repeatedly asked the same question "How can we humans be so cruel? How can we do that to our own species?" Carl Crassasius had lost several layers of enamel due to all the gnashing of teeth. The accursed powerlessness filled him with furious madness.

XVII. The Viper

It had not taken the kidnappers particularly long before they had located our friends' camels at the foot of the mountain. The camels had their feet loosely tied together, so that they could move but not run away too far. In the desert, you did not want to get rid of the camels. For nomads in general, and Tuaregs in particular, camels were their most valuable belonging. The camels gave them milk, meat and combustible material, and were on top of all water-efficient means of transport. At weddings, the gift to the bride's father was counted in the number of camels. In return, brides from wealthy families were able to bring with them a considerable number of camels in dowry. However, among many nomads, a camel was worth more than a woman.

Upon arrival, Calle and Company had not had time to examine the mountain around the rock shelf, where they had camped. They had therefore never discovered the terrorists' weapons cache and food warehouse very close by. It was there, the two attackers had been deployed as guards. Now their camels carried the terrorists' weapons in wooden boxes and water in plastic cans. The villains were a total of just over two dozen people.

They all went on foot. By following the movement of the sun across the sky, Calle concluded that their movement was largely in a southerly direction. If they were on their way to the ancient city of Agadez in Niger, they would have more than a thousand kilometers of inaccessible desert in front of them. By foot! The family's feet were already broken, chapped and began to bleed in some places. But two days later, they arrived at a larger camp with several military tents, as well as motor vehicles of various kinds. Trucks with tarpaulins and open off-road Chinese-made military vehicles. Several of them were equipped with similarly Chinese-manufactured machine guns.

The terrorists had not yet given up the plan to extort a ransom for the three prisoners. They threw them on the bed of one of the trucks, which too was "Made in China" and even had a large star, together with four smaller ones, painted on the tarpaulin. Under this rubber blanket it was probably over fifty centigrades hot and the thick acrid air completely unbearable. The journey on the platform became very uncomfortable, which was a severe understatement. The truck's poor suspension and the non-existent "road" in the middle of the desert made them fly around like autumn leaves in stormy weather among all sorts of goods on the flatbed. The fragile Hiri got bruises all over hir little body. Calle tried with all his might to keep Hiri as still as possible, while he had difficulty keeping himself in place.

In addition to the injuries to their aching feet, Calle, Hiri and Sofia had dry, bloody lips and cracked skin on the backs of their noses. Taking care of their hygiene was but a dream and they stank worse than the International Space Station, the ISS, of the "glorious" past. The wounds from numerous bites of sand fleas had become infected and were malodorous spots of pus. No one in the bandit gang cared about them. They began to understand that the kidnappers' demands for ransom had been met with a cold hand and the three felt utterly abandoned.

In the midst of all the misery, Sofia developed a vicious form of amoeba dysentery with violent abdominal pain and bloody diarrhea. She had to "go to the toilet" for countless numbers of time. She was unable to keep anything she had taken into her mouth. She quickly became scalded by a very high fever and for the most part was no longer conscious. Calle and Hiri were terrified. They saw Sofia slowly fading away. It had been a little over a week and now she was just a skeleton with loosely hanging skin. Due to starvation and dehydration, her usually lush bust had now been transformed into a pair of lifeless shrunken cocoa beans.

Sofia tried to climb up from her scanty emergency camp. Calle tapped his hand on the small window of the cab to make the truck stop. Hiri gently helped to get Sofia off the platform. There was not a bush or a rock to hide behind and Sofia stumbled away about thirty meters, before she suddenly lifted her shalaba, crouched down and let it rush out of her. She was turned away from the truck and its gazes. She looked dazed in front of her.

Suddenly, she froze. Around her, s-shaped tracks appeared in the sand and they were all aimed at her. It was as if she were sitting in the hub of a spoke wheel. Sofia immediately understood what she was seeing. It was the traces of a sidewinder, probably a horned viper, and one of the world's most venomous snakes. With its cover mimicking the environment, the snake usually lies buried in the sand and is basically impossible to detect. Before leaving home, Sofia had tried in vain to see this aggressive viper in the zoo's terrarium. No matter how intensely she had stared, she had been unable to detect it, even though she knew the animal was there somewhere.

Terrified, Sofia rose extremely slowly from her sitting position. She was afraid that "she had shit on the reptile's nest and that it would bite her in the ass" at any second. Sofia felt an uncontrollable will to live grow inside her and she just wanted to get out of there. She would not die of snakebite today!

But what would she do? She could not call for help. That would be completely meaningless and also risked alerting the reptile. Beneath her? She stepped extremely slowly, as in slow motion, into her own footprints to get back to the truck. After a time that felt as long as the age of the universe, she finally reached Calle and Hiri unscathed, who helped her back to her mattress. She was bathed in sweat. Completely leached. And fell asleep on the spot.

Hiri lay next to hir mother, with hir head level with Sofia's and hir feet reaching right down to hir mother's navel. Hiri whispered in Sofia's ear that s-he wanted to tell her that s-he had met a boy s-he was very fond of. His name was Søren Svaalby. He was a youngster from the Norwegian North Calotte and with his 155 cm in stockings, he must be described as short grown, but next to Hiri he looked like a giant. Hiri felt very safe with him. Most recently, when the annstruation had arrived, Hiri discovered that s-he felt like a woman and decided to belong to that sex from now on.

The pronouns *s-he* and *hir* would henceforth be changed to *she* and *her*. She wished to keep her name Hiri. She hoped she would meet Søren again. Sofia only faintly sensed what her daughter had told her.

Calle fed his wife very carefully first with broth, then with canned tuna and after four weeks she had regained most of her life force. Sofia had developed a huge appetite and could eat a whole loaf of bread for breakfast, cut lengthwise, breaded with lots of peanut butter and filled with bananas. She regained her former weight within a few weeks.

Under the circumstances, the three of the Crassasius-Werdhem family were in relatively good spirits. What was missing from them was their freedom. They had wandered around, seemingly aimlessly, in the desert and did not know, if they would survive the next day.

For how long would their kidnappers drag them around?

Main Act

I. Morals of Faith

In the hands of the Islamist Liberation Front, Hiri had plenty of time to think. She thought of virtually everything. For example, of what is called religion, which was something she had learned in school. Her parents never visited the church, the synagogue, the mosque or any other sort of temple establishment, for that matter. Nor were they interested in all sorts of fetishism, schamanism, voodoo and similar creeds.

That thing with the Decalogue, or the *Ten Commandments* as it was also called, she thought was strange. Very strange, actually. Killing someone came first in fifth place, 5(10)! But working on the weekend came in third, 3(10). So it was more sinful to work on a Sunday than to take the life of another soul. With a full two places, *sic!* Only one step worse was not showing respect to one's parents. Hmm..., sort of okay 4(10). But to brutally take someone's life was thus in fifth place and hence in all essentials relatively *harmless*. Killing in Place Five !!! A religion that did not consider it extremely reprehensible to kill another individual was not a religion for Hiri.

Another thing she remembered was that the disciples had been instructed by their master to "walk barefoot and clothed in the garments of poverty..." As she understood it, the present disciples showed not many signs of compliance with these words of their Savior. One of the worst in that department was the pope himself with his golden robes, the diamond-studded tiara, the flashy stone on the ring that people had to kiss, and his custom-made golden velvet pumps. With them *he*, because the pope had always been a male, strode around, boasting in his magnificent castles and grandiose palaces. The shear amount of jewels and art treasures kept in pappa's *castelli* would make the director of the Louvre fade with envy.

Really terrifying, however, was that time, when she witnessed a priest blessing the weapons of soldiers that were about to go to war. The meaning of the act was "May these weapons kill as many as possible!" And that's fully understandable and okay, it's only in place five. Right?

But completely incomprehensibly odd is the tenth commandment 10(10) which speaks of lust for slaves, oxen and donkeys! Is this a joke? Hiri asked herself that question, but also wondered if this, in today's modern society, has lost its timeliness - or was it still in place? Slaves? Oxen? Donkeys? "Seriously!?", she shook her head and sighed deeply.

But worst of all was probably that there was no mentioning of the atrocities on small choire boys. The gross pedophilia committed by priests, bishops, cardinals, popes and the like *men* throughout the centuries was apparently not a breach of commandments.

The ways of the Holy Church are unfathomable.

II. The Revelation

Something completely different, that Hiri had also been thinking of, had to do with this infinite universe. The theory of relativity and space travel. And the events in the extremely small microscopic quantum world. In her mind she went through all these different arguments that people had put forward and the equations that were meant to describe what was happening.

And then she got stuck on one detail. "I must have misunderstood something," she thought. But the thought, or the wrong track, had stuck and gnawed at her. "When you say that space is curved ... Hm, curved in relation to what, how does space know that it is positively or negatively curved? Relatively an absolute space? When you want to deviate from the curved path, do you then need to travel faster than light?"

She was familiar with the theory behind the *Miguel engine*, commonly also known as "Alcubierre's warp drive", for strolling around at superluminal speeds. But Hiri never felt really convinced of the correctness of the theory. Finally, she decided to prove her possible mistake by proving its opposite. She would be very technical with all equations and do it from scatch. In a thorough and solid Einstein spirit. First a *Gedankenexperiment*, then the mathematical formulation of the same. If it proved useful.

She asked her dad Calle to bribe one of the guards, "he who looks kind of kind", that the next time he would go to a market, he should buy some sheets of paper and a pen. The guard who looked kind thought that this could not be dangerous for the brotherhood in any way and two weeks later he had returned with the ordered goods. In addition to paper and pencil, he also brought with him soap and lice repellent, the total cost of which was far above the normal market price. So much for the kind look.

Calle, Hiri and Sofia all had lice and it itched something really awful. Treatment with the purchased powder required access to water, something they did not even have enough of to meet their daily needs. They rubbed in the dry lice remedy anyway and felt a little relieved.

During one of those liberating moments, Hiri pondered something she had long been fascinated by. It was this fantastic *Möbius band* that looked like the sign of *Infinity*, but did not have to be more than a twisted strip of paper whose ends had been glued together. This Möbius band has two sides, an upper and a lower side. When you follow the "road" on one side, the front say, you will find that after a while you come to the same place, but on the back side of the band. Hiri realised, like so many others before her, that the quickest way to get to that other side would be to pierce directly through the paper.

This meant that, for a moment, one had to leave the two-dimensional world of the Möbius band and step through it via the third dimension of space, that is the one we live in. She asked herself the obvious question.

"Would it be possible to move, and this at a pace much slower than light, to a place that could seemingly be very far away in our universe?" She answered herself "Yes, of course, but that would require a dimensional penetration."

The next day, when Hiri could finally forget the annoying itching for a while, she took out her pen and thought of writing formulas in a tiny style, which would be just readable to an eye with exceptionally good eyesight. She only had three sheets and these had to last all the way forward. She had therefore started with the first steps of the theoretical derivation in her head, that is without any paper. She used the formalism that had been developed, independently and for three decades, by the three extremely talented mathematicians Martin Muntsch, Katarina Bergdorff and Svetlana Shakovskaya. In different parts of the world, these curious people had dedicated their lives to something called *topology*.

However, this subject had nothing to do with the science of mice, as might have been believed due to the Italian prefix *topo* and its ambiguous meaning. It is worth noting that, despite its mathematical complexity, this Muntsch-Bergdorff-Shakovskaya metric describes something as seemingly trivial as the distance between two places or events in spacetime.

Hiri worked well and already made significant progress. Good as well, but then she had to decide on an assumption that was based on how matter is distributed in the macrocosm and microcosm, respectively. In the great universe, the scholars said, matter was very evenly distributed, and the whole thing looked the same in whatever direction one looked. On the other hand, it is very clumpy and grainy in the small-scale, Hiri thought. And she decided not to make the assumption of the universe's "homogeneity and isotropy" - beautifully complicated words for very banal things, she also thought. However, allowing the world to be non-homogeneous and non-isotropic made the equations she arrived at much more cumbersome and more difficult to solve than those in the case of "homogeneity and isotropy".

Hiri had previously read the unpublished work of a Swiss mathematician. This Guido Nachtmeier had suggested that one could connect the theory of relativity, which was responsible for the universe, with quantum physics, that is, the theory of the microcosm, with the help of a Frommsmann bridge. The Frommsmann bridge was an advanced mathematical tool that was distinguished by its incredibly calculable elasticity.

The bridge could be twisted and crumbled or also expanded and shrunk as needed. It was formable and followed the bends of the local space at one end and joined this maze of unpredictable tunnel roads at the other. The application led to the dimension penetration theorem.

Quite pleased with herself, Hiri completed her equation building. In the last sentence of the paper, she suggested that the theory of dimensional penetration should be named after Frommsmann and Nachtmeier, that is, be described in the Frommsmann-Nachmeier metric. As she put it herself, she had "just put together the work of others and shown that these led to exact solutions to the extended Einstein field equations." Hiri was very timid in nature, a very modest being.

All of this was difficult mathematics to master and therefore probably quite boring for many. Besides, it was just theory.

III. Fabulous Friends

They wandered apparently aimlessly around in the endless desert landscape that changed in shape and color, from pointed alpine-like mountain ranges over endless fruitless plains to gently undulating sandy dunes and from dirty gray-brown over a juicy mustard yellow to a deep cinober red. The further south they came, the redder the ground became.

After four long months, they finally arrived in Kano, a city in northern Nigeria, on the border with the Sahara. There was vegetation here, not much, but still an occasional shrub here and an occasional overgrown chubby tree with hard leaves over there. The grass was sparse, dry and yellow and its straws were fewer than the vultures that sat all around the rooftops and stared at the life below them, impatiently waiting for this soon to end.

The day before it had been the last Lent of this year's Ramadan and today would be a party! Kano is widely known throughout Nigeria for organising Eid al Fitr's carnival-like festivities with food, drink, music and dance. There, daring equestrian games are displayed by magnificently dressed warriors on their slender thoroughbred Arabs. Most of the riders belonged to the Fulani people and these were all Muslims. The Muslim holiday of Eid al Fitr began early in the morning with a prayer by the Emir of Kano in front of thousands of believers. The emir's shrill voice cut through the morning cool air and his guttural sounds sounded strange and frightening to the foreigners.

But it was not because the festivities in Kano that the terrorists had dragged the Crassasius-Werdhem family to the outskirts of the city. Their kidnappers' plan was to sell them as slaves. They would end their journey in bondage! The three sat tied up on the dusty ground and saw how the terrorist leader gestured talking to three men in long caftans and with fez-like caps on their heads. After a long line of interludes, where people walked away, screaming and waving apparently despairing with their arms in the air, only to return after a short while with a more collected face. And then the performance and the spectacle began all over again.

After an unusually long round of negotiations, even for Oriental traditions, the three merchants and the leaders of the terrorists had agreed. A considerable bundle of money changed hands and Calle, Hiri and Sofia were thrown on the platform of a pick-up truck. They were now slaves to the three fez-wearing individuals in their long caftans. Gold gleamed as they opened their mouths.

It was getting late and the slave traders decided to stay overnight and take part in the partying in town. They left their recently made purchases chained to the car body. At the next morning's first dawn light, however, they set off. For the three passengers on the platform, the journey became at least uncomfortable and sometimes even very dangerous, when the car drove into potholes and they flew high into the air. The road pits were many and the bumping never stopped. They only halted for emergency services and the number of pee breaks could be counted on one finger. They went all the way east and Calle said "They might be transporting us to Niger or Sudan. What is worse of the two I do not know." Hiri and Sofia just looked trumpeted and shrugged. "Shit the same," Sofia thought. The pick-up truck rolled on for twelve hours, between sunrise and sunset.

After three days, the car stopped in the middle of the day in the square in a small "town", God knows where. Should they be auctioned off now? Should they be divided and would they end up in different places? Calle, Hiri and Sofia were scared. Hiri whispered, turning to her parents, "Do not worry. I will find you wherever you are. I love you", and she hugged them tightly.

There was no large crowd gathered in the square waiting for an auction. There was nothing that could indicate that something special, out of the ordinary, would happen. They were ordered to step off the platform and sit on the ground. After a while, an ordinary dusty car drove up next to them and a tall man stepped out, perhaps in his upper forties. Unlike the three bronze-skinned fezars, this man was clearly black. He was wearing a dark western suit, with a white shirt but no tie, and was wearing black leather shoes. He went over to the slave traders, gave them a large bunch of money and then came to the three prisoners.

So this was their new master. He looked quite nice and at least had no whip with him. They should be together, what a relief! “Hold on to your hat,” Calle joked, grumpy. The newcomer said in nearly perfect English that he would free them from their bondage and that they should then get in the car. There was water and fruit for them. They drove away from there.

After a couple of kilometers outside the village, the man stopped the car and turned off the engine. He turned around to face the three in the back seat, and looked at them. They stopped chewing and looked back. The man smiled and said in a gentle voice “I am Wonokwu N’Barku, but you can call me John. My organisation has paid the ransom for you and we are now on our way to what I call home.” The three were completely taken aback and speechless. After a while, when they had gathered and regained their speech, they bombarded John with questions. What type of organisation it was, if they were now free, where they were going, why his organisation had paid for them and how much, *et cetera.* John calmly answered all their questions, except the one concerning how much he had paid for them. He also did not want to go into detail about what his “organisation” was about.

He told them that he belonged to the Ibo people of southern Nigeria and that he would take them to Enugu, the capital of Iboland. When he was a little boy, civil war broke out in Iboland, as the mostly Christian Ibo people wanted to establish their own sovereign state, called Biafra. That part of Nigeria was the country's most developed and prosperous province. There were more and better schools, more paved and better roads, more developed infrastructure and more modern and better healthcare. Illiteracy has long been a thing of the past, everyone could read and write. Although the majority of the black Ibo population was Christian, they were tolerant of other religions and there were, for example, many mosques in Biafra. The intention was to introduce a democratic system of government, with the permission of several political parties and free elections.

The military government of mainly Muslim Nigeria opposed these aspirations for independence and tried by military force to make Biafra to re-establish itself as one of the states in Africa's largest nation. In the armed conflict, Biafra defended bravely and the war dragged on.

The violence escalated and was increasingly perpetrated against the civilian population, ordinary people of all ages, men, women and children. John witnessed how soldiers of the government forces beheaded his father. Then they killed his mother with a machete. He himself had kept himself hidden in a half-full water barrel.

John had suddenly become orphaned and wandered in despair among all these corpses that lay scattered everywhere, on the road, in the houses and in the square. Only a few of the villagers were still alive. An old hunched woman saw the little screaming child. She wrapped her gnarled arms around the boy and hugged and tried to comfort him, patting him gently on the back. He remembered that he woke up in her arms and felt a tender security. After all these terrible days. John stayed with her for what he thought was several weeks. One morning she was lying lifeless on her sleeping mat and he was alone again.

Biafra did not want to give in and join the large military-controlled confederation. There was no cease-fire. In any case, no one held. The military government went to extremes to bring the breakaway nation to its knees by brutally starving them. An unprecedented famine broke out, resulting in millions of starving people, especially children.

John was among the few happy survivors. He had been taken care of by a couple of nurses who took him to a Red Cross station in the middle of the jungle. With the help of what they called "välling", they made his emaciated skeletal body recover. Eventually he felt better and was able to run around again and play with the other equally fortunate children who lived at the station. Best of all, he thought, was playing football. One of the sisters named Lena showed the children how to kick a ball. Lena was very good at it. The children shouted for joy. Lena was also good at telling stories and she described many adventures of a little girl. It was like this, through Lena's persistent perseverance, the children learned English. And that the girl, whose name was Pippi, lived in a country, far, far away called Sweden.

John took a break. Then he continued, "People

from your country helped the people in my country, when they were in their greatest need. You were our best friends. And we want to show you now that you still are. We wanted to help you get back to freedom."

On the not always completely navigable roads, the two-thousand-kilometer journey from Nokou in Chad to Enugu in Nigeria took several days. There was a lot of yam stew or cassava sticks for dinner along with very good beer. In even the smallest African village, consisting of say three huts, there was at least one bar, where wonderful pilsners were served. And that for a trifle. The trucks they encountered on the road were mostly loaded with trays of beer bottles. People here seemed to understand how to live life. Calle shone, "I did not think I would live long enough to be a part of this. That's lovely. And so great beer!" Sofia and Hiri agreed and they laughed something really violent. John shook his head with a smile.

Once in Enugu, they were greeted by a whole crowd of people who spontaneously began to clap their hands when the Cassasius-Werdhems got out of the car. The cheerleaders were both adults and children and they had come from a school nearby. It turned out that John was one of the teachers there. He had driven them to his home. His wife and their three adult children stood in front of the entrance and laughed happily. The reception was dizzying. They felt an all-encompassing warmth and love and their gratitude knew no bounds. They mourned Ali and Beli and wished the two of them could be here with them.

John drove them almost a thousand more kilometers, to the Cameroonian capital Yaoundé. From there, the three flew via Khartoum in Sudan to Frankfurt in Germany and then on to their home country. They had no luggage to check in. Their belongings and backpacks had been confiscated by their kidnappers long ago. They arrived at the airport with only a couple of plastic bags to take on board. In Nigeria they had bought a giant jar of the world's tastiest peanut butter and in Cameroon several bars of the world's nicest chocolate.

The parting from this amazing friend Wonokwu N'Barku, alias John, ended in tears.

IV. The Strongest Man on Earth

Life at home had changed and could not be recognised. In the great country of the West, many had completely lost their minds and chosen a fat clown as their political leader.

He reminded Hiri of the Strong Man on an old-fashioned amusement park, skinnyfat in a red-and-white cross-striped tight-fitting swimsuit, with loose bingo wings on the porky upper arms. “Mister President” looked ridiculous with his silly hairstyle, but at the same time dangerous with his narrow pig-staring cold eyes and his cynically down-pulled corners of his mouth. He pretended to be one of the richest men in the world. At the same time, however, he was extremely stingy, towards his employees and co-workers, but also towards his own family.

A Christmas anecdote from the time when his children were still small describes him in a nutshell: his children had complained that the Santa Claus who had come to their home was a woman. He then replied that they got a female Santa Claus, because women are cheaper than men. “Thank God they have lower wages.”

Another little anecdote tells of a thing that happened during the great pandemic period, when nearly a million of his subjects would die as a result of a terrible viral infection. He explained that, since *Pan demi* had to do with flying half-boys in green tights, one would not have to be vaccinated: “What harm could flying half-boys do?” After falling on his nose himself, he changed his mind, however. “Boys can’t fly.”

Despite his clown-like demeanor, this man was not a funster. At his many, according to some too many, stunted public appearances, he had innumerable times shamelessly called himself “genius”, after which his followers had cheered in drunken ecstasy. He proclaimed his message in a monotonous sluggish voice like a grumpy child who had lost his pacifier.

Standard phrases were of the type
“There are nice black people out there”
pause
“there are nice black people out there”
longer pause
“but they are very few”
pause
“but they are *very very few*, I tell you.”

Wild white cheers. And in that style it continued. For many years. Too many, thought too few.

After being re-elected by a good margin, he considered that he had been given a mandate to carry out his plan, as he had long intended. Anyone who wanted and had the energy could have read about the man’s ambitions in his book “I, the Strongest Man on Earth”. There you could read, among other things, that he considered the woman to be clearly inferior to the man or, as he put it, "The woman’s most interesting part is her pussy, whereas the man’s most interesting part is his brain”.

In the same spirit, he profiled himself with his pure

unpolluted German blood and called for the supremacy of the white race. The brown, black, yellow and red, although there were not so many of them anymore, were vermin and he had been commissioned by God to put an end to them. "I am the Chosen One! I am your Matthias!"

Did that man's ignorance know no limits?

When someone confronted him publicly with excerpts from his own literary exploits, he refused to respond and waved away the criticism with nasty and ridiculous personal attacks on the offender. His hallmark was the lie. And, therefore, many of his followers refused to believe in what they called his opponents' slander.

His latest move was to insult France and its "abuse of its right to *veto*" in a very vulgar way at the UN Security Council. The dispute concerned the final decolonisation of Western Sahara, which was occupied by Morocco. France, an old cruel colonial power itself, supported Morocco and denied the people of Western Sahara the right to self-determination. France's motives were, of course, completely selfish and focused on Western Sahara's rich mineral resources and gas and oil deposits.

Similar considerations governed the actions of the man in the White House. In particular, the large deposits of uranium, a hot-coveted element, were of great interest to many states, especially the totalitarian ones. The first research reports from Camp Hiri, which began to seep in, said that the propulsion of spacecraft ultimately needed nuclear power. If you wanted to get somewhere. And he wanted that, among other things to seize other, mineral-rich, celestial bodies.

One thing that had caught his attention and approval was that Western Sahara had a long wall that stretched several hundred kilometers from north to south and divided the country in two lengthwise, like a cut-up baguette. He thought this was very interesting, because he himself was also building a wall. In Western Sahara, the “wall”, a pile of sand and rubble, had originally been built as protection against the Islamist Liberation Front Police, who poured in from the Sahara and harassed the population. Nowadays, however, the danger came from the other side of the wall, the fertile and rich part of the country towards the sea, which was occupied by Moroccan military forces.

Referring to the “provocation of foreign power”, France sent military troops to Western Sahara to “assist the rightful administrators of the area”, that is Morocco and its military. This one was extremely well equipped, with the best and most modern weapons on the market. The nomadic defenders were equipped with surviving repeat rifles from the Second Boer War. The White House reacted strongly to the “abuse and rape of the poor defenseless people in Western Sahara” and sent an aircraft carrier with other naval squadrons to the Atlantic coast of Western Sahara. The strong man showed his muscles.

Now, it was France he had to show that he really had balls. But Frenchmen are Frenchmen and Frenchmen are stubborn. And had a long-cultivated inferiority complex vis-à-vis the great country in the west. France expanded its military presence and began bombing the dunes and nomadic tents in the eastern parts of Western Sahara. That was too much for the White House and the strong man's navy started shelling the western side of Western Sahara from the sea. That's how it all started. And eventually escalated.

Thousands of miles away, others seized the opportunity and began to quarrel. The bombings took place within a minute of each other and it was never ensured who it was who had first pressed the button. The 20-kilogram bombs had exploded in Tel Aviv and Tehran at the same time, causing enormous destruction and death. Now more "great powers" came to life and a great war with devastating consequences began to take shape.

V. Two Thousand Hiris

Hiri had finally seen her Søren Svaalby again and the two were sitting in the bathtub in Søren's bathroom. The water was steaming hot and the two discussed the world situation. "That damned man is a complete moron," she pressed frustratedly between her teeth. In her anger she strained so hard that small bubbles appeared in the tub's water, as if there were goldfish there. "Oops, sorry!" she shouted in horror. Søren's answer came immediately, but deeper and more like a bass tuba. Hiri felt less embarrassed and they both laughed heartily. "But we do not let it become a habit," she remarked.

After getting out of the bathtub and drying off, they went out on the evening-warm balcony. "We're on the verge of the last world war, damn it!" Hiri swore, "I must go to my sisterbrothers immediately," she said firmly. Søren added, "I'll come along!" Hiri gave him a loving look and nodded gratefully.

Hiri contacted her parents and asked, in fact ordered, them to immediately get to a place far away from all human settlements. Preferably somewhere in the wilderness. Hiri did not know if this would be enough to put Calle and Sofia safe. Hiri was afraid that if there was a war between the "superpowers", there would be hardly anywhere you could be safe. The radioactive fallout would kill almost all life on Earth. And the prolonged cooling would lead to a new snowball planet. In short term, this would mean the end of what nature had created and nurtured for hundreds of millions of years, with the possible exception of a few microbial survivors.

Calle and Sofia were hesitant at first and did not want to leave, but Hiri was so determined and assertive that they finally gave in and started packing their backpacks. The two were on the same wavelength and had agreed to return to the mountain with the Crassasius-Werdhem cave. "If we're going to have to hide, far away from everything, it's a good place. There we can at least do some good. We can always hope. But we have to keep in touch with each other - promise us!" "I call every day," said Hiri, hugging her parents tightly. She hoped her parents had forgotten that there was no coverage there. Calle started "But Hiri darling, there is no", but Sofia interrupted him, "And we look forward to it!"

The next day, Hiri and Søren arrived at Camp Hiri outside Phoenix, Arizona. They were dead tired, there had not been much sleep in the uncomfortable airplane seats. But in the camp it was an overwhelming reception, with many happy shouts and endless laughing and clapping in the many small hands. When the first euphoria had subsided, the hiris began to discuss the serious political situation on the global stage.

They had previously been commissioned to investigate suitable methods of conducting space activities. At first the hiris had not understood what they could contribute. They were only a couple of thousand individuals, while the "normal humans" were close to ten billion in number. If these billions, like the hiris, were able to function mentally as a single organism, they would be able to gain an enormous collective consciousness and would be able to solve virtually any problem.

The hiris had concluded that man as a species was underdeveloped. Where humanity was headed was not easy to predict. If you looked at today's individuals around you, you were not directly met by a hopeful sight. Everyone behaved completely unsocially, staring silently and blunted at the mobs in their palms. There did not seem to be any physical communication between the people. The human species had degenerated into a heap of zombie-like solitaires.

The military leader at Camp Hiri had announced that this was a purely scientific project with the aim of exploring the solar system. In order to carry out the project, they wanted, above all, to receive proposals for technical solutions regarding the propulsion of the vessels intended for this purpose. They counted on the good will and interest of the hiris and looked forward to a fruitful collaboration. After all, they had made a decent *quid pro quo* offer, providing free housing and food in return for a "simple engineering job".

After some deliberation, the hiris announced their well-balanced conclusions. They had looked at a number of different possibilities and their technical feasibility and concluded that in the current situation, with the existing technology, a three-stage program would be the most realistic alternative. The program was based on three cornerstones, which consisted of a trip to Mars, one to the asteroid belt and finally a large expedition to the Kuiper belt. The different distances gradually increased, from one and a half times, via three times to fifty times the distance of the Earth to the Sun. The first two stages could be completed with the help of the Sun, but the third would require electricity production and propulsion by means of a motor powered by a nuclear reactor.

The hiris had developed the proposal for an industrial-scale manufacturing process of square-kilometer solar sails. These consisted of graphene with a film of crystals and weighed no more than a kilo per piece, a significant, if not entirely decisive, factor in space travel. Apart from the kept-secret nature of the crystals, the innovation in the technology of the hiris was above all the ingenious packing process, both in terms of the stowage in the nose of the vessel during launch and then the roll-out in space.

The hiris also claimed that the application of completely newly developed technology, on the other hand, would be several decades, even several centuries, in the future. The careful hiris did not convey all their thoughts and knowledge to their "hospitable" hosts. Unfortunately, the hiris' recommendation meant that the strong man's country looted all the uranium it could get over. They were looking for nuclear fuel around the world. In cases where money was not enough, rifle bullets would lead to results. The message the hiris had left had, however, been a diversionary maneuver, as the hiris considered that *homo sapiens sapiens* was not sapiens enough to populate space. It was most likely that this self-proclaimed double sapiens would only pollute space, as it had done with Earth.

VI. Clusters of Holes

The most important research result that the hiris had really come to was based on Hiri's previous theoretical work which had led to the realization that it should be possible to use Frommsmann bridges for dimensional penetration. Qualitatively, this picture was comparable to theories about wormholes in rotating black holes, but with the crucial difference that in the Frommsmann bridge you did not have to travel close to the speed of light but could "ride" at a more comfortable pace. In order to put the theory into practice, however, it was necessary to find suitable places where Frommsmann bridges actually existed. The next step would then be to construct a physical adapter for the bridge through which the hiris could be sluiced to the equivalent of the "back side" of the Möbius band.

The hiris had become aware of one of the hottest, current results on the ultimate astronomical research front. Led by seemingly very reliable data, which had been collected with a very sensitive telescope in space, astronomers claimed that there is something as bizarre as invisible matter. This matter did not emit any light at all and was therefore "dark", or even transparent. But as matter normally does, regardless of whether it is bright or dark, the dark matter also obeys the law of gravity and should tend to clump together, forming accumulations of such invisible "holes" in space. The hiris thus considered that there should be globular clusters of holes, invisible and transparent, which could function as Frommsmann bridges.

The professional stargazers had also discovered areas in the sky, where bright arcs had formed around something that was not visible. Earlier, such arcs had been noticed around bright objects in the middle. The light phenomenon was called gravitational lenses and was well explained by the theory of relativity. What was not visible could be a very massive black hole. In a few very carefully investigated cases, however, the astronomical observations were not consistent with the black hole theory and these were described as enigmatic mysteries. The experts called these Black Conundrums, BCs.

The hiris had realised the significance of these new scientific findings and put them in their proper context. It was concluded that the "enigmatic mysteries" corresponded to the expectations of the globular hole clusters, which the hiris called GHCs. Since the creation of the universe there should exist almost infinitely of them. But where the nearest hole cluster, and thus the Frommsmann bridge, was, and how far it would be, one could not answer. A journey to this "GHC 1" could take a long time. But for the hiris, this would not be a major problem. It was probably okay.

VII. Civil Brigades

If you ignore the millions of people who died and were maimed at the first two detonations, which you can not do - ignore them, that is - it was the fifty million on the run who were now in greatest need. In various places, mainly in the Middle East, the refugee camps were overcrowded and lacked the most basic things. There was neither potable water nor food that was not spoiled. And no medicine, nor bandages for the wounded. There were no toilet facilities, no toilet paper and people had no roof over their heads. The children in particular were grossly malnourished and dirty with abscesses full of pus and wounds that did not want to heal.

From Iran, the people had sought refuge with their former arch-enemies and arrived in large numbers in the central parts of the Arabian Peninsula. The Ayatollah had been neither heard nor been seen and the terrified masses of Persia also poured into Azerbaijan, Afghanistan and Turkmenistan. The People from Israel, Palestine and Jordan had fled to Egypt's almost unpopulated Sahara. The influx of refugees could be likened to the return of the Israelites to the land of the Pharaohs, an Introdus, so to speak. Added to this was the still massive migration from poverty and misery in Africa and Asia, which was dammed up by the high walls of Hungary. Latinos gathered in the hundreds of thousands outside the strong man's repulsive wall. Off the coast of Florida drowned almost as many as in the Mediterranean Sea. The human catastrophe was total.

The aid organisations stood helpless and the UN issued a "resolution", number 126082. The wise statement was made that the warring parties were asked to immediately resolve the conflict and to begin peace negotiations. *Sic!* Both Russia and China argued that they should not interfere with the war and used their *veto* to reject the UN resolution. These self-righteous men sat in comfortable, air-conditioned rooms and decided the lives, or rather death sentences, of others while they distractedly munched on cookies for tea.

And at the same time, millions of people were on the run and, on top of all the misery, were completely left to the whims of nature with persistent droughts and sandstorms. Tsunamis and floods. Devastating earthquakes and volcanic eruptions. Ironically, in the end, man himself had caused these catastrophes. Man as a species was finally on the verge of its self-inflicted extinction.

In a contemptuous act of *"formidable arrogance"*, France had declared war on the United States. In any case, this was what the strong man verbatim announced on his electronic website

BigBoy$$$Beaver.com

He added that he had laughed to the mild degree that he almost choked. It seemed like he was living in a dream world.

In fact, laughter had stuck in his throat when he

was informed that the French had just sunk “his” aircraft carrier that had been off the coast of Western Sahara and shelled the French positions. He had an insane fit of rage and with an angered red head, where his eyes seemed to swell out of their sockets, he shouted with a scream, an angry voice “I’ll kill that cat!” a phrase he had heard on television. He also mixed up the French symbolism of “coq” and “chat”, which he thought stood for “cock” and “pussy”.

The strong man had always been deeply impressed by A. Schicklgruber’s skilful conquest of France. His intention was to trump this feat in an even shorter time through a *superblitz.*

He sent there seven divisions from the reopened military bases at Mannheim and Stuttgart, with air support from Ramstein, all located in the western parts of Germania. This exposed the back of the country, whose capital was less than 50 miles from the eastern border. With the locks open, revenge-hungry masses poured in from the east. They had not forgotten what had happened to them before these many bygone decades of cold peace.

After only a few days, in the streets of Berlin one could hear once again people shouting

Ivan ante Portas!

At the same time, the strong man’s boys were stuck in the mud outside Dunkirk. His great ambition, to light the fireworks of the century on the Eiffel Tower, had been thwarted. Now it was a matter of taking care of the enemy in the east.

However, he was not entirely sure how Napoleon had fared. Had it ended well or badly? The strong man did not remember. It would all turn out to lead to an unfortunate development of his French adventure.

VIII. The Cassasius-Werdhem Cave

Calle and Sofia were on their way to “their cave”, but this time without Ali and Beli. The absence of the two faithful and dear friends made them depressed. “It feels like wrong to go there without them,” said Sofia, “it’s because of us that they are dead.” Calle made an awkward attempt to appease her, but he failed to hold back her tears. She cried bitterly and he had a hard time letting go.

Without Hiri and the Tuareg friends, they did not worry so much about the means of transport and their comfort, but intended to rent a ragged, rusty “furgone”, that is an Italian van, which had a handwritten note with the noisy text “Machina Rent” and a phone number in the windshield. It turned out that the owner was an Italian archaeologist.

The Italian was named Luigi Buonafortuna, who absolutely wanted to invite Calle and Sofia to dinner. The couple felt the emptiness in their stomachs and said yes. Together with Luigi, they went to his home, near the new El Badr mosque in Tamanrasset. Luigi offered pasta, *farfalle all‘amatriciana*, very good. During dinner, he said he had been to the cave on several occasions looking for historical clues. He did not know what he was looking for, but thought he might be able to find something that others had missed. As for the depiction on the grartstone slab, he did not think the three figures looked like they were dancing, but he could not put his finger on what it was that made him believe this.

They returned to the cave via the road on the back side. Luigi was with them. The furgone had only two seats in the cab, and that would have been enough for Calle and Sofia. Now they needed to take turns to share the rear of the car with all sorts of junk. Since he was coming along, Luigi did not think he would charge for the furgone, but they agreed to share the petrol. Calle and Sofia gratefully accepted Luigi's generous offer. They also pulled the shortest straw and filled the car and the plastic cans to the width.

Luigi was well acquainted with the "road". He was a skilled driver and avoided the worst tire-threatening obstacles. The desert was strewn with pointed stones that protruded everywhere like thorns on the back of a dragon. However, they did well. In fact, not a single puncture, and the journey progressed quite quickly. When they reached the "oasis", that is, the lone little tree, the Sun was still high and they decided to press on.

Sofia had a question and said "Luigi, I have a stupid question." Luigi seemed upset. With raised eyebrows he said louder than normal and fell into Italian "Non ci sono le domande stupide!" And then he added with further sharpness in his voice "soltanto le risposte stupide!", which means something like "there are no stupid questions, just stupid answers!" Sofia apologised, but also came to the matter and wondered how he could have known where the cave was. The explanation was simple. Before the closure by the Algerian authorities, the place was a very popular tourist destination. Lots of people got on buses through organised excursions from Tamanrasset. There were even points of sale for entrance tickets and refreshments. So the location of the cave was no big secret. Calle and Sofia were disappointed and smiled embarrassed. They thought they had kept their secret well.

When the party had reached the mountain, they found, probably because of the endless tourist streams that were perceived as clearly disturbing, that the bandits' hiding place had been abandoned and had probably not been used for years. They decided to name the bandit cave their "home". There were a lot of utensils left, which could come handy and useful. They unloaded the furgone and then hid the van as best they could behind a cairn. Luigi pulled out a camouflage net from the cargo hold, and the fact that the rusty vehicle was not shiny brand new also helped to hide it reasonably well.

The next morning they set off on foot to the very destination of the journey. Calle and Sofia were surprised to see that electric lighting had been installed in the cave. They were also very upset about all the rubbish that lay there, soft drink cans, crumpled pieces of paper and plastic bags. All this graffiti on the rock walls made them furious. This is not how archeological treasures were preserved! Luigi then informed them that it was he, together with representatives of the World Heritage Committee on Monuments, who had persuaded the Algerian government to close the place to the public. The two long-distance guests looked at him gratefully and Sofia said "First of all, we must start by cleaning up the pigsty." They filled the plastic bags with all the rubbish and tried to wash the graffiti off the walls. They were only partially successful with lots still there. But what they had come here for was fortunately undamaged. By pointing the lamp at the right angle, the three figures appeared on the smooth surface of the grartstone slab.

With a glass of tea each, they sat down by the wall on the opposite side and watched the hexagonal plate in devotional silence. Suddenly Calle broke this contemplating silence and shouted out loud "Think, if it's not what we call dance! Imagine if it symbolises something completely different!" Was it possible that the figurines just pointed upwards, that is, towards the roof of the cave. Was there anything significant there in the rock? Gold, Uranium? "Symbolise? You said", interjected Sofia, "these wave-like movements, could they represent the Schrödinger equation and point to quantum fuel in the rock? It could be a guide for posterity, a little helper to get on with the journey. Or something." Sofia held her breath and waited for a violent laugh from the two men. But this did not happen. After a moment of silence, Calle said "Darling, that was absolutely brilliant! Of course, it could be something like that! "

Luigi sat petrified, looking as if he had received a deeply religious revelation, as if he had seen an angel with white wings and a shining wreath above his head. "I knew it! I knew it! You're right! Something like that! Perhaps the nature of the painting tells us what it is all about. Could it be a soft nuclear fuel, such as rhenium?" He thought, somewhat naively perhaps, that rhenium would not leave any long-lived and difficult-to-control radioactive waste as in the use of fissile uranium or plutonium. Then no heavy clumsy nuclear reactor would be needed. Energy could be generated via low-risk radioactive processes. But would there be any energy to speak of? For the operation of a giant spaceship? Perhaps. Doubtful. More than a billion years ago?

Calle and Sofia told about Hiri and inaugurated Luigi in the top secret existence of her two thousand very smart cousins, and that they as a collective "were a whopper of encyclopedic knowledge and phenomenal solvers of all kinds of problems". They suggested that they consult them. They would themselves start by taking samples from the rock to determine if the rhenium content would be significantly higher than in the general earth's crust. Rhenium would be found mainly together with molybdenum, but also in platinum ore. Was it a platinum vein, and not a gold vein, they had above their heads?

Any occurrence of rhenium larger than one atom in a billion would mean a jackpot. It was important to find it. Therefore, samples were taken from a variety of locations of the cave's ceiling, which were to be sent to various laboratories around the world for examination. The samples were marked with the same code as the places in the cave, so that you knew exactly where the samples were taken. A practical problem in the beginning had been, how to reach the ceiling five, six meters up. It all became a little difficult, when the lightest of them, Sofia, had to climb up on the sparsely carved table, on top of which stood an even more wobbly chair. It turned out that all this wonder of ingenuity would not suffice, Sofia did not reach.

Fortunately, she was not injured either. Luigi recalled that he had seen a pile of tent poles or something like that in the arms depot of the Islamist Liberation Front. In fact, they found plastic sticks in different lengths. The longest ones were two and a half to three meters long and were easy to tie together. For each rod it took several sticks for the sake of rigidity, but these were still not as stable as real rods made of steel, but they served their purposes. Although you had to redo the whole device several times and tie the rods together again. At one end, a tent nail, the tip of which had been sharpened extra carefully, and a small bag of cloth, from Sofia's skirt, were attached to collect the material that had been scraped off.

After a couple of days of tricks, gimmicks and scrapes, the friends had collected several dozen samples from as many places in the cave, neatly cataloged them and finally stowed them in old rifle boxes for transport in the furgone. All sites were marked with the same code as the samples from there. "Professional" markers were in the archaeologist's van. Six of the samples were taken from randomly selected parts of the cave, on the walls and at its bottom. These samples constituted “control material” and were labeled like the others and were to be treated in the same way by the laboratories. They therefore did not tell anyone that the consignment contained “a bunch of fake samples”. Implicitly, they assumed that no significant amounts of rhenium would be found in these. But would it be different in the samples taken from the ceiling?

On the way back to Tamanrasset, Calle, Luigi and Sofia talked a lot about what they thought of their samples. The speculations were many and some of them quite wild. But one thing was for sure, the three were all very excited and tense. It would be unbearable to sit and wait for the lab results. And these could take weeks to produce.

IX. Threepointfourteen Squarekilometers

The Hiris presented a part of the first of their proposals to Camp Hiri's commander. This applied to a communication and research station on the dark side of the Moon. From there, one could communicate undisturbed with the colony on Mars, whose structure was, after all, phase one in the hiris' draft. This plan was much more elaborate in detail and took advantage of the fact that a telescope would always be in the shadow of all the disturbances and noises from the Earth. A large telescope could thus reach unimaginable sensitivity and therefore required only small and extremely energy-efficient transmitters on Mars and especially in the future on the planned interplanetary spacecraft. There were several relay satellites in orbit around the Moon, which would transmit the signals to the mother planet Tellus.

Another, very exciting, aspect of the enormous sensitivity was that one could see all the way to the "edge" of the universe. The idea of a large, fully manoeuvrable telescope on the dark side of the Moon was by no means new in itself, but the practical implementation needed new technical solutions. Conventional shipments of thousands of tons from Earth to the Moon were excluded for financial reasons. The proposal by the hiris for a controllable telescope of just over three square kilometers was based on their ingenious production and use of large doped graphene films. A telescope diameter of a couple of kilometers was no longer a technical impossibility. Since the huge "primary mirror" itself would weigh less than five kilograms, its transport to the Moon was no longer an obstacle. The much smaller "secondary" should weigh far less than half and would follow *pro bono.* The mirror's support structure could be made of balsa wood and not weigh more than five tons. Due to the absence of a thick atmosphere and strong winds, which would deform the telescopic surface, this lightweight construction of the giant telescope would be definitely possible. The material for the entire telescope would thus require only a single launch of a cargo ship. With such good financial conditions, the project would clearly be feasible.

The construction of the "research station" was thus also carried out quickly, as the military were in a hurry. As a basis for new knowledge, the project was by no means classified. In this way, the generals could openly justify the high costs and expenses for Congress. The information about the great work had a great impact in public media such as newspapers, radio and television broadcasts, and was spread in a huge edition via the all-encompassing internet. Several members of the government took credit for this grandiose monster building. However, the role of the hiris, and in particular their mere existence, was not mentioned.

The real intention of the hiris with the construction of the telescope was that they could always, over huge periods of time and wherever they were in the Milky Way, be able to know exactly where their own solar system would be. Things in heaven are not immutable but ΠΑΝΤΑ ΡΕΙ, *everything flows*, as some wise man so beautifully said long ago in the city of Ephesus.

X. Realm of Clones

Since the hiris were the results of the cloning of a single individual, they would theoretically all be completely identical and in the strict sense exact copies of their mother. In the real, Darwinian world, however, there were, here and there, small errors in the copying of the triple helix. Mostly insignificant, but in its entirety there could be almost imperceptible small deviations from the original.

However, some external mutations could be clearly noticeable. Some hiris were longer, others shorter than average. Some weighed more and others less. The hair color could differ slightly from individual to individual. The hiris were well aware of their individuality and cultivated it with pride.

Instead of the numbers they had been assigned by the camp management, they used names of themselves. They had chosen the names mostly for aesthetic reasons, names that they thought suited their personality. Most people were content with a single name, usually the first name, like the blonde Nina. While others also invented surnames and some even middle names, such as Elizabeth Rosamunde Sailor. There were those who had been nicknamed by their comrades. Beany really wanted to be called Astrid, but was called Beany, because with her ninety-two centimeters, she was clearly the tallest of them all.

Most of them dressed individually, had different hairstyles and some used make-up. But as for their hirishness, they were in complete agreement with each other and united in this overwhelming sense of community of their warm collective togetherness. Getting all these inspirations, new ideas and “Aha” experiences was something wonderful and almost like a religious revelation. To achieve this Nirwana-like feeling, the hiris needed both spiritual and physical contact. They used therefore to attend a common assembly hall, the so-called realm of clones. This realm had no kings nor queens.

The ships to Mars, the asteroids and the Kuiper belt were built on the “Shipyard”, some four hundred miles from the GLT, which was the acronym of the Giant Lunar Telescope. The shipyard had grown into a huge facility and construction had been going on for five years. The “solar system exploration” vessels were designed for four hundred hiris each and gradually became larger. Extra personnel for the vessels’ crews were not needed, as these tasks were handled by trained hiris. The large ship to Mars, Colony 1, was already on its way for a while and would reach its destination any day.

The finished construction of the four belt ships used pre-produced modules. The conveyor band production was done at elltoo, a place in empty space, several Moon distances away. “Everyone” wanted to go to elltoo, although not many people knew what the name meant and why they were going there. As the asteroid belt approached, the sails would be repacked and stowed down, and the two spacecraft would then be dismantled in lots of smaller “boats”. This to minimize the risk of collision with the myriads of boulders that were in orbit beyond Mars and formed the asteroid belt itself.

A similar system was applied for Kuiper 1 and Kuiper 2, but with a much larger number of modules. It was thought that these two ships would be finally assembled beyond the asteroid belt. Although they were intended for the little hiris, who only needed a fraction of the necessities of what a corresponding number of "normal" people would have been dependent on, these spaceships would be gigantic. The hiris' own spaces would be in a little over a kilometer long ring around the more than one hundred meter large meeting room with a transparent dome on each side. These would be the passengers' large windows to space, so that the hiri collective could observe the amazing splendor of the Milky Way and have spiritual contact with the universe.

The construction of the two flagships continued in parallel, required enormous resources and would take another six years. To ensure access to the building materials, the United States had entered into wide-ranging global alliances, except with China and Russia, both of which had refused. Most countries contributed voluntarily and even made their deliveries to the solar system project available free of charge. The lithium was so important, and found primarily in China, and you had to pay expensive money for it. The Chinese were as stingy as a Gothenburg professor and had raised the world market price by several hundred percent. “Very communist, very supportive, extremely lovable”, Hiri said.

The Russians feared the escalation of the raging wars and crouched behind a mountain of missiles. They supported the Palestinians, who were supported by Hezbollah, who were supported by Iran, which was at war with Israel. Syria saw its chance, after decades of humiliation, to recapture the Levantine Golan Heights. Israel managed to launch a nuclear missile at Damascus, but the city had been in ruins before that. “So no damage was done”, someone remarked cynically. But now millions of Palestinians were killed in the Syrian refugee camp. In addition to the devastating explosion in Tel Aviv, two other Iranian missiles had struck Haifa and Besheba. Israel was in ruins, milk and honey had stopped flowing, and half of its population had been killed or maimed. Most of them had Arab roots. The other half were on the run. The well-offs fled to America, but the majority went on foot to seek asylum in Egypt.

Most of Iran had been spared direct nuclear hits, as Israel did not have time to carry out its entire planned retaliation. However, the old city of Susa, now Shush, was literally pulverized. The entire population of the country was exposed to heavy radiation doses with terrible damage as a result. The illness was horrible and extremely painful. People died like flies. Mounds of corpses grew every minute to stinking, unimaginable heights. The plague lurked around the corner. Many went to Iraq, hoping to find Shiite friends there.

XI. Devastatio Telluris

The international political situation had recently deteriorated considerably and the polarising quarrels between East, West, North and South had, if possible, even increased. The confident and assertive general secretary of the Communist Party of North Korea was convinced that "his time" had come. He ordered his comrades at the rocket bases to nuke-equip and refuel intercontinental robots.

To make it difficult for foreign spies to identify North Korea's nuclear targets in the United States, North Korean IT comrades had encrypted the homes of randomly picked individuals in said target areas. The address in Washington D.C. happened to belong to a certain Vladimir Ostok, "senior computer system analyst", it said on his business card. Due to a small arbitrary auto-correction in the programming of the target coordinates, which were performed autonomously by the supposedly intelligent AI software, nuclear-equipped missiles from North Korea were sent instead of to Washington D.C., to Vladivostok, not far from the border between North Korea and Russia. The Russians did not have time to see what was coming.

The Russians became, to say the least, very angry and did not wait for the generally accepted time in higher diplomacy, but immediately sent a full load of similar gizmos to the Capital of the Dear Respected Leader. People in the Kremlin had for some time seen unfavourably at China's protective attitude towards

North Korea, and China was not Russia's friend. The Kremlin provided a "preliminary declaration of war" to the Chinese embassy, but delayed taking up arms.

In the north, the next generation of Kamchatka crabs had been given nine legs, a circumstance that was liked and welcomed by the world's gourmands. Only they avoided dining in the intimate light of only the candles. The crabs gleamed faintly green. In the south, the very last remnants of the Beluga Sturgeon Population had disappeared, a circumstance that was disapproved of and noted by the world's gourmets. The total extinction of an entire species, which has survived the whims of nature for hundreds of millions of years, was now an irreversible fact. In the central parts of Russia, the tigers lost fur and teeth and slowly withered away. Another species was disappearing from the face of the Earth forever.

In the northern part of Korea, the large statues of the great leaders had been turned into scrap metal. Pyongyang was an empty gravel heap, without the happy, cheerfully singing masses in their red pioneer scarves, which had been seen on television in reports from there. The ugly, and in contrast to his countrymen and ditto women, fat rocket man had crawled under the Earth and was nowhere to be seen. He had hidden thirty floors down in his private bunker and spent his windowless days watching Walt Disney's cartoons.

U.S. intelligence agencies had not lain on the lazy side and found out fairly quickly what had happened.

The fact that the explosion in Vladivostok was intended for the District of Columbia's Washington made people in the White House very upset. From there, the Chinese ambassador was told that he would inform his North Korean friends that the United States would declare this aggressive criminal state a "preliminary declaration of war".

This had never happened before, to submit a "preliminary declaration of war". What would that mean? A declaration of war is usually a definite, final thing. But the wording "preliminary and definitive, final" indicated a poor knowledge of semantics. Would this gibberish so typical of politicians be an attempt to hide a perhaps less childish message "Naughty, naughty! Do not do it again, otherwise so...", yes, otherwise, so... what?

In Pyongyang, they did not wait for the answer but reloaded. The Dear Respected Leader declared to his generals "The Americans are afraid!" And most broke out in cheers and applauded excessively long. A few were skeptical, but said nothing. You did not speak against your God. You do what your God commanded.

The North Koreans fired some more intercontinental nuclear weapons, but these were intercepted by the US space force and all were defused. This act of North Korean hostility was resolutely answered with large-scale bombing from the air and violent shelling from the sea. The artillery pieces were highly explosive but conventional weapons without fissile material.

Because the subtropical country lacked comprehensive rainforests, North Korea was a much easier target to destroy than Vietnam. The Chinese felt compelled to assist their cheeky ally and, somewhat awkwardly, submitted a note of protest to the United Nations General Assembly.

Due to their newly acquired dependency, several countries, most of them south of the equator, joined China's protest. The voltage in the world had reached several hundred thousand volts and the slightest spark would be enough to make this whole gunpowder jar called Tellus explode.

The irony of this development was that in the first half of the twentyfirst century, much discussion was put into discussing the theme of the "climate crisis" and how to "save our planet". There was a lot of talking and a lot was done. Not enough, but still. They succeeded in reducing the increase in the global temperature average. However, the ice on the polar caps continued to melt at an alarming rate. So did the inland glaciers. The storms increased in number and strength and destroyed the homes of millions of people. The spread of the Sahara was doubling and its population was starving to death due to the persistent drought.

Some people thought it was outrageous that there was no snow in the mountains, so you could not ski. Hm, different people then have different priorities.

Sofia had intended to spend her silver wedding with Calle on one of the Beldive's fabulously beautiful islands. Unfortunately, the atolls in the holiday paradise had disappeared in the Indian Ocean. Things did not go much better for large parts of mainland Pangla Pech, whose population suffered from the aftermath of heavy rains that led to widespread flooding and colossal landslides. Many lost their homes and, worse, their lives.

Mankind was finally on the verge of its own self-inflicted extinction, completely under its own auspices and without any external help. So sapiens, sapiens: What would happen first, a global nuclear war or a global climate catastrophe?

XII. Sahara Miracle

It had become almost unbearable for Calle and Sofia to remain at the cave. The same was true of Luigi's home in Tamanrasset. The catastrophically hopeless supply situation had made it impossible to stay, there was neither water nor anything to eat. They took Luigi's van and drove two thousand kilometers straight north, towards Algiers. From there they would take a boat to Genoa and then on to Gothenburg. Luigi was going home to his parents in Milan and the Crassasius-Werdhems back to Anna, Letitia and Hubertus. All the parents had come of age and some were perhaps no longer alive.

The three desert travelers had virtually no water with them. The little that was left in the plastic can was becoming foul, something that not even the countless chlorine tablets could hide. This warm sludge was simply disgusting to both smell and taste. Sonja took a sip, did not get it down and vomited over Calle's favorite sweater in Luigi's trunk.

After several miles, they came to a small village, some houses in yellow-gray clay bricks by the road. The village's *Supermarché*, a small dark space with a simple bar counter, was run by a middle-aged man.

Sofia asked in an almost silent, creaking voice for water. The man behind the counter smiled, turned around and opened the door to something that could be a refrigerator. He took out a small metal jar and handed it to Sofia. The jar had mist on the outside and in some places it could be seen that it had previously contained Libby's coffee cream. Sofia nodded gratefully, accepted the jar and drank the deliciously cold water in a single swipe. Then she looked around, rolled her eyes and said, "this was the best water I've ever drunk in my whole life."

She turned to the shop owner and asked for two more, a jar each for Calle and Luigi, and wanted to know what she owed. The shop owner just laughed and made it clear that in Algeria the water cost nothing, "where there is, there is for everyone, that's the law in the desert". Unfortunately he had nothing more. This had been the only water in the house and he wanted to keep it in his refrigerator until the evening. During Ramadan, one was not allowed to drink during the day, not even to swallow one's own saliva. "But then Allah had sent this foreigner in need of water! And she got it!"

Sofia became very dull and dumbfounded. So she had drunk up the man's only water, the man who longed to drink after sunset. She had received this valuable gift completely unknowingly, but was so ashamed that she began to cry. Calle and Luigi had been waiting outside, but now rushed into the store. When they heard what had happened, they absolutely wanted to give this good Samaritan some money, but he stubbornly refused to accept it. "Here it is forbidden to charge for water, it is everyone's property."

As they continued, they tried to sing a song of joy, but the men had lost their voices and could not make a sound out of their thirst-dried and constricted throats.

Hundreds of miles away, fifty miles outside In Salah, they came to a gas station, out of nowhere. In addition to diesel and petrol, you could buy bottled water, which was obviously allowed. They filled the furgone's tank with fuel, loaded two dozen of water bottles, and drove the two hundred miles back to Sofia's "watering hole". When they arrived, they could witness a colourful, immensely beautiful sunset. Luigi said he had seen the "green flash", but in that he was alone.

They surprised the Samaritan in his shop and pointed to his refrigerator. The Samaritan shook his head apologetically, there was nothing. But Calle and Luigi filled the refrigerator with water bottles and in this way they expressed their gratitude. The Samaritan's eyes shone with restrained tears. The three travellers spent the night in the Samaritan's house, together with his family. They drank a considerable amount of sweet sweet tea with fresh mint. Now they had water and everyone thanked Allah for this miracle.

The next morning they left early, during the people's morning prayer, and the rest of the journey went smoothly. During the boarding in the port of Algiers, the customs officials wanted to know why they had so many glass ampoules with gravel in them. Did they want to steal and smuggle out the Algerian people's mineral assets? Had they encountered a gold vein? Valuable uranium?

Many hours of discussion and many bribe-dinars later, they finally got on board, with the mineral samples in undamaged condition. What had decided the successful conclusion of the negotiations was the customs officials' strangely limitless interest in aliens. Sofia had taken advantage of this weakness of the customs office's representatives and told fairy tales taken from Erich von Däniken's collected works.

The boat trip was then quite unremarkable, rather boring, like reading the Dead Sea Scrolls. Back in "civilisation", Calle and Sofia provided various labs with cave samples, which also contained materials from the control group.

The analyses confirmed what they had expected and hoped for: the samples from the ceiling typically contained many billion times more rhenium atoms than those from the bottom of the cave.

XIII. Off You Go

Calle and Sofia immediately informed their daughter about the positive test results from all laboratories. Hiri was overjoyed by the news and the whole hiri collective broke out with her in celebration. Many danced. In elegant wave movements with raised arms.

Hiri's conversations with her parents were initially a bit artificial. Hiri was currently at the construction site for the Kuiper ships and it took over an hour to get an answer to a question. For example, the response "We love you too" to her farewell words "I love you" felt unnecessarily unnatural. They changed their thought exchange to written correspondence which was sent via the Moon. There was then at least no time delay between the sentences, but at the same time gave a premonition of how the postal service would take shape on the day Hiri would finally give way on a long journey.

A basic question that preoccupied them all was "What does it all mean? Had someone or something left a message? About a billion years ago?" This was a dizzying thought that could not be accepted without further ado. Not flippantly in any case. Consequently, the discussions among the hiris were in full swing. On Earth, Calle, Luigi and Sofia tortured their brains without reaching any credible conclusion. However, the hiris had a couple of sensible suggestions. The starting point was that this grartstone tablet could not have a natural origin. It should be some kind of artefact, but not necessarily made in the literal sense of the word, that is, made by human hand. Would the age determination of roughly one billion years or older be correct, then the human race is obviously disqualified, or any other race, for that matter. On Earth, absolutely.

Creatures from Mars? From distant worlds? There, the hiris' opinion differed. A large crowd believed that life in the solar system could be a realistic possibility and preferred real visits from either Venus or Mars, when the Earth was still uninhabitable. But the star dust fans had got water on their mill. In the cosmic perspective, a billion years is not so violently much and a billion years ago, the Milky Way was already old and mature enough to have had several generations of starwalkers or their messenger machines.

The only thing that was clear was that no single common explanation could be agreed upon. The fact that opinions differed, however, would not be reason enough to disagree so much among the hiris. They loved each other and different perceptions of this or that could not change it. As for their mission, this relationship would not change anything in practice either. In any case, the inhabitants of the settlements on Mars would soon begin to look for signs of past life there. And within ten years or so, many samples would have been taken of the debris floating around in the Kuiper Belt. As it was so succinctly expressed in a live television interview by paleozoologist Professor Isabel Martinez-Svensén from Vaduz in Liechtenstein "if there is something interesting out there, we will know this after seven quick hours."

Hiri made it clear to her parents that the hiris needed the cave's rhenium. After a brief deliberation, which took several hours due to the interplanetary distances, they suggested that Luigi should be the one to handle the contacts with the Algerian authorities and also be the site manager at the cave.

The authorities knew Luigi well, as he had on several occasions been granted excavation permit applications. He argued that it was an absolute must that he was personally on site to ensure that the archaeological treasures were not damaged or even destroyed. He would also bring with him guards he trusted who would ensure that no one stole any of the precious metal. The plan was to mine the platinum ore on behalf of the Algerian state, but secretly extract the rhenium for their own use.

After lengthy discussions in Algiers' governmental buildings, they finally agreed and signed the necessary documents. All parties considered that they had made a good deal. And that was thankful. Luigi proved to be extremely efficient and initial mining started after just a few weeks. The ceiling of the grartstone cave contained the extremely high content of the coveted rhenium isotope of almost half a gram per tonne of ore. Such huge abundance was completely unique.

However, the salvage of the treasure was by no means non-dangerous, as the removal of the ore above the cave posed a risk of landslides and threatened to bury the miners. And the murals. And the grartstone slab. This just could not happen! Luigi looked very seriously at this risk. He did not want to rely solely on his "buona fortuna" and took a series of precautions to stabilise the rock. His workers first supported the walls with pillars and braces and then cast the inside of the shaft with reinforced concrete. Gradually, it was then free to also install an elevator device for transporting people and ore. But it was crowded. Very crowded. And oxygen-poor.

To extract the necessary amount of rhenium for the two longsailers, it was necessary to mine hundreds of thousands of cubic meters of ore, more than a hundred meters obliquely up inside the rock, like the passage to the royal chamber of Khufu in his pyramid. Hopefully, the abundant deposits of platinum and rhenium held up.

After years of building the ships, which included the testing of new concepts and the trying out of completely new technologies, it was finally time for a roofing party. The two flagships had fitted colorful wreaths fifty meters in diameter and braided from recycled construction waste. After the wild feast with "home-brewed" beer, sails were set and the ships slowly began to slide out of elltoo on their joint maiden voyage. Some hiris called the trip a male virginity voyage, invoking gender equality. Otherwise, the hiris were normally not particularly prude. It happened that the lust just suddenly fell on them and that they could copulate where they were right now, in the public or in the private space. They also lacked common prejudices about sexual preferences. These only concerned the parties involved.

As the ships approached the asteroid belt, the hiris dismantled the ships, resulting in a considerable fleet of smaller "boats" that were easier to navigate through this sea of various large boulders. At Jupiter, the spacecraft were reassembled and, with the help of the planet, took charge to be thrown out of the solar system, far below its plane, thus reducing the risk of collision with Kuiper belt bodies.

When the solar wind calmed down and the radiation pressure became too low, the hiris used their specially developed nuclear power operation with softeners, without explosive chain reaction. This is what they needed the rhenium for. Another delicate, novel detail concerned the solar sails, which were made of thin layers of reinforced graphene sheets. The hiris changed the straight, flat shape of the sails to almost perfect concave spherical surfaces. They would henceforth be used as giant telescopes, so that they would always point towards the Sun. The hiris would know in the future where their home star Sun is. Or rather, has been.

XIV. GHC 1

When Kuiper 1 and Kuiper 2 passed Pluto, the hiris found that this tiny miniplanet was surrounded by far more than the five moons known. They performed various measurements and calculations and cataloged their results in detailed and concise tables. The digitized results were then sent to Earth. Hiri and her sisterbrothers were surprised that even after more than a day, they had not been reached by an affirmative answer that the Earth had received the message. Not a beep, not a thank you, nilch, *nihil.*

The hiris swept over every conceivable and unimaginable frequency band, with little consoling success. Apart from occasional disturbances, probably noise from the Sun or Jupiter, no meaningful signals were found. Despite persistent and renewed calls, their receivers remained silent. The hiris feared the worst: had at last the Last World War broken out and devastated the "blue-white pearl"? If this was the end, the apocalypse, homo doublesapiens could have calmly continued to burn fossil fuels and not have had to do anything about the threatening climate catastrophe.

The doublesapiens had themselves managed to come up with their very own fabricated ultimate nuclear disaster. Excellently done! But maybe it was time to call henceforth this hominid *homo stultus stultus.*

Hiri was completely desperate and hollow inside. Not knowing what had happened to the world and in particular her parents put her in a state of apathy. She was unable to perform her duties as the hirimother and handed over the leadership to Gudni Helgedottir. Gudni was stationed on the sister ship Kuiper 2 and was considered extremely suitable for the managerial job. She was an energetic little creature, small in stature even for a hiri, but with an enormous brain capacity. The length of her elongated head was almost half her body length.

Gudni immediately set to work. Above all, you needed to know in which direction to go. Elizabeth Rosamunde Sailor had found a recent interesting article in one of the top astronomical journals. She showed it to Gudni Helgedottir. There was an "anomaly" in the southern sky. This hemisphere was not as well studied as the northern one, as most astronomers had lived and had had their telescopes on the "upper part". And, as planned, Jupiter had thrown them out in the "lower" direction.

Near the star ω Pan in the constellation Frying Pan, a small area in the sky had been found that was completely empty of stars. The area was not large, just a few thousandths of a degree, but totally black. Not even the monstrous space telescope Hubble 4 was able to detect a single small distant galaxy. This was very remarkable, because it used to be crowded with them. For the hiris, this news meant that a globular hole had probably been found. They called it GHC 1, an acronym for *Globular Hole Cluster* number One. The distance to the star omega Pandellae was well determined, but it was impossible to figure out how far it would be to GHC 1. Equally far? closer? farther?

that was impossible to determine. Being next to each other in the sky did not have to mean anything, since it was just a two-dimensional projection of their real locations.

Thanks to the grandiose space project STELLA at the beginning of the twenty second century, there was a detailed mathematical model of the dynamics of the Milky Way. STELLA, the Satellite Tomographic Equatorial Longitudinal Laser Astrometry, which now comprised the twelve vessels STELLA 1 to 12, had mapped one hundred and twenty billion of the Milky Way's stars, and discovered and measured vast quantities of planets. With the help of complicated simulations of the ever-changing local gravitational field, it was possible to determine how the stars moved and where they had been in the past and where they would be in the future.

At the occasionally quite stormy hiri meeting, it was discussed what to do henceforth. After much back and forth, it was decided that most of the hiris on the two ships would be in hibernation mode. On each ship, at least two hiris would always be on the bridge for one year. At the end of the shift, all would be woken up to eat and drink, go to the toilet, shower, brush their teeth and so on. Some might have time for a quickie. Then there would be a changing of the guard for another year. When everyone had been on the bridge once, they would have traveled for two hundred years in the direction of ω Pan. If they would not have arrived at the destination by then, one would start on a new round. If one encountered GHC 1 before that, the guards would of course wake up the others. The same applied in the event of major repair needs, breakdowns or other emergencies. Being two people on the bridge was an entirely precautionary measure in case there was a prolonged power outage. Like all other chores, navigation could also be left to the large number of self sufficient robots on board the two spaceships.

After almost three changes of the guard, it started to feel like they were approaching GHC 1, although the impenetrable blackness in front of them did not grow much. It did not even fill their field of view. But they felt its irresistible gravitational pull. The engines of the ships had fought in vain and the guards on duty shut them down. They drifted into the blackness. After a little while, it was completely black all around them. It was “black” also in the electronics on board, and the Sun had been lost sight of. There was not even a hint of noise from the radio receivers, not the slightest Heisenberg fluctuation from anything. It all felt very secretive and inexplicable. The hiris’ experience was similar to that of going into a dark tunnel, but they could not perceive any walls, no bottom, no ceiling. No up nor down. They saw no light ahead, nor the end of the tunnel. They could not describe, express in words, what they experienced.

The Frommsmann bridge did not look at all like Hiri had imagined it. In her mind the bridge would be like a tunnel where the entrance would be a hole and the cave could be likened to an extended condom that would taper forward. And that they would literally go through it, one by one, in a single file. To then step out into something that looked pretty much like what they had stepped into, an infinity of stars and galaxies. Now she was no longer so sure that they had actually done a dimensional penetration. They were still in their spaceships. At least that was what she thought.

They had not had any contact with the other ship for a while. Was Gudni Helgedottir and all the others still there? Hiris' comrades looked at her with wide-open mouths and large eyes, waiting for some kind of statement from her side. After all, it has been Hiris' idea to come here. So, what happened now? Hiri was hyperfebrile trying to come up with something sensible to say. But there was no enlightning. She tried to determine whether they were standing still or moving. It was impossible to say, it felt nothing.

Suddenly it felt as if they had stopped. Had they hit an invisible "iceberg"? Then the ship was snatched and rocked violently from one side to the other. The beam of the ship's headlight was not reflected by anything or anyone. It was still pitch black everywhere as well as unpleasant, creepy. Was there something outside that rocked the ship? Were there invisible giants?

XV. Touching the Dark

Hiri and her sisterbrothers had become frightened and most of them were pale in their long faces. Hiri opened her mouth to say something, when she felt something invisible seemed to grab her and pull her away. Hiri had not experienced any real physical contact with this, whatever it might be. She waved her arms like Don Quixote's fighting the windmill, but it was as if she was hitting empty space. At the same time, she did not feel attacked by anything dangerous. Was there a kind of consciousness around her and her sisterbrothers? A consciousness that was invisible to them? Then Hiri raised her voice and said, "Dear sisterbrothers! I think we have done it - we have made a dimensional penetration via a Frommsmann bridge or we are about to do it. We have succeeded!" Cheers erupted and many laughter of relief was heard. Then Hiri added "I think we are in the realm of dark matter, which is called DM by the scientists. It is apparently completely harmless to us all. It seems as if we are surrounded by a great and gigantic consciousness. Completely in line with our own consciousnesses, this consciousness is also invisible."

Suddenly it jerked again, stopped abrupt, jerked, stopped abruptly, rocked gently, stopped dead, rocked faster, stopped dead, jerked and then there was a halt. The ship did not move. What was this? The words flew through the room. Everyone wanted to say something. A voice was heard from the far rows. It was Bella Amanda who said "It's similar to Samuel FB language - could it be something like that, that is Morse code?" Most people fell silent at once, as if they had had a common Aha experience "Sure, it could be such a thing", thought the devout crowd. "Let's try our own variant and see what happens," said Hiri, beginning to look for something to pound against the ship's walls. One of the hiris found a wrench and handed it to Bella Amanda with the words "Bella Amanda, do your thing". The Beautiful Loveable received the wrench and pounded on the floor, "donk kriiiish kriiiish". She continued with a "donk", "donk kriiiish", "donk kriiiish donk", "donk", "donk donk donk donk", "donk", "'donk kriiiish donk" and finished with a "donk ". She smiled and said "*vi är här*", (we are here).

"Do you think they understand Swedish?" was someone wondering.

Bella Amanda, who had thought the same thing and therefore expected the question, quickly replied, "No idea. Does it really matter? I do not know what language they speak, if they speak anything at all. We will have to wait and see." They did not have to wait long, but the ship suddenly made rock roll roll, rock, rock roll, rock roll rock, rock, rock rock rock rock, rock, rock roll rock, rock and then it paused. The answer was exactly the same message that the hiris had sent and was basically just a repetition, but in terms of boat rockings and seasickness rollings. Athough the content of the message was most likely not understood by the Dark Men, that is the DM creatures, but this was proof of their existence and that they had a consciousness that was able to perceive other consciousnesses.

Or was it really that? The answer was identical down to the smallest detail. The rocks, the rolls and the breaks were exactly as long as theirs. Even the different sound volumes had been mimicked as the degree of softness in the rocking or rolling. It all seemed very artificial. As made by a machine. Which in turn was made by whom or what? Hiri and her sisterbrothers were at a loss. What would you do? Hiri turned to her comrades, “we need to get a clear indication that the answer has been given consciously and that the intention has been to try to communicate with us. In order to communicate, we need some kind of language. That both parties can understand. Communicating our thoughts can be difficult. For example, when we look at a painting, we see the whole image immediately. We perceive all the details of this two-dimensional creation simultaneously. But describing what is on the canvas in words would take a long, long time. Because our language is one-dimensional, one word after another, not words above, below, next to each other, not everywhere. Would *we* understand a two-dimensional or even multidimensional language? How should we go foreward? Any suggestions?”

Bella Amanda revealed a certain impatience when she exclaimed “I want to remind you of the anecdote about the two old men sitting next to each other in their isolation cells. In complete darkness. One was a Swede from Haparanda and the other a Tibetan from a suburb of Lhasa and their language had no similarities at all. Indo-European versus Mongolian. In addition, there was a whole universe of experiences between their different cultures. They simply had totally different frames of reference. They could knock on the wall that separated them, but could they communicate with each other?" The question was rhetorical and she did not expect an answer. "But the important thing is that they both belonged to the hominid species. Their language, though so different, had been developed by a common denominator, namely that they were based on how people perceive their surroundings, they had the same senses, especially sight, but also hearing and feeling, and then smell and taste, of course." Another long artistic break. "So, the two who could not talk to each other, however, had a common base to stand on. They could concentrate on what they had in common and not on their differences. Over time, they jointly developed their very own language. Not entirely different from the Morse code. When the guard came with food, one of them knocked once, which meant "food". Two knocks meant "good", three "not good" and three plus a scraping "disgusting". Then they built on that and expanded their vocabulary."

"But as you said, they belonged to the same biological species, the same genes!" said Danne Daneson in the first row. "Exactly!" Now Bella Amanda looked triumphant. She took a deep breath and bubbled up "Philosophers like Bertrand Russell and Kurt Gödel, for example, and scientists like Erwin Schrödinger and Frank Drake and several others before and after them believed that there is a universal language, which all intelligent beings in the universe would understand, regardless of what they were made of. And this language would be mathematics. With this argument, Carl Sagan justified his messages on the Pioneer and Voyager probes. These were intended to leave the solar system, to fly out into the space beyond and perhaps be picked up by "someone". We can test this, with the mathematics, that is. That way we could find out, whether the Dark Men understand or not. What do you say?" A widespread mumbling in agreement accompanied by a collective nod was the respond.

Bella Amanda, who was still holding the wrench, said "we can do this" and hit the floor "donk donk donk", pause, "donk donk donk donk donk", pause, "donk donk donk donk donk", long pause, "donk", pause, "donk", pause, "donk donk donk".

Many looked bewildered, but Hiri had immediately grasped the meaning of the thumps. She declared "if you interpret the number of thumps as natural numbers and if you divide the number before the long pause by what came after, you get an approximate value of π. And this with an accuracy of one in ten million, that is, $355 \div 113 = 3.14159292$. This number divided by π itself gives $1.0000000849\ldots$, pretty close right?" She was really smart, that Hiri. (Oh well, this is actually a natural number approximation by S. Ramanujan.)

Hiri had barely had time to finish her sentence, when there was a violent rocking of the ship with the speed of a machine gun and with very short pauses between the "firings". The hiris flew around the hall as if they had been thrown by a giant hand and landed higgledy-piggledy. They were completely dazed. However, some had perceived that it had all started with three shots, a break, a shot, pause, four shots, one shot and then they no longer kept up. They were not entirely sure of their case, but guessed that the answer symbolized the numerical value of π, probably with hundreds, maybe thousands, millions of decimals, before this damned rocking finished. This was extremely strange! How would the hiris interpret this? Was it evidence of intelligence? Awareness? Willingness to communicate? But were not extremely fast calculations that machines were very good at? Could it be a question about advanced AI they were dealing with? Such machine intelligence as was called *Life 3.0* in a book by *"The world's smartest Swede"*?

In that case, the machines would have taken over and the doublesapiens' worst nightmare would have come true.

Bella Amanda was embarrassed but spoke up again "maybe, numerical language was not the right method to find out, after all, whether we visit spiritual beings and not soulless machines. Can we come up with something better?"

"Love!" Someone exclaimed and everyone agreed "Love! Love! Make Love!" Big waves in a sea of warm emotions washed over them. These feelings embraced the whole collective and once again conveyed to everyone what it meant to be a hiri. The word *love* lacked a rational explanation, a definition, but everyone knew what the word meant. Everyone felt love, in depth, for all their relatives. To nature. To Earth. Which they had not seen in ages.

But now the hiris on the ship had to concentrate on developing a common language with its "hosts" and then establishing renewed and deepened contact. The hiris wanted to follow the example of the Swede and the Tibetan and start with concepts around the word "food". But here no prison guard came and served food. How should one proceed?

Hiri shook her head and said "I think we have to start from scratch. We must first understand who they are we are dealing with. I guess we are in the realm of Dark Matter. Light or other radiation are not used there, but only the law of gravity. But to do this, that is, to handle and manipulate it, one needs to understand gravity. These DM figures understand gravity at the simplest, subnuclear, even sub-JamesJoycian level. They understand the laws of the universe infinitely better than we do. We need to construct a common language based on the laws of mathematics. I think Bella Amanda is right there."

XVI. Love Play

Their common alphabet expanded as time went on. The hiris carved triangles and squares of different lengths and widths. The size was described by the number of blows with the wrench, the direction of the carvings described the shape. This led to the old Greek guy Pythagoras and they were able to expand the realm of numbers beyond that of the natural ones. And so they already knew Archimedes' constant, the number π. It was natural for the circle to make its entrance, followed by the sphere, trigonometry and spherical geometry. The rest then followed quite naturally. Eventually it was quite easy to communicate with each other by means of mathematical concepts, but it turned out to be much more difficult to convey words that referred to everyday things, such as food, drink and hunger. In an attempt to introduce the word *satiety*, they were asked what kind of number system is a "satan". The hiris made several fruitless attempts to explain, but then gave up.

The hiris wanted to know who they were dealing with. When asked how many of their invisible hosts were, they received an incomprehensible answer, the meaning of which they had interpreted as "one many many". If you looked back in time, where did their host come from. The concept of "backwards" seemed completely unknown to the interlocutor. That made it clear that it knew only "forward". However, they eventually established a mutual understanding of what things they should not bother to discuss, or even try to do so. Eventually though, they were able, after some laborious and lengthy work, to converse with each other reasonably satisfactorily.

Hiri still did not know what this mysterious conversation partner was. However, she felt it was time to do something about it. An insane idea crossed her brilliant mind. To visualize the concept of *love*, the hiris would put on a big love party. There would be music, dancing and a lot of beer, but above all hugging, kissing and maybe even a little moofky-poofky. The main thing was that there was contact, a lot of contact, *warm contact.* With the help of this performance, Hiri hoped that they would "unmask their host and see its true face". The other hiris were catching on immediately. The love play what the best play they knew. They sang with beautiful voices like fairies

to be naked, I said,
is nice, so you get laid.
get naked, I said, get laid, I said,
yeah yeah yeah yeah.

and in several places people began to cuddle and kiss. After a while, the performance intensified into pure coital activity. The scale of the ganghumping would even have blushed the Italian Member of Parliament Cicciolina. The acrobatic positions displayed were not even seen in the first edition of the Kama Sutra. The hiris gave evidence of refined seduction art and Eastern Mongolian yoga at the very highest level.

The scene resembled an overcrowded northern German nudist beach and the widespread nudity confused their "host". Who wanted to know why the most valuable organs of the hiris, that is their genitals, were so close to their cloaca. There, such nice things should not be! They should be next to the mouth, because the hiris apparently showed up a show to describe the word *food*.

DM had noticed that several erected hiri penises stood straight up like rods in a bamboo forest and had concluded that the copulating crowd wanted to convey the concept of *hot sausage*. It got that with heat right, but hardly the rest. That thing with *food* was weird and suspicious. Did the host consider the "invaders" to be some kind of fresh Wiener-schnitzel? In principle, all hiris looked the same and this crowd resembled a herd of some kind of copulating animal. Slaughtering them would therefore probably not raise moral concerns. It would just be felt as "at home", quite naturally with the obvious right to make sausages out of them. Understood, of course, that their host acted as people at home. The realisation made Hiri very frightened, but also thoughtful. She still had no idea where they were, and with whom or what. How long would this cat-and-mouse game last? What had happened to the other ship? Would they ever return? Anxiety, bewilderment and despair washed over her.

Hiri came to think of her parents. The parting had come suddenly and become very hasty, as if it should be quickly shoveled away. No heart scenes. Hiri longed for them violently, so that it hit her flat breasts. Tears ran down her long cheeks. "They probably died a long time ago," she thought in pain. "According to the on-board clock, we have been living for more than six hundred years. Except for the twelve who are no longer with us. Even though we are so many, we have lived in harmony with each other, without jealousy, ridicule or bullying. And, above all, without Svante's Law. This is a powerful feeling." Incidentally, they had spent their six hundred years without the stock market crashes of corruption, without emotionally cold bullies or greedy speculators in the money-hungry culture on Earth.

The long separation from their parents had made Hiri depressed for a long time. She was also so desperately unhappy that she had not met her beloved Søren for ages. The Søren Svaalby she remembered was a cheerful guy from the High North. They had not been allowed to grow old together, but they had known that and accepted it. At least on the pretence. Søren was only equipped with double helix cells and they did not last that long. The ends of the double helices shrunk more hastily. She would never see him again. It hurt a lot.

Throughout the love party, Hiri had stood still like a pillar of salt. She had cried herself dry. But in her head the thoughts flew around in a swirling dervish dance. She and the other hiris had always considered that after the passage through the Frommsmann bridge they had ended up somewhere else in the big black space. In their own universe, or possibly in someone else's. But at least in space. Was there any way to find out if that was the case, that is, how it actually went with that thing? An enlightening flash passed through her, when she realized that they had their large telescope always aimed at their own sun. "As a six-hundred-year-old, you easily get distracted and can forget one thing and the other" she joked to herself. She rushed to the observation platform. She wanted to know right away.

Hiris' intense thinking activity had also been felt by many other hiris, who followed her with their eyes. Of course, they were also tense and full of expectation. It took a long time before they heard Hiri saying "Can't see anything. No Sun. No other star either, for that matter. However, we receive radio noise, so it is not completely hopeless." That with the radio noise aroused general interest, because it meant that they were not inside a DM cloud, that is, a cloud of dark matter. There it would be "very quiet on all frequencies" as 813 put it. 813 was interested in electron technology and had read about DM's presumed properties. 813 had not been interested in changing names, but retained his number assigned by the Armed Forces. "To remind me forever of the humiliation of the concentration camp."

Others, however, were already in the process of locating the origin of the radio noise. Where it came from and if it had a particular wavelength. Like, for example, the one at 21 cm, which was the supposedly universally known wavelength of the hydrogen atom's spin flip. Or was it not just a special, but something completely different, distributed over many frequencies? The noise did not seem to come from any particular direction, but seemed to be the same all around. Hiri stood up and started saying “we do not know where we are and who or what surrounds us. And it does not seem like we would find out. Not in the near future, anyway. But we all seem to agree that we need to do something. What I can come up with is the following. On the way here, we have filled in our log on a daily basis. There are our exact coordinates. So, if we're just going backwards, in our own “footsteps” so to speak, we should get out of the predicament. Eventually or maybe quite soon. What do you say?”

“Turn around! Turn around!” was shouted resounding in a unanimous chorus. Going back seemed to be the wish of all and the hiris set off immediately with the departure preparations. They got the engines up and running, but the ship barely moved. It stamped on the spot with roaring machines. Suddenly it seemed to come loose. Just a little. It was as if a giant rubber band was holding the ship. The rubber band stretched more and more and the ship moved slowly forward. Until it came to a halt. Then the ship was suddenly thrown out with a violent force and flew backwards like an arrow from a taut bow. Three hundred and eightyeight souls exhaled. “We are not there yet”, but Hiri was cautiously optimistic.

XVII. Weighing Anchor

After two more annual guard changes, a faint shimmer began to be seen outside the ship. More and more stars appeared, and after a while they found themselves in something resembling their own universe. They did not recognise the groupings of shiny dots in the sky in what could represent constellations, however. The large telescope pointed in a strange direction, and their sun was not visible.

Meanwhile, the "radio operators" had scanned a large number of frequencies on the telescope's receivers and concluded that this from-all-direction radiation resembled the Cosmic Microwave Background, the so-called CMB, as it had been measured on Earth. But it was remarkable that now the apparent temperature was higher. The hiris had found that this was rather exactly three Kelvin. This corresponded to the CMB over a billion years ago. Would they really have passed a Frommsmann bridge and made a dimensional penetration?

Beany exclaimed delightfully straight out "have we come out again in *our own universe* from the past?" Hiri put her forehead in long creases and mumbled, "darned!" She did not like swear words, but used diminutive forms like "mother's little effer" instead of the f-word, "tiny buggerlet" and so on. Did it make any real difference? In any case, she seemed astonished and tried to gather and digest what had happened.

"Beany has a point", she thought, "yes, that must be it."

"Hello, my dear sisterbrothers! I agree and believe that Beany has hit the nail on the head. In some unknown way, we were locked through a Frommsmann bridge and ended up in a place with new four dimensional coordinates. Space and time are intimately connected. A new place in space also means a new time." Hiri took a short break. "The whole thing is immensely exciting and we have a lot to study and to understand. Very much, in fact. I suggest that we divide into smaller study groups and work on it. About twenty sisterbrothers per group seem good. After three days we can have a first reconciliation. Then we will get an idea of whether we are making any progress. Maybe, we need also to regroup. Does this seem okay?" General approval of the working plan.

Pretty soon, however, it became clear that the number of groups was too large, and that twenty members per group were perceived as too small. It was decided to have four groups of ninety-seven hiris in each. The themes to be studied were: *i.* Find methods to figure out where one was at this time, *ii.* make suggestions of what type of destination to visit next, *iii.* draw up an exact roadmap, including the manning of the spaceship and the hibernation routines of the hiris *et cetera* and *iv.* calculate the fuel consumption for the different scenarios. A general wish was also that one would have more time, maybe six months or so.

There was great agreement on this and the hiris began, as so often when it came to important things, with a joint meditation. This lasted for sixteen days.

After that, they all felt pleasantly refreshed. Now they were alert and full of creativity and they immediately set about their respective commitments.

The first group had a really tough task to deal with and they were not at all sure that they had a good solution to the problem. The hiris had concluded that they were probably on the edge of a galaxy, which appears to be of the spiral type, not entirely unlike the Milky Way. Apparently, they had determined the position of the centre of this spinning wheel of shining stars, colourful nebulae, and streaks of dark clouds of dust and soot. Their greatest difficulty lay in choosing a reasonable assumption regarding the galaxy itself.

Using Occam's razor, they chose the simplest of the myriad of hypotheses, namely that they were somewhere in their own Milky Way. In that case, they would have a whole arsenal of high-class observations and analysis tools at their disposal. Above all, a detailed mathematical model for the dynamic evolution of its hundreds of billions of stars. Using this model, they were able to calculate where their sun is at a given time. Like, for example, just over a billion years ago, where they themselves were at present (*sic!*). Then they could fast forward the model to the time of their departure from their solar system, compare the result with its true position, adjust the input parameters and run the model again. Until they got a good match between model and "reality". That was what they had come up with so far. The best value for their present time was one and a half billion years BC, that is before the birth of Christ (hm ...), meaning their "own original time". The calculations had been extremely machine-intensive and for this reason they had not been completed until after four months of hard work.

This was in stark contrast to the time it took to decide the next destination. This took less than three hours. An overwhelming majority in group two had voted in favour of returning to Earth. Despite the risk that they might not recognise their home. Therefore, it was decided to stop at suitable planets "along the way". There, they would find out if any of these planets had produced organic life forms.

With the results of groups one and two in hand, the two remaining tasks were very easy to solve. The model computations showed in which direction to go and the engineers found that the fuel supply was sufficient, and this by a comfortable margin.

From now on, they had kept the Sun steady within the telescope's viewfinder. "It's now about eighth magnitude in V", came the message from the telescope's operating console. "We are barely one hundred and fifty lightyears from home," said Hiri, "so I suggest we go into hibernation and steer toward Earth."

Most of the hiris went into hibernation. Only a few were awake. These were busy keeping a constant eye on all events on and off the ship. They headed for the Sun, but also scanned other stars' planetary systems. After a considerable journey, they discovered a very promising planet around a star not entirely different from the Sun.

The planet was slightly larger than the Earth and was also covered for the most part by water. Liquid water, that is, oceans. Big white cloud systems indicated a favourable atmosphere.

XVIII. Ecce Terra Nova

The hiris, who were on guard on the command bridge, put the ship in orbit around the planet and then woke the others. A general expectant tension spread among the dazed hiris. Hiri herself was very excited when she discovered a landmass on the horizon. Just minutes later, they floated high above the solid ground, which was distinctly black-brown against the bluish-black shimmering sea. There were patches of green, but not so many and so large that one would gaze in awe. "There is no Amazonia in this America," thought Hiri. A chain of active volcanoes engaged in eruptive activity. Hot lava flowed in a black-and-red reindeer down the slopes to the sea. Fountains of evaporating water were followed by a roaring noise along the coast.

When Hiri asked who wanted to go down and land, almost everyone shouted "I want too! I want too! I too want to go down!". Transporting everyone down at once was an impossibility. The ship's ferries only accommodated up to a hundred individuals each. Max. And they were almost four hundred in number. Hiri suggested that they should go in four turns and draw the order in a virtual raffle containing ninety-eight digital tickets with the number one, another ninety-eight with the number two and so on for the numbers three and four. 813, the unnamed hiri, had already started programming the raffle, which was basically an antique random number generator by IBM, and the most eager hiris had already begun to form an orderly queue. The seats were allocated by pressing any key, after which one of the four departures was displayed on the screen with its number.

Janne Bereit, a stately hiri with long black hair and continually erect penis, asked to speak and then said “maybe we should not all go down to one place, but spread out to more locations. In this way, we can collect information from different premises. Then we can meet here again and tell the others what we've seen.” Bella Amanda added “in order to always have someone on board, the first party should return, before number four leaves.” Both proposals were received with general approval.

UV and infrared spectroscopy was exploited to analyse the molecular constituents of the atmosphere. The atmosphere was saturated with water vapour, nitrogen, methane and ammonia and weighed twice as much as Earth's. The volcanoes contributed sulfur containing substances such as foul-smelling hydrogen sulfide and corrosive sulfuric acid. There was not much carbon dioxide as it disappeared into the sea immediately after formation, like the rare oxygen that joined the iron on the planet's surface and coloured it red. Hiri thought that the landscape, yes the whole planet, looked like it might have looked on Earth billions of years ago. She felt that the other hiris shared her thoughts.

Mainly due to the very low oxygen content, but also in view of the caustic sulfuric acid, all hiris were asked to put on their spacesuits. When the first contingent was ready to leave, the remaining ones commented that their sisterbrothers looked like an army of invading aliens. But these strangers did not intend to invade this planet that lacked a larger moon. On the contrary, the hiris came with peaceful intentions. They were simply curious. What it looked like on other Earth-like planets. Was this moonlessnes important in any way?

XIX. Secrets of Life

To have a moon, or not to have a moon has long been the question. However, if Life on Earth emerged from hydrothermal vents on the ocean floor, the tides, far up at the surface, did probably not matter much for the *origin* of Life. However, it seems plausible that the moon did have a crucial importance for the emergence of land based organisms. So, having moons was perhaps not a particularly important issue. Unless one was valuing the Moon for its esthetic beauty, of course.

The green kilometer scale patches that Hiri had seen from the spaceship turned out to be lifeless remnants of dehydrated organisms from the sea. They resembled stromatolites on Earth. These sinks with green must have once been filled with water and then the ground has been raised and formed these formations that resembled giant tubs. Because of plate tectonics? There was no major flow and ebb that could have filled and emptied the tubs. But one thing was quite clear: There has been life on this otherwise so desolate planet. Wherever it may be, *life originates whenever the conditions are right.* Now this far-reaching hypothesis had finally been proven! Through the general cheering came a squeaky voice "could it possibly be a matter of life in a hibernation phase? If we add water from the sea, will the withered spinach come to life again?" Danne Daneson held his breath, a little afraid that he had done away with himself and was found to be ridiculous by the others. Hiri spoke loudly,"what a good idea! We will try and wait and see what happens."

The hiris speculated if there were seasonal changes, winter and summer, dry and rainy periods. In that case, it would not be entirely unreasonable for the green organisms during the rainy season to go into some kind of rainy season seam. Standing in the sulfuric acid rain would definitely be unhealthy. But, then spraying water on the "greens" would not be a good idea, would it? But it turned out differently than they had expected. As soon as they had emptied some canisters of water, it started to grow big green fingers that sought the sea, they sucked in lots of sea water and the flat green carpet became rounder and fuller with each passing minute until it resembled a trembling jelly pudding, though a much larger portion than that served at Aunt Erna's home. The kilometer-sized "pudding" began to move slowly towards the water. This was reminiscent of newly hatched turtle cubs that in thousands all rushed towards the sea. After just crawling out of their buried nests in the sand. How did they know which way to go? They were never wrong. Did they smell the sea? And, how did the green, several-kilometer-long lump of gel know the way? It had no nose. How did the various constituents of this being communicate? It seemed to consist of only a colossal amount of unicellular organisms. But it definitely seemed to be alive now. There was *Life* on this planet! What a discovery!

But some obvious and vital questions arose in front of the hiris. How could the different parts of this giant green creature know what they were doing or would do? How did it "talk"? with itself, with its environment? could it "se","hear"? perceive smell? vibrations, feeling? did it have something resembling a brain? several such?

It actually looked as if it was making some attempts to capture several hiris by rolling over them, but these were too fast and escaped unscathed. "That was a sly dog", someone said breathlessly as he ran for his life. "Oh, that was the biggest bugger I've seen", remarked another, adding "if it's some kind of carnivorous plant, we should probably watch out."

The world around them felt strange. It was completely quiet, there was no wind, there was total silence. There was no noise from the sea, no waves crashing against the shore, not even the slightest ripple. The parts of this colossus that sank into the water caused an inverted tsunami, which pushed a giant, kilometer-high wave out to sea. When finally the whole green mass had disappeared below the surface of the ocean, they were amazed to see how the giant creature, just minutes later, threw itself out of the water like a sperm whale of the Arctic on Earth, but this "whale" was immense, a hundredfold times larger. It created a huge surge of waves that now rushed towards land. The hiris had to run for their lives to save themselves from the rushing masses of water. After a while, they saw how the drained pool had been filled with water again. The water in the pot shimmered beautifully green and at the same time aggressively black.

When the hiris had returned to the shuttle, which stood a good five miles inland, they saw with astonishment that it was surrounded by green jelly. It almost seemed as if the green mass was waiting for them! You could imagine big green fingers drumming on an imaginary table. The whole thing was clearly uncomfortable!

The hiris were now cut off from their vessel. How would they now get back to their ship high above them? Janne Bereit would prove brave and explain to the others his daring plan. When the night had settled over the bare landscape, he would calmly and carefully wade through the green grunge and then go into the shuttle, start it up and pick up the others. He hoped that the "greenling", as he called the algae mass, would sleep and that he, Janne Bereit, would not wake it.

When the time came, he left. Janne seemed to be almost there, when a green arm shot out of the water and grabbed the terrified hiri. Janne Bereit disappeared into the green mud. He had been swallowed, become algae fudder. The hiris mourned their beloved friend in silence.

Still sobbing, Hiri wondered "is this really a carnivorous algae? They're plants, aren't they? Single-celled creatures", she paused and then continued "maybe, they are cannibals?" The crying and sobbing stopped immediately and someone exclaimed "we lure another monster out of the sea and trick it into following dinner, that is, us. When the two meet, they hopefully feast on each other and not on us. What do you say about that?" A general chatter erupted, but it also seemed that everyone thought this was an excellent plan. Hopefully better than the previous one.

By splashing in the sea and making a lot of noise, they actually managed to attract another green monster. This immediately went to attack and a couple of hiris who stood too close could barely escape the slimy arms. This stimulated the algae mass' hunting instinct even more and it became quite easy for the hiris to trick it into persuing them. When the two algae creatures finally met, things did not go as planned. Instead of starting to munch on each other, they united in a friendly way to an even bigger hulk, if this could even be possible. A single giant greenling, as big as Manhattan.

The hiris ran terrified in all possible directions, which completely confused the greenling. It suddenly could not decide in which direction to send its arms. Their undersides had a coating of sticky slime which made their arms excellent fishing gear. The greenling's only short-lived bewilderment was enough for the hiris to wedge away. They ran up a hill. At a safe distance, they watched the green giant, now visibly resigned, slowly retreat to the sea.

The shuttle was ready to start. They had just enough time to lift off the ground, when a violent earthquake shook the entire bare landscape. "That was close," Bella Amanda said, startled, and the others nodded in agreement. They became emotionally aware that the other two hiri groups were also returning to the ship. What would they have to say?

After the usual, cordial hirish welcome ceremony with many hugs and kisses from the various groups that had been "ashore", all the hiris were gathered again in the great hall of the big spaceship. Their stories were somehow similar, but at the same time also very varied.

The landscape around them became black again and mostly porous. Individual islands of young granite protruded from the colourful volcanic soil. Elsewhere, further afield, new, viscous rock masses began to solidify into bizarre formations with sharp edges. Silicon in all its forms, in combination with oxygen and metal. A planetary crust in the making. The hiris looked at the spectacle with speechless reverence. "Did it look like this on the young Earth?" someone wondered. Maybe a couple of billion years ago, but not today.

This led to the big question that had occupied Hiris' brain for a long time now. "What time are we living in now? We seem to live in *our own* room even after the passage through the Frommsmann bridge. This is the universe we know, but has the Frommsmann passage twisted time? So that we have ended up in a same-space-another-era? Have we possibly bent the time? Curled it, stretched it, or moved it along an unknown, imaginary axis into another dimension?" There was a general lack of understanding and considerable confusion. No one had a good answer.

Afterplay

I. Glacies Dulcis

Calle and Sofia Crassasius-Werdhem had since long given up hope of ever seeing their beloved daughter again. Today it was twenty-five years since Hiri disappeared into the night-black space. As usual, the Crassasius-Werdhem couple would also celebrate this anniversary, especially this twenty-fifth anniversary. On the anniversaries, they used to cook Hiris' favourite dessert, namely homemade vanilla ice cream with hot chocolate sauce. Below is the recipe.

Homemade Vanilla Ice Cream with Hot Chocolate Sauce: 3 - 4 servings

ice cream: the recipe is for Italian style, *gelato*:

2 eggs
1 1/4 dl caster sugar
1 vanilla stick
2 1/2 dl milk
2 dl whipping cream

Cut the vanilla pod lengthwise and place it in the saucepan with the milk. Let simmer. Take out the vanilla bean and scrape out the seeds. Put the pod back. In a bowl, beat the eggs and sugar until fluffy. Then pour in the warm vanilla milk while whisking. Pour back into the saucepan and simmer, constantly stirring until the cream thickens. Allow to cool to room temperature. Take up the vanilla bean and stir in the cream. Start the ice cream machine and pour in the ice cream mixture. The machine stops when the ice cream has a creamy consistency.

sauce: *chocolate flavor*:

2 dl whipping cream
2 dl caster sugar
100 g butter
3 tablespoons cocoa
1 teaspoon vanilla sugar: NOTE !!! The vanilla sugar is added after cooking!

Mix the cream, sugar, butter and cocoa in a saucepan. Bring to the boil and then simmer for 5 - 10 minutes on low heat. Remove the pan from the heat and add the vanilla sugar while stirring. Can be served hot or cold.

Hiri's parents sat each on a stool outside the house and lapped up the divine ice cream. China's best gift to humanity. In addition to pasta and fireworks.

They ate the vanilla ice cream with hot chocolate sauce drizzled over beautifully shaped quenelles. Nectar and Ambrosia! Like sitting on Mount Olympus. They sat cozying up in the warm sun.

Harald Heldan, who absolutely did not want to miss the ice cream party, came out of the kitchen door with a bowl and spoon in hand. Harald Heldan was the son Sofia and Calle had born nearly twenty years ago. He was conceived a beautiful morning in "their" cave in the Ahoggar Mountains. They were both sleepy, and they didn't feel much about the fuck. But they made love. Loved with deep affection. Eros sat and watched really pleased. In short, Harald Heldan was a real love child. In contrast to their first love child, Hiri, he was a completely "normal kid", not too long and not too short. Sofia and Calle had baptised him Harald Heldan in honor of his sister Hiri's boyfriend Søren's North Norwegian father Harald Halvdan Svaalby, who had died the same day Hiri went into space. That day, the despairing Søren suffered a double loss. Calle and Sofia took him under their wings and helped him get back on his feet.

II. K S C

Of course, Harald Heldan had never met his sister. Hiri had left before he was even born, but her parents' stories about her fascinated him so violently that he had got the crazy idea that he would go out and look for her. That's why he was now at the Kennedy Space Center, KSC, to train as an astronaut. In the USA, it was enough to be eighteen years old to get an astro card, while in Europe you had to wait until you had turned twenty-five. In China, they even took fourteen-year-olds.

Harald Heldan was called "Harry" by his classmates because they thought his name was too complicated and too long. They could only remember short words. This morning they wildly discussed a news item that had traveled around the globe like an oiled lightning bolt. The Moldovan investigative journalist Zinaida Pandu had revealed what was happening at Camp Hiri. The secret had been shrouded in complete obscurity for decades, but had now been brought to light. Nowadays, the facility was deserted and closed. Not a hint of physical evidence could be gathered that could testify to the events at this desert site. So, it was argued from an official point of view, Zinaida Pandus' allegations were based on pure speculation. What was not speculation, however, was that Scotland *de facto* had abandoned the Hiri cloning program, because it had leaked to the public that the US president had insider-bought shares in the Scottish cloning industry. The president's business led to the entire industry going bankrupt. On a global scale.

The President, on the other hand, couldn't care less and continued to preside.

But no hiris could be found on Earth. And since more than half of the Earth's population now comes from China, most of the astrocourse participants were Chinese children. These constantly played, without looking up, on the mobs in their palms. The teacher had long since given up trying to get their attention. There were a lot of people nowadays, but unfortunately the number of animals on that front looked different. Rhinos, elephants, tigers, among others, and most shark species have been extinct for a long time. All that was left of this once magnificent fauna were a few old-fashioned two-dimensional things called "movies". Those responsible for the disappearance of the animals were mainly old stupid goats who thought that Chinese vaginas would care about tiger penises.

Harry sat engrossed in his thoughts when the teacher asked him, "how long would it take today to go to Proxima Centauri?" Harry stepped out of his dreams and replied, "it's a bunch of years, but I would go anyway. Absolutely." In his red-checkered apple-knit trousers with black braces and his fishbone-knitted canary-yellow-striped long-sleeved curling shirt, Harry looked a little cheeky.

"Can you give me a more detailed answer, kind of with numbers", the teacher did not allow himself to be provoked.

Harry fired back, "but doesn't it depend on how fast you drive?"

"I said *today* and meant *with today's technology,*" the teacher refrained from showing his growing irritation.

"Proxima Centauri is just over four lightyears away, so if we went subrelativistic, say with one percent of the speed of light, it would take at least four hundred years. But since our technology can not handle even a tenth of that, it would probably take more than four thousand years. That's what I meant by *a bunch.* The acceleration and deceleration times would make it even longer."

With a motionless stone face, the teacher was heard saying, "thank you, Harry! This was about our *nearest* star, besides our Sun of course, and it's well worth considering, when we talk about space travel. The moon is only a good lightsecond away and it was very hard to get there, the great achievement of the twentieth century - *...a giant leap for mankind*, as they then said. Giant leap! Ridiculous." The teacher paused, then continued with "so, ladies and gentlemen, we really need to work on it. Come back with good ideas."

Shortly thereafter, the lesson ended. Harry sat motionless staring in front of him, "finding Hiri is probably not going to be that easy", he thought. Then he went to the parking station and got into one of the training vehicles there. Harry called the traffic management, which by old tradition was still called *the tower*, and requested a start permit, as well as approval that he would enter a 600 km high orbit. Or rather 600 km low orbit, a so-called LEO. One would have a good view both downwards and upwards. In addition, up there, it would be slightly sparser than at lower flight levels with the reckless driving of the youngsters' space toys. The radiation values should also be lower than on the ground due to the continued radioactive fallout.

Previously, the originally smaller skirmishes had degenerated and escalated into a large-scale armed conflict. The war had been short, but ruthless. Countless millions of people had died. From his high vantage point, Harry saw that large parts of North America, India, China, and virtually all of Europe were in ruins, black, and burned. Most of the few survivors had migrated to South America, Central Africa and the interior of Australia. To areas where usually no one lived. And that lacked any form of organised infrastructure, no houses, no electricity, no toilets, but screaming water problems. However, some facilities, such as KSC, had been rebuilt, due to their advantageous or strategic locations.

The totalitarian rule of the citizens of the great country in the east included all conceivable, and unimaginable, areas. Among the more bizarre interferences in people's private lives were questions about their reproduction. Not so much about the act itself, that is, how to do it, but the injunctions that concerned parenthood as such. It had been stipulated by law that the state-permitted number of children per woman should be limited to a maximum of one. This in connection with the ever-increasing life expectancy of the population made the dependency burden on the country's seniors increasingly difficult to manage, as fewer and fewer people in society worked productively. This was solved in an equally cynical and effective way, namely to spread a viral, untreatable disease that specifically targeted non-able-to-work-people over the age of sixty-five, that is retirees who burdened the state's finances. The oldies died like flies and the land gave way to a marked rejuvenation. For the state, this meant more welcome income and less costly expenditure.

One odd thing in this context is that those who had instituted the laws themselves had gone far over time. They did not want to die, like most human beings. But above all, they did not want to die of any targeted viral, untreatable disease. They therefore lived separately in closed, guarded areas outside the capital, without transparency for outsiders. Intrusion by unauthorised persons was punishable by death. The execution was carried out immediately by the area's guards. To make it more difficult to see from above, with drones or spy satellites and the like, these political complexes were hidden under large camouflage nets. Harry would not have been able to see them, even if he were right above them.

III. The Shanghai Plan

The thought that constantly gnawed at Harry was, "how can I get to Mars and Hiris' siblings?" The exercise school-craft he was sitting in was, of course, completely out of the question; it could never get up to the speed needed to free itself from the Earth's gravitational pull. He would have to snitch an interplane. But they were very well guarded. Even if he managed to refuel the interplane without attracting attention, it would be futile to think that he could start it and get away, before being shot down. But even if he was prepared for a chance, would the others in his family - Sofia, Calle and Søren - want to take the risk of dying in the coup? He had not even talked to them yet.

But there was also the banal difficulty that he alone would not be able to lift an interplane even an inch from the ground. A crew of at least six trained persons is required. A crew of people who knew what they were doing. His thoughts went to his classmates at the astro school and he invited his best friends to an innocent beer party in his room. Although from Thailand, the twins Somporn and Somsak Pornakrap were not Siamese twins. They were immediately in, and so were the Vietnamese My Dîk and also Bernardo Bernucci from what had once been Rome. After a while, the Austrian prodigy Helga Schulze also joined. Lahore's son Dilip Singh from Punjab, Pakistan, was still hesitant to attend, as he drank only juice for religious reasons and was at first not present at this simple bacchanal. Eventually, however, he joined and sat down among the others.

Harry raised his bottle, toasted and then cut to the chase, “I would like to ask you to help me go to Mars.” He was answered with open mouths. “We would snitch an interplane and drive straight to the red planet. I can not steer the ship alone.” Ten seconds of silence. After that, a jumble of surprised exclamations and loud questions. “Yes, but how? Should we just steal an interplane and leave without asking permission? How did you plan to fix that? What about us, on Mars?” And so on. Harry raised his arms gently and said, “we are not going to steal anything, just borrow. I also do not want you to risk being expelled from school. To avoid punishment, just say I threatened you and hijacked you. I will probably stay on Mars, but you can take the shipwreck and go home with it afterwards. What do you say? Do you need to think about it? It would be a wonderful adventure.”

Dilip was the first to say, “if you are friends, you are. Of course, I’m in. My dad will kill me.” Then he jokingly added, “but you need to stock up on juice for me.” Laughter from the others and then, “yes, damn it, we’re going!” They pounded each other on the back and swore happily. Helga said cautiously and in a low voice, “this will probably be the absolute highlight of the year. Gosh, so cool!” Nods from the others, they would all be in.

“The planet is currently in the seventh house and on its way down, into Aquarius. So, in other words, it will take almost a whole year before we arrive”, remarked one of the Pornakrap twins who were jointly responsible for the navigation. “Hope it’s okay with you”, said Somsak, twin number two. The others shrugged - what choice did you have?

Bernardo filled in, “we probably need to make a plan on how to get over and away with an interplane. Does anyone have a brilliant idea?” Then the otherwise so prudent and shy My came forward, who until now had stayed in the background. “The best and most effective way would probably be that we girls flirt with the guards and distract them, so that you guys can sneak past and snatch the tin can from the hangar. Does that seem a good idea to you, Helga?” - “It’s probably a really good proposal, but maybe it will need more than just a flirtation. Would you be prepared for that, My?” Helga probably had a point there. My answered surprisingly carefree, “of course! One for all, all for one.” This was it, and decided. Helga’s creases in the forehead became smoothed out, “This can become a really fun trip”, she concluded.

IV. An Interplanetarium

Preparations were in full swing. Two weeks of intensive work came to an end. The biggest difficulty had been getting enough fuel. But then Bernardo came forward. His mother's family, Salva-Agrippa, owned in Florida one of the world's largest factories for the production of rocket fuel. Bernardo was a Bernucci, but a Salva-Agrippa on his maternal side and thus a potential successor to the current leader of the Salva-Agrippa Group, which in addition to rocket fuel also manufactured fifteen different sizes of crotchless nylon socks and *one size fits all* jockstraps for ice hockey players.

Bernardo had taken his driver's license for one thousand sixty-plus ton trucks at the age of sixteen and used to work at the factory as a driver during his summer holidays. He was a well-known face among the employees and therefore would not raise much attention, when one fine day he came driving a large tanker on his way to the entrance of the factory area. The gatekeeper saluted for fun and raised the barrier. Bernardo smiled at her and blew a kiss. Then a breath of relief. "Easy as pie", he thought aloud.

At KSC, there was feverish activity in one of the hangars. For security reasons, they had closed the large electronic gate that could now only be opened from the inside. There were the astro mates who were fully occupied with going through the starting protocol, loading supplies, making the berths and emptying the latrine of the "millipede". The nickname of this type of ship indicated that it was a kind of myriapod, that is, that the ship had a length one thousand feet, that is more than three hundred meters. It was of an older model and with a maximum diameter of sixty meters, it belonged to the middle class. They said *she*, when they talked about the ship, and had named her *Antonia*, because she with her six engines in a way reminded of the ancient piece of art *Antonov 225*.

The plan was to leave the following night. It was low season at KSC and not many people on the move. At night there would be hardly a soul out. KSC has long been a civilian planetodrome and its military presence with its heavy weapons was thus extremely limited. A now rarely used runway was to be used for take-off and landing from the time of the "flying frying pans". Admittedly, the track had been significantly expanded in both directions, but the pavement was of the old variety and not particularly hardy.

On one side, the track stretched all the way to the ocean. The idea was to take off towards the sea and then fly low over the water until they had reached international territory. The very low pitch angle required all the knowledge of a well-trained pilot. If everything went according to plan, after just over eleven kilometers they would be only two hundred meters high, from which they would then ascend steeply to a short-lived parking orbit of two hundred kilometers, before taking the leap to Mars. This was the plan.

To everyone's surprise, things went as planned. No problems at all. No guards alerted. No artillery shelling.

No engine trouble. *Antonia* slipped away like an albatross and then flew completely unhindered into space.

Now they had already been “on the road” for just over two months and admired the beautiful double planet in the panoramic windows. At this distance, the Earth and the Moon were most beautiful together. Thus far, Mars was an inconspicuous little dot. My Dîk exclaimed with a hoarse voice to a tune her mother used to hum

I’m coming, I’m coming - I’m coming,
I’m coming, I’m coming - I’m coming,
I’m coming, I’m coming - I’m not coming,
I’m not coming home to Mars tonight.

The others laughed and sang with delight. The joint cantata constituted a small, but very welcome interruption in the boredom on board. Because on board the *Antonia*, it was generally boring. Very boring. Not much happened from day to day. Outside the small windows, it was evenly black, embroidered with small dots of light.

The colouring of the spaceships was ample and the interplane was not at all reminiscent of the sadly monochromatic white or black fantasy ships of ancient *science fiction* movies. The colours were very intense with bright tones of red, yellow, blue, green, ocher and purple. The purpose was not only aesthetically conditioned but would above all be helpful to assist passengers in finding their way. Upon boarding, they were each given a coloured bracelet which was the key to their accommodation. The bracelet bore their room number. The rooms were located on both sides of the corridors on the hexagonal housing wheel. The colourful elevators went to the corner points of the hexagon and the length of the six corridors corresponded to half the diameter of the housing wheel, which was considerable at one hundred and twenty meters. The housing wheel spun incessantly to accomplish something resembling gravity on Earth, stopping only briefly to drop people on or off the elevator. You simply had to wait for your colour.

Those who remembered their Hellas-history would describe the interior design of the rooms very spartan. The walls were smooth aluminum gray arched surfaces. Only a few rooms had any form of wall art or other decoration, most breathed bare fatigue. The floors were very natural-faithfully painted in different parquet patterns of oak or ash. The thin layers of paint weighed much less than the kind of wood they imagined and this made it more suitable for space travel. Carpets of wool or the like were strictly forbidden on board due to the dust they would produce.

The six astronauts from Mother Earth killed time with mental and physical training, such as reading and powerlifting and running, with or without music. With two of the one and five of the other variety, there was an obvious gender imbalance. As for their respective abodes in the sexual landscape, none of them showed obvious homosexual preferences or clear tendencies to other non-“normal” inclinations. The static hormone charge that made the fine hair on the arms stand straight up was felt throughout the ship. The boys became increasingly desperate, but even the girls behaved prurient. The sweet heavy air became saturated with erogens. Everyone began to feel that it was time for pairing. With the unfavourable male odds, the choice layed with the girls.

Helga Schulze was a Viennese prodigy, who, like Amadeus, had composed sonnets as a four-year-old. She had since won everything there was to win in competition contexts when it came to young people's piano play. Her hands, with her long, narrow fingers, could literally fly over the keys, but her touch was full of empathy and sensuality. Although at the moment the four crew members did not look so much at her musical qualities as at her long shaved legs, large breasts and firm buttocks.

My Dîk's breasts were small, but she was not by far as flat as Hiri. My would enjoy their breasts right up to old age, for they would still stand up and not hang down like that pair of gourds, a common phenomenon in senior women's circles. In her tight underwear, she looked extremely well-proportioned. She wore no bra, and the warts were clearly visible. Her minimal thongs almost exposed her private parts, due to only the thin fabric of the undergarment.

Neither Helga nor My had any personal favourite among the guys, they were kind of okay, no *grande amore*. They would all serve as playmates for them. With regard to the question of "who's first?", Bernardo had suggested drawing lots. However, there was no greater enthusiasm for this in either the girls or the three other boys. While they were discussing, My suddenly said, "I can imagine a threesome with the twins, but prefer to take Bernardo, Dilip and Harry one by one." After an astonished silence, Helga reported, "apparently, we seem to be in on this, but I would like to add that we girls only show up when we feel like it and that it is up to us who we want to mate with. Because this is hardly burning love and you should not become fathers to our children."

The guys thought this was a generous offer and of course accepted. My nodded to Somporn and Somsak, "after you take a shower, you can come to my room." The twins disappeared immediately.

The Pornakrap brothers surprised My. They were rather well-equipped in relation to their body length. My was admittedly small and resilient, but not particularly cramped, she had clearly been in training before. Her bushy hair around the fleshy blue-black labia confused the twins at first, but soon contributed to their prolonged stiffening. Both she and the brothers eventually became wildly excited and they indulged completely in mutual enjoyment. Afterwards they sat on My's bed, exhausted but happy. They had found each other and felt neither shame nor embarrassment. They went to the sauna together and relaxed.

Meanwhile, Helga had taken care of Bernardo, who grinned triumphantly at "the next man". Harry had been in the sauna with My and the twin brothers and was now sitting clean and freshly showered in a white bathrobe in Helga's bedroom. Helga came out of the bathroom. She was already, or still, naked. Harry was very captivated by what his eyes provided his brain with, "what a bombastic figure! what a chick!" replied his brain. Helga's body was entirely to his liking, absolutely. But when they began to kiss and play, she seemed stiff and remained cold and dry. Harry interrupted the act of lust, as he would have felt like a rapist if he had continued and penetrated her. Helga looked up and said "Thank you. We'll take it another time, when we both feel like it." Then she gave Dilip Singh a nice rub with her long narrow soft left hand. Dilip bit his lips and sighed loudly, when his semen ended up between Helgas breast.

When they were gathered again, they felt like celebrating the great union. They invited Calle, Sofia and Søren to join in and have some space food and drinks. These consisted of powders dissolved in water that had been recovered from their urine and feces. Even if one ignored, that is, tried to suppress, the idea of the source of water, these dishes were hardly any culinary delights. But they were easy to prepare and hardly required Auguste Escoffier's big cookbook or Paul Bocuse's imagination nor Heston Blumenthal's scientific approach. For those who were born gourmet, space travel was not recommended. The three guests had come on board with the large tanker, hidden in the cabin behind Bernardo, who was standing at the steering console of the large monster. In the hangar they had then hidden in the back quarters of *Anto-*

nia and stayed there from the very beginning and almost throughout the journey. Occasionally they had strolled around on the giant ship, but for the most part they stayed away because they thought they would be in the way and distract the astronauts in the forebody.

But now they had joined their hosts. The three had taken with them two bottles of a pre-war vintage of Dom Pérignon to celebrate fifty days in space. The young people did not really know what was in the bottles, but they suspected that it was some kind of prosecco.

Helga disappeared to find some goblets in real glass, but returned empty-handed, "things like champagne glasses do not exist here. We only have these paper cups." Calle replied that in that case they would drink directly from the bottle, using cardboard cups was out of the question. The bottles went around the team and there were many surprised exclamations. "Wow!", "Yeah, yeah, really good stuff!", "Lord, what is this?" and the like.

Calle told them that for twenty-five years he had saved three bottles of these angelic tears. When he and Sofia were to be reunited with Hiri, they would toast properly, "one bottle each, we thought. In any case, there is now only one bottle left". Sofia broke in, "we have not given up hope, but deep down we may not think we will see our daughter again - we will probably not live that long. Until she comes home, that is."

V. Welcome to Hiristan

During long times in space, social strains among the crew members had in several cases contributed to almost unsuccessful missions. But since an acceptable arrangement had been found on *Antonia* between the members of the group as to their sexual life, it had remained possible to curb the strong tensions and to avoid discharges. They all have lived in reasonably good harmony with each other.

Søren had joined the astroboys and he too was given a treatment by the girls. Considering their relatively old age, Sofia and Calle were nevertheless still very active in their relationship. On all levels.

As they now approached the end of the journey, everyone was expectant and looked forward to having solid ground under their feet again. Everyone longed to avoid the constant humming of the engines and to get rid of this incessant tinnitus. You could go insane for less.

The landing protocol required the fully concentrated attention of the entire crew. The checklist contained one thousand sixty-three points, each of which had to be completed before the actual landing began. They then spent four days in orbit around Mars, ticking off the checklist, which would take another day to complete. When they finally finished entering all the data, they ran through the simulator to ensure that all parameters had their correct values. Then it was finally time.

Landing on Mars was not the same as landing on Earth. With hard-set eyes and white knuckles, Harry held the ship steady, as this, like a giant fireball, rushed through the thin atmosphere. Harry headed for the twenty-one-kilometer long runway in Utopia Planitia. The onboard electronics announced through speakers everywhere in the ship the countdown to touch down. Everyone was seated in the front passenger seats with their belts on and were holding their breath. Thirty seconds more ... then they felt a dull thump and then violent g-forces forward, when the ship braked in with screaming tires. Finally, they rolled out reasonably softly along the dirty red-gray ground.

The crew and their three passengers stepped into their spacesuits and then boarded the bus. They rolled out of the stern hatch of the interplane and then began the six-hour drive to Hiristan, the capital of the hiris. The "capital" was the only settlement of Hiris' offspring and they were all in all barely five hundred people, including the few refugees who had escaped from the Earth's apocalypse.

After several hours, the people in what was called the bus were tired and bruised. The view offered an outstanding monotony that had quickly become dull and sleepy. But the eternal bouncing of the bus meant that they could not fall asleep but just sat drowsy and unwilling.

Suddenly someone shouted, "we have arrived!" And everyone got up to their feet to see what it was all about. The giant graphene-made dome was visible from miles away in the flat landscape. It was surrounded by a large number of smaller ones. The domes were actually large balloons that held a higher pressure inside than the surrounding atmosphere and were filled with Martian air and nitrogen that had been made and added by the hiris. Green plants contributed in the large central dome. There was a forest of twenty, thirty meters high coconut palms that bloomed and bore fruit all year round. Adjacent was a small grove of date palms and citrus trees. All plants were grown from planted coconuts, date kernels and lime pips that had been part of the hiris' travel provisions on their move to Mars. In addition to the forest of bamboo and banana plants around a small pond filled with water, there were flowering plants grown from brought seeds from Earth. There were no natural pollinators like bees and other insects, but the hiris had made small insect-like mechanical flying things that do the job. In a similar way, it had been ensured that artificial worms loosened the earth, or rather, the mars. Lush plants, swirling "insects" and digging "worms" were found in each of the domes. This was the first step in the "terraforming" of the dead red planet.

Outside the large dome in the center of Hiristan, crowds of hiris had gathered to welcome their unexpected guests. Curiosity hung like a thundercloud over the square, which was built as an annex to the great dome. Who were they and what did they want? Apparently they were not hiris, but such creatures as Hiri's parents, Carl and Sofia Crassasius-Werdhem. But these were not visible among the people at the front of the bus. A young man, however, had an appearance that reminded of Hiri. One of the small settlers came forward and asked Harry who he was and what his errand was on Mars and, above all, why he had come to the hiri's settlement. Harry tightened his back and said, "Hello, my name is Harald Heldan Crassasius-Werdhem, but I'm usually called Harry. Hiri is my sister and our parents Sofia and Calle and her boyfriend Søren are also here with me. My best friends from the astronaut school risked suspension and maybe even imprisonment to help us get here. They will return to Earth with the interplane we came with." Harry paused, then continued, "we who are Hiri's family would like to stay with you, if you will allow us to. We will be looking to find Hiri. I have never met my sister and long to hug her."

Johanna Schmelzenegger, the hiri who had first spoken to Harry, turned her head and looked around. All the hiris nodded and smiled and suggested that Johanna continue. Once again Johanna spoke, "we felt that you came with peaceful intentions and you are very welcome. That you are Hiri's family and want to be with us makes us very happy. And proud. Thank you for coming!" A wild cheer erupted in the square.

"Now we're having a party!" was there someone who exclaimed and immediately received a resounding response from the others, "now we're having a party! Now we're having a party! Now we're having a party!" This party was far less sexualised than the previous one. Instead, the hiris concentrated on friendly company with the guests. Speaking, not screwing, was the motto of the evening.

VI. Mars, God of Peace

Harry, his parents and Søren Svaalby had of course come up with peaceful intentions, but not much more - they had no presents nor the slightest contentment with them. It was really bad and embarrassing. All they could contribute to the party was the bottle of Dom P 2008, which Calle had saved. Most of the partygoers would not even get a drop and the main person, Hiri herself, was not there. Now would have been the right time for someone to know that old Jesus trick. Which nobody did, of course. However, in the end, there was no lack of drinks.

The guests had noticed that all over the place, there were long piles stretching towards the sky. On these piles one could see green climbing plants. Hop! If there was hop, there was hope, that is there was beer. Very plentiful, too, beer in large barrels was stored "outdoors", outside the large dome, where it was cool even in the middle of the day. The food served by the kitchen hiris was based on what was grown in Hiristan. There were no animals and the hiris were vegetarians anyway. Harry and the others were very hungry and devoured the cabbage soup with pleasure. Sofia asked the chefs for the recipe. Here is what they told her:

Hiri Cabbage Soup: 4 copious portions

day 1:

1.5 l water
2 bouillon cubes

700 g cabbage
6 potatoes (normal size)
2 carrots (normal size)
2 bay leaves
5 allspice grains
1 dl finely chopped parsley

Boil the water with the allspice, bay leaves and bouillon cubes. Cut the cabbage, moroots and potatoes into fairly large cubes and place them in the boiling water. When the soup has boiled again, lower the heat and cook under a lid for 30 - 40 minutes (feel with the potato picker). Set cool and let rest overnight.

<u>day 2:</u>

Boil the soup and serve with fresh bread and butter and/or cheese. Sprinkle with the finely chopped parsley just before serving. If additional liquid is needed, beer would be good with the food. And traditional.

Harry and his family wanted to know what it was like to live on Mars, didn't the hiris long for Earth? The hiris told with empathy what had happened. They had set off with their interplane and lay in a parking orbit around the Earth, before entering the transfer track that would take them to Mars, their final destination. As they looked down and admired the beautiful blue and white planet, something completely devastating suddenly happened. Everywhere mushrooms grew after violent bomb blasts. The mushrooms looked from above like the flat tops of cumulus nimbus clouds. Below, fires spread in all directions.

This disgusting spectacle lasted for over half an hour. Then it was suddenly over. With the bombings. But the fires multiplied at a furious pace. In the places where one could see through the smoke and the huge clouds of dust, the eyes were met by the sight of an indescribable destruction. The cities were wiped out. The landscape was perforated by huge craters. Forests were flattened. The earth's cities and settlements had been turned into a single great ruin.

What had happened off the coast of Africa, far out in the Atlantic, was extremely strange. A powerful atomic bomb explosion had taken place far beyond the territorial waters of Mauritania. Did anyone want to nukebomb the Cape Verde Islands ??? Whatever the goal might have been, it would have been missed by a colossal margin. Even if they had aimed at the Mauritanian capital Nouakchott, which would just as well have been completely inexplicable. The accuracy of this missile was not one of the wonders of modern technology. The whole of Nouakchott had been spared and the city had remained intact. However, shortly thereafter, the tsunami the bomb had created destroyed the entire city, killing hundreds of thousands. Corpses and debris were swept far up on land.

The hiris were on their way to Mars, which since ancient times had personified the god of war. But they promised each other that they would make the planet a place of peace. The Earth had shown its true face. Tellus was the god of war.

VII. Space Whisper

They lay under the large dome on bast mats and sipped the good beer. Calle wanted to know where the hiris had found the yeast: there were no mushrooms on Mars ... or? Johanna Schmelzenegger laughed and told that they, that is the hiris, had in samples of the Martian soil found freeze-dried spores of some type of fungal culture. They contained DNA, whose molecules also had the same chirality as organisms on Earth. Therefore, this DNA did most certainly not belong to Mars.

One of the amazing miracles of life had occurred when the hiris on a petri dish added water to one of the Martian soil samples. Fungal spores that had lain dormant on Mars' icy surface woke up from their hibernation and immediately began looking for food. They literally threw themselves over the added sugar solution. The sugar had been extracted from the cultivated coconuts.

The hiris stubbornly experimented with the dizzying single-celled creatures and finally succeeded in producing a full-fledged beer yeast. They adopted an Australian invention to get rid of the mushroom-produced carbon dioxide. They placed a filter of Australian green algae on top. This released, as an added bonus, a welcome addition of oxygen. It was not long before the hiris filled their first beer keg and breathed fresh air.

Toward the end of Johanna's narrative, a thin voice was heard a short distance away. "The fact that the fungi have DNA does not in itself prove that they are not genuine Martians. They may have come from Mars to Earth, and not the other way around." It was a hiri child who had spoken. Aniyra was one of the fifty-eight children born on Mars. "By the way, Aniyra was the name." Cell biologist Calle felt compelled to say something, as a kind of expert in the field, so to speak. "Aniyra is probably right. It is by no means easy to determine how and where different forms of life have arisen. The fact that it would be difficult to understand how plants and animals, based on fungi, would have come about, makes the transfer hypothesis less likely. But the probability is not zero."

The hiris were overjoyed: they had a real, non-trivial problem to solve. Had Life been delivered to Mars? That Life had originated on Earth was a long told truth. Or was it possible that Life had actually been transferred from Mars to Earth? To find an answer to that question the hiris would all gather in the annex of the great dome bubble and meditate together until they attain the great collective consciousness. Then they would solve the problem, in a frenzy of feelings of happiness.

The hiris sat still and slowly began to fall into a trance. They felt their nearest neighbour, then the next and then they sensed everyone sitting around them. This perception spread in increasing circles until everyone's consciousness was interconnected in perfect harmony. They had achieved the supra-brain and its outstanding capacity. They had become a single organism. They all longed for Hiri, their mother, the genetic origin of all hiris. Waves of well-being, warmth and boundless love washed over them. After a while, they sensed a form of reverberation, an extremely faint vibration, like a small tuning fork two miles away: Hiri! had they gotten in touch?

Hiri and Bella Amanda sat on the ship's bridge and dozed. They had the guard, but not much happened. The hiris on board had for a while put themselves into deep sleep to dramatically lower their metabolism and thus save on resources, such as food, water and oxygen.

Hiri and Amanda suddenly felt at the same time a vague little ripple in the sea of the infinite universe. They tried to understand what it was they had felt. There it was again. They were immediately awake. It was a cry in space after them! Bella Amanda awoke the sleeping hiris, while Hiri concentrated deeply to determine the direction of the signal. She alone was not able to get a clear sense, but for this everyone's collective ability was needed. Her sisterbrothers on board did not need persuasion, they were all immediately eager and expectant. Hiri thought that at the same time one should try to reach the other ship as well. "We are also thinking of Gudni Helgedottir and her crew." Everyone agreed and prepared for the common great silent cry into space.

After a long time, the loving hiris had finally reached the collective consciousness. They thought of all their comrades out in the vast universe and were carried away by the warmth and bliss of happiness when all the world's hiris responded. A powerful thought grew stronger in Hiristan "Come to Mars! Come to Mars! Come to Mars! "

VIII. Black Mystery

Harry and his gang had set off for Elysium Mons. It was thought that Harry's friends would take the interplane back to Earth, but for the return they had to wait for a more favourable position of the planets. After several weeks of waiting, they had become idle and life in Hiristan had become boring. That's when they decided to go on an adventure. They had set out to reach one of the giant, but long dead, volcanoes. Of all the great Martian volcanoes, Elysium Mons was the closest and that was where they were headed. In size, it is admittedly only number four on Mars, but its considerable height still corresponds to a Mont Blanc stacked on top of a Mount Everest.

They had been driving their red Mars bus for several days, before they finally began to discern the contour of the massive mountain on the horizon. As they got closer, Elysium Mons showed all it's majestic grandiosity. They were literally overwhelmed by its beauty and stared dumbfounded with open mouth. The wind had picked up. The mighty volcanic cone was disappearing at an increasing rate in an opaque cloud of red dust. They had been surprised by a sandstorm and thought of the warnings the hiris had issued. Now it was time to seek protection. At the foot of the mountain they were looking for some kind of pit in which they could endure the storm. There was no time to dig one. After a while, they saw a flat furrow that had probably been dug out of running water billions of years ago. There they dived down and pulled a tarpaulin over themselves. Their space suits made sure that they were not bothered by the sand. They tried to take the opportunity to sleep. If at all possible.

The wind calmed down as suddenly as it had reached hurricane strength the day before. They managed to crawl through a small opening. On top of the tarpaulin lay tons of fine-grained sand. They looked around, but nowhere could they make up their bus. It was like engulfed. Helga Schulze then said, "I crawled in last and looked for our vehicle, to sort of remember where we left it. The bus should be about here", and she pointed with her hand a few meters away. Harry, the Pornakrap twins, My Dîk, Dilip Singh and Bernardo Bernucci looked appreciatively at Helga and started digging with their hands in the soft sand. It did not take long before they had found what they were looking for, the bus was where Helga had pointed. They had to start the engine immediately, as the oxygen supply in their suits was reaching a critical level. They would probably not be able to continue today, but would have to wait until tomorrow. They camped in the shallow ravine, after first completely digging out the bus and then clearing the tarpaulin of sand and stones. At the same time, one stone attracted everyone's attention. It had a different color, shape and structure than what was common on Mars.

The stone was not red but gray, varying in colour to black. It was not round but flat and hexagonal like a honeycomb. And it was not rough but one side was smooth and well polished. In Harry, lightning struck: that stone looked like the one Hiri and their parents had found in the middle of the Sahara desert. On Earth. And he was on Mars! Was this a copy of the grartstone? or was it even the original? He picked it up and turned it over and looked at it from all directions. He waved it a little and held it against the Sun, swaying a little back and forth. And there, quite rightly, he saw the shadow of the fine exact drawings! There were four long, narrow figures with outstretched arms that appeared to dance in a wavy motion.

He told his friends what he had seen, what he had experienced and what he thought it was. Dilip Singh, Somporn and Somsak Pornakrap, My Dîk, Bernardo Bernucci and Helga Schulze were all silenced and had to sit down. Harry followed, with his hand over his forehead, his legs bent under him. They all sat in a circle and did not say a word for a long time.

Then Somporn opened his mouth and then closed it again. Somsak took over and said, "on the stone from Ahoggar there are three figures, and here there are four."

"What, if they are not little old men? Just because we like to see little dancing individuals, they do not have to be. Maybe something completely different. Anything, except elephants, of course." Helga really thought outside the box. Then she added, "*ceterum censeo* that Kilroy has already been here."

Harry rose from his confused thoughts and exclaimed "I'm giving up! I'm going crazy! I do not understand!

I think we should consult with the hiris. Maybe they have an answer." The others nodded in agreement. They abandoned the mountaineering plans and prepared for their return to Hiristan early the next morning.

IX. The Reunion

Gudni Helgedottir and everyone in her crew on Kuiper 2 had felt the weak vibrations in the brain and the light, pleasant tingling in the neck. And on Kuiper 1 it was understood that the message had arrived. The individual hiris had grown together into a single multicellular organism, the abilities of which far exceeded the sum of those of the single beings. In their minds, the hiris now lived in a hyperspace.

Now they could communicate with each other, seemingly outside the fettering framework of physical laws. The thoughts of the hiris were not ripples in any field, they were not oscillations of electromagnetic or gravitational waves or rays of small weightless particles. Their abode was elsewhere and the thoughts lived in a different geometry, where distance in time and space were meaningless concepts.

The closest one could come to human imagination was possibly the parable of an existence within a singularity. Well, if you could imagine something like that. Compared to so-called "ordinary beings" of a double helix nature, their thoughts were orthogonal and had no obvious interface with what is called reality. They did not have to use human language to dissect the phenomena of reality into a sequence of elementary pieces such as letters and morphemes. In a summer meadow, the triplehelixed hiris collectively would know all the names of the beautiful flowers with a single glance and in a savant way how many they were. But the hiris did not count, they just knew. Or rather, perceived.

However, the physical reunification of the hiris on Mars would take another four years. Wherever they were, the hiris now spent much of their time pondering the mystery surrounding the two grartstones. These rocks appeared almost identical, if one ignores the fact that one had been embedded in solidifying magma and the other laid loose in the sand. And the number of figures depicted. These stylised creatures actually resembled the hiris themselves. Their wave movements brought to mind Erwin Schrödinger's wave equation, as well as the works of his respected colleagues. Were the stones about quantum physics? After all, in the quantum world things were possible that are generally believed to be impossible. The guesses were many.

But the number of figures, which were also different, had no apparent direct connection with this theory. On the Ahoggar stone, three were depicted. Two equal in length, and one shorter to the left of them, if what looked like the head indicated what is up. On the Elysium Stone there were four creatures, one smaller to the right and one even smaller to the left of the two equally tall in the middle.

Aniyra, the hiri child who had a veritable intelligence and colourful imagination, suddenly exclaimed, "what if they symbolise the planets in the solar system! The smallest, Mercury, on the far left, the larger Venus and Earth in the middle, and at the far right end the slightly smaller Mars. The number indicates where the stones had been found. In other words, it's not about dancing little guys but planets. The dance may symbolise that they are living beings. That is, those who have made the stones. And that they should be treated with care and respect." After a short pause, she added, "does that seem crazy?" Aniyra wrinkled her nose a little and stood with legs crossed.

A jumble of thoughts, sensory impressions, sensory expressions, and multidimensional images of memory fluctuated in the heads of the hiris, so that it became too much even for the hiris themselves. Hiri said in a soft voice, "I hear you. I see you. I know you. With every fibre in my body. But let's take it a little calmer, at least for a moment, please." The imaginary cacophony turned into a restrained murmur. "Thank you! Thank you very much, my sisters and brothers, my children. Bella Amanda wanted to say a few words. Please, Bella Amanda." Figuratively speaking, Bella Amanda cleared her throat, a little embarrassed, before saying, "hi, yes, thank you. I just wanted to say that I have been trying to find some clues regarding the nature of the stone creatures. For example, do the stone drawings reflect the creatures in natural form and size? Or do any of you know the right scale? Are they still alive in our midst or are they extinct long ago? Is our solar system their home or do they come from far away? Unfortunately, I have not come up with much and have really no answers."

The hiri without a name, 813, launched a slightly curious thought, "if they are kind of termite-like and live underground, but much much smaller, they could still be around. To us they would be completely unnoticed. For the most part, at least." Someone wondered, "do you have any evidence for your termite hypothesis?" 813 did not answer and withdrew in embarrassment. He should not have been ashamed, there were more other rather bizarre suggestions. They were mostly just wild guesses, with no real basis, and one had not come much closer to a plausible theory.

X. Red Wedding

The Siam twins Somporn and Somsak Pornakrap, the Vietnamese girl MyDîk, the handsome Bernardo Bernucci, the Lahore-son Dilip Singh and the god-gifted Helga Schulze from the *bratwurst* city Vienna had held a pow wow and decided that they would fulfill their promises and take back *Antonia* to the John F. Kennedy Astrodrome, as KSC was called officially. Saying goodbye to friends on Mars was painful and many tears rolled down on many cheeks.

The one-year journey took them back to the planet that had once been a blue and white jewel. They had returned the interplane safely and parked it nicely in the hangar they had "borrowed" it from. Afterwards, they were taken care of by the military police and then fined the equivalent of three years' salary. This was a very lenient sentence and nothing to worry about. They slept and ate at the base and did not have much use for money, there was still nothing worth buying. Like food for example. On Earth there was a global catastrophic famine outbreak. Being NASA students, they were still very privileged and were given a meal every other day, consisting of porridge, bread soup or crushed beans. Once a week they got a small piece of meat or sausage. Where the meat or sausage came from they wanted to avoid knowing. Rat was a good guess. Not only because of the lousy food, the friends longed to return to the warm community of Hiristan on Mars. But it was clear, a bowl of cabbage soup would be something to die for. And then, they had very nice pilsner too. The friends planned for the return.

In Hiristan on Mars, Harry had previously been informed about the plan of his Earthly friends. With his full name, he contacted the commander of the Moon Base. He signed up as Harald Heldan Crassasius-Werdhem, so that the Moon-hiris would understand who was calling them. The answer was also very, very friendly, "hi Harry, may I call you Harry? We're related to each other." Harry replied, "of course! And I am really grateful for your instant reply. However, I have, hm, a *problemino* and I wonder if you on the Moon could help me with that." The speaker voice calmly said, "of course, if it's in our power, we'll help as best we can." Harry explained what it was all about.

From his hiri friends on Mars, Harry had understood that their sisterbrothers on the back of the Moon had secretly extended their working hours and improved a couple of moon ferries for long-haul purposes. In normal ferry traffic, the lunar ferries ran daily back and forth between Earth and the Moon. Most of the ferries had now come of age and several used to stand in the hangars for repairs. Grabbing one of them would not be difficult and in the end had not even triggered an alarm. Several of the Moon-hiris had long planned to go to Mars and be reunited with their relatives.

Now that Harry had made his "little" request, the inhabitants of the Moon did not need much time to think. They understood immediately. They decided to take care of the humans. At the same time, they intended to escape themselves as well. Harry announced his astronaut friends who were overjoyed, they would get rid of this miserable half-alive half-dead on the ruined Earth. Would the planet ever recover, perhaps sometime in the future, with future generations of hiris. *Homo sapiens sapiens*, however, would be very very dead very very soon.

The "filching" itself was actually legitimate. The commander of the base had provided a bill of lading for the "emigrants" and they had loaded the supplies ordered by the lunar base. With this old ferry, the journey took almost twelve hours, so the friends had ample time to relax and make plans for the future.

There had been whispered rumours among them for quite a while now, but no one really knew what it was all about. But now Dilip Singh spoke up and said in a low voice, "when we get to Mars, we want to get married, My and I." He waited anxiously for the reaction of the others and glanced in My's direction. She smiled. "This was about time, come on!" exclaimed Bernardo Bernucci. "And, by the way, this was no news." Everyone laughed. Congratulations whirled through the air. Dilip bowed and thanked and My curtsied very courtly, but also a little embarrassed.

The friends did not want to stay on the Moon any longer than necessary, and after only two weeks, the ship to Mars weighed anchor and shipped the hiris and their guests out to Earth's red neighbour. The long journey was largely uneventful. The hiris had entered a state of deep contemplation. Of the hiris there was not a whimper and it was difficult to imagine that there were as many as four hundred small people. Those who hissed and buzzed were Harry's friends. They engaged in various activities, such as now, for example, playing round table tennis. There were no ordinary ping-pong racks, so they used everything, such as palms, flattened aluminum spoons and the screen of a baseball cap. They had a lot of fun and laughed something really violent. But eventually it came to an end and the discouragement of boredom simmered again.

Their situation for the previously so liberating and unforced intercourses had changed. After Dilip's proposal to My Dîk with her consent as a sanction, there was now only one person left for the other three testosterone-sturdy men with whom they could have enjoyable sex. One in three, so Helga Schulze never had to be bored again. Many of her back-on-Earth peers must have been jealous. Helga said kindly but firmly, "I can take Bernardo tonight. And remember, tomorrow is my day off." Disappointed grunting from the boy's shelf, the twins looked a little sour. Although they realized that it was no longer possible for them to hump sweet My with the nice firm little boobies. They sighed silently in mind.

Before bedtime, they sat and planned the wedding together. This would be quite different from what one imagined a wedding celebration on Earth. Before the great destruction, the great killing, the last and greatest mass extinction. My and Dilip, however, wanted it to be a party, they ignored the ceremonies. The actual wedding ceremony was, after all, different in Vietnam and in Pakistan. Although they thought that in Hiris' absence, her mother Sofia could be the officiant. They would be going to ask her for this.

The hiris loved to have a party, but they did not always want to be completely placid and had therefore also brewed a non-alcoholic beer. It looked like the real thing, but came as a nonalco lunch drink. Dilip, who was not allowed to consume alcohol on the basis of the ordinances of his religion, would try this drink after landing. He would find it quite tasty, neither too bitter nor too sweet or sour and with just the right carbon dioxide content. The nonalco was belch-friendly, but lacked the fullness that even an ordinary pilsner could muster. Of course he did not know this.

Dilip wanted Harry as marshal and he would ask him as soon as he had landed. But this would take another four months. But he did not want to do this over the open intercom line. My, on the other hand, had already agreed with Helga that she would be her bridesmaid. Helga had felt flattered and immediately said yes. They discussed what music they would play and what dance they would perform. Dilip voted for waltz (*An der schönen blauen Donau*), while Bernardo thought that breakdance, such as Trixie, would be fine ("to jazz up the party, sort of"). The others did not like any of the suggestions. After a long, sometimes stormy, palaver an ancient piece, actually from the previous millennium, *Only you* was agreed upon. This was by someone called Elvis Presley they had never heard of. Everyone thought this was an acceptable compromise. My smiled lovingly towards Dilip.

On the actual day, the wedding went undramatically, but the hiris sang *Only you* so beautifully, so sweetly and devoutly that the bride and groom got goosebumps all over their bodies. Their friends were relatively unaffected. For them this crooner embarrassed them to the point of being unbearable. But when it was finally over, the party got off to a good start, with fast, rhythmic music, wild dancing and unbridled laughter.

The beer frothed in the glasses and freshly baked bread and white beans in tomato sauce were served for dinner.

XI. Ad Martem

Hiri sat leaning back in her recliner on the bridge and pondered in confusion what she had just experienced. That her double-helixed relatives, and also her fiancé Søren, were still alive. And in safety on Mars. But, how was this possible? Hiri had been in space for over six hundred years. According to accepted theories, the clocks would have run faster on Earth than on their ships. And on Mars too, for that matter. On the planets, more than a thousand years should have passed. This just could not be understood.

Unless... a dimensional penetration would have messed around with their understanding of space-time concepts. That must have been the case, Hiri could not see any other logical possibility. In addition, it would also be completely in harmony with the known laws of science. It was just that the peculiar spatial geometry of the Frommsmann bridge had not previously been studied by the experts. These theorists had not even been aware of its existence. As the room seemed to expand, time seemed to shorten. Just the opposite of previous thinking and experience. Very strange, very interesting.

Startled Hiri went up with an explosive Aha experience: "ἐυρηκα! (heureka!) And that goes without saying!" And she ran her hand over her forehead. She would meet her parents and her beloved Søren again. And her "baby brother" Harald Heldan for the first time. What a bliss! Her ebullience was so intense that it was also immediately perceived by the other hiris.

Warm honey floated deep in their consciousness, with the sweetness of the all-pervading love. This emotional phenomenon also included the hiris aboard the Kuiper 2. Gudni Helgedottir and her sisterbrothers immediately put themselves into deep metahypnosis to communicate with the others. They received a "loud" cheer in response. All the hiris had become one.

On Mars, the hiris understood that the two Kuiper ships would arrive in the near future and they immediately tackled the new construction of homes for their fellow sisterbrothers. Hiristan would grow with a large number of newcomers. But also of the highest priority was the preparations for a thunderous welcome party. Lots of food and drink would be needed. The entertainment with music, dance and magical performances would be provided by talented Hiristaners.

Individually, the hiris were not significantly much more intelligently gifted than ordinary people. Some were even equipped slightly below average, while some had an iq clearly significantly higher. Many hiris, in fact, were rather mediocre in all respects. However, it was their ability to work together in an interconnected collective that distinguished them and made them special. To give them unimaginable power of thought. Ordinary humans lacked this ability. Would evolution ever lead them to develop this unique talent? To satisfy their emotionally cold desire for power? Hopefully, natural selection did not work this way.

But, had it not already done so before?

XII. De Bello Martico - Pars I

On Earth, the democratically elected American president engaged into an alliance with the non-democratically elected Russian president to curb the global hegemony of the equally non-democratically elected Chinese president. All the presidents were men, awful ones too. The non-democratically elected Chinese president had by lie and cunning seized large parts of Africa, Asia and Latin America. The weight of the Chinese yoke made any attempt for economic recovery of these countries futile. Having lost their independence to foreign interference had enslaved them again. This time forever.

Every sensible person would point out that there was not much to argue about - a takeover of *Nada-Land?* All countries lay in smoldering ruins, without infrastructure and without any valuable resources such as food and unpolluted drinking water. Despite persistent rain in most places, radioactivity had not yet diminished and despite the fact that it had been several years since the war had formally ended, the humans' condition was still devastating. They were hungry, frozen and thirsty. Longing for drinking water. For sunshine. For edible food. And for the infected wounds, that were inflicted by radiation sickness, to heal.

However, the presidents, whether democratically elected or not, had completely different concerns than meeting the physical needs of their subjects. Their round body shapes gave clear evidence that they lacked nothing in the way of food and drink. In the underground presidential bunkers, they forged plans to emigrate and colonise the planet Mars.

By this time they were aware of the hiris' settlement and they intended to take advantage of it. And to punish them for their betrayal of abandoning the Moon, for having deceived the generous governments who had made possible the hiris' shameful exodus. A lot of presidential teeth were gnashed on "Mother Earth".

The Americans' cooperation with the Russians was based on pragmatism rather than warm feelings of friendship. The Americans provided the service modules for long-distance travel, while the Russians contributed with their powerful launchers that were capable of sending up six modules at a time to the parking orbit around the Earth. From there, it was no match to reach the escape speed for the flight from Earth. Their common equipment bore with capital letters and fully visible the common cover

USSR

When Republican Steve McMutchel in the US Congress protested against the naming, which was reminiscent of an old foreign communist's immoral erotic and musical activities, the female Democratic senator Ann Pelzing replied that U stands for United, SS for Solar System and R for Research. And you had to accept that.

The Chinese, the new flag bearers of colonialism, did not feel the need to cooperate with anyone else. Due to their favourable "trade agreements" with countries in the "Third World", they had acquired access to the necessary natural resources. After their scientists and engineers had been trained for free at American and Russian universities, the Chinese now had the technical knowledge required for successful space operations. Their flagship, the Long March 186P/R, *Chang Zheng 186P/R*, would be capable of sending troops and military equipment to any planet. "Not a problem," according to the non-democratically elected Chinese president.

Who would first make it to Mars with his military units had developed into a frenetic race against time. On both sides, USSR and CHN, work was done feverishly to ensure a first arrival and thus the occupation of large parts of the red planet. It was planned to land near Hiristan, take "the city" in one day, and immediately establish one's own administration. A prevailing assessment was that the hiris were peace-loving hippie-like creatures who would not offer serious resistance.

A total domination was equally accessible as crucial. An important strategic aspect was also to intercept the competitors' ships already in space, where warfare could be considered easier than on the ground, and strike out the opponent's forces once and for all. Apart from the eight months that the crossing would take, it was calculated that the campaign outside Mars and the invasion of it would be over in a few days.

Neither USSR nor CHN had reckoned that the hiris had feared that this would happen. And would carefully prepare for this. They had hoped until the bitter end that they would be left in peace, but then saw the merciless truth in the cold presidential eyes: man seemed incorrigible. Always eager to fight since time immemorial. Killing machines.

The hiris were not hannibals, they would not lead elephants over any Alp, but they were as cunning as the ancient Punic warlord, if not even more so.

They invested in something that no one would expect. Their double-helixed guests should basically have no qualms about the use of force in selfdefense. They would ask them, Hiris' parents and the others, if they were willing to train the hiris in martial arts. Because the hiris wanted to be prepared to fight for their right. To Exist. To Live. They had realised the inevitability and that they had to resort to tangible action. But they promised each other that they would use the least possible amount of violence. An absolute minimum. At best, none at all.

Of course, the double-helixed friends would line up. There was no question of anything else. But fighting hiris? They were hesitant. "We have to come up with something else," Harry explained. "With me, brother-in-law Søren, Mamma Sofia, Pappa Calle, my buddies Somporn, Somsak, My, Bernardo, Helga and Dilip, we are ten able-bodied and battle-ready people. Not much against a whole army. But you hiris must figure out how you want to place your ten pieces in the best way on the chess board." General applause rewarded Harry's well-worded speech.

Mars resident Johanna Schmelzenegger wondered if it mattered whether the Americans, along with the Russians, arrived first or whether it was the Chinese who did it. After a rather lengthy discussion, it was concluded that it probably did not. Aniyra remarked in her somewhat precocious way, "one would assume that both parties will choose the nearest optimal date for departure. Thus, they should arrive with us at about the same time. It would be thankful, if we could persuade them that they neutralised each other." Well spoken. Thank you, Aniyra!

The hiris were at once completely absorbed in planning different strategies in different scenarios. Which tactic would be best in the individual cases. For example, to leave Hiristan and head out into space and hide on the back of the planet? Or to apply the tactics of the scorched earth and destroy the whole of Hiristan, with all that it entailed?

Now it was the prodigy Helga who came out with a trump card, "I remember that you hiris and the AI machines had a well-functioning collaboration in Camp Hiri. Wasn't that so?" A unison nod of the elongated heads. "Hm," Helga continued, "maybe, we could build on this. I imagine you could possibly agree with the AI machines where to maneuvre their respective fleets. Would you be able to direct them on a collision course? In that case, there would be no need for any use of force by either you or us. The bandits can handle this themselves." After a brief pause she added, "in short, can you hack the AI software and send over some code changes? New coordinates and stuff like that."

A long moment of silence. Then it broke loose. Wild cheers erupted, as all the hiris began to shout and moan, and talk all at once. Even though in this noise it was not possible to hear what was being said, the spirit was clear: Of course they could do it. Piece of cake. But what a brilliant idea this was! Why had they not thought of it themselves? And, how nice that you yourself did not commit acts of violence! And similar. The hiris, who indulged in strict pacifism, became blissful and began to sing. An old song, *We shall overcome*. Harry's parents were old enough to recognise it and they sang along. Harry looked admiringly at Helga, who just smiled contentedly.

After a long journey, the two "longsailers" Kuiper 1 and Kuiper 2 were reunited near Pluto's orbit. That was where they had once parted. When the crews entered each other's ships, it became a very heartily hugging and kissing. The hiris slipped into a joyful euphoria and were boundlessly happy to be seen well again. After a while, however, they mourned the seventeen who had fallen and were no longer among them. One of them was the always cheerful Janne Bereit who had sacrificed his life to save his friends.

Hiris' story of the voyage on Kuiper 1 was very detailed. Gudni Helgedottir listened very attentively. Hiris' memory of DM was like gel, which could not be caught and held, but flowed through her fingers like water, and when she tried to catch it, it fell apart into smaller and smaller pieces until these disappeared into nothingness. Her memory image was dark, formless, indefinable.

Gudni responded that this was not entirely different from her own experience around the black hole they had happened to end up at. They had not found any GHCs, but had come close to a black hole.

What happened was that at some point during the journey, it seemed as if they were slowing down. Almost imperceptible at first, but the small reduction in engine power had clearly been registered by the ship's instruments. This deceleration increased steadily with time and Gudni realised that they had to do something. They ran the engines at full throttle for several minutes and finally managed to free themselves from the force field of the black hole, which was still relatively weak. After all, they had still been at a reasonable distance. Gudni described the surroundings of the hole as completely unrecognisable and unrealistically distorted. She would like to return to "her" hole and study it more closely. Hiri said she felt the same way about "her" Dark Men. They decided that, after the trip to Mars, they would follow their instincts and together travel back to these strange phenomena.

The crews of the two ships had so much to tell each other. But they had still a long way to go to Mars and there would be enough time. Kuiper 2 joined Kuiper 1 to go along to their new home.

XIII. The Battle of Deimos

The hiris had come to the conclusion that they would try to solve their problems with the impending invasion at a reasonable distance from Mars itself. In particular, as far away from Hiristan as possible. They had chosen an area in space outside Deimos, the smaller of the planet's two moons.

One would take advantage of the fact that military camouflage technology had been pushed to near perfection. Nowadays, one could expect that one's own armada would remain largely invisible to the enemy's constantly sweeping ν-echo search system. The contours of the warships would apparently not be drawn until they were at a fairly close distance. And then it was mostly already too late.

But the enemy had his own invisibility cloak. So, in the end, no one would be able to see anything, until the cannons towered right in front of your nose. In order not to lose valuable minimal fractions of a second, the weaponry was completely autonomous. They would not have to wait for an order from any sinister commander, but would fire their entire arsenal of weapons the moment they became aware of their antagonists. If both sides' ships were on a collision course, so the hiris reasoned, these combatants should contribute to the hiris' own welcome party with an outstanding fireworks display.

The hiri-hackers made contact with the computers onboard the armadas relatively easily. The necessary changes to the navigation and attack protocols were made quickly and smoothly. The AI software had been surprisingly benevolent and proved to be very willing to help. This felt a bit creepy, but the hiris were too busy at the moment to care.

Then it was just a matter of waiting. Until it was high above them and far above the Martian atmosphere, the silent fireworks of a wand were visible. The color leaned towards black and white and mostly a down-dying killer gray. The glow of the silent colours was far more brilliant in its dazzling intensity than the surrounding stars. After four minutes and seventeen seconds, it was all over. Dark night settled over Hiristan. Both Phobos and Deimos gave off their cold blue and white glow as usual and the stars had regained the dominion of light over the sky. The hiris and their friends stared in amazement at the abrupt end of the play.

Then the beer glasses were filled with foam-drink and the dancing came into full swing. The intoxication of happiness was stronger than that of the beer. A miracle had happened on Mars. The hiris had won a war without a fight!

The colonial masters had annihilated each other.

Mars would not become anyone's colony! Never! Not as long as there was a hiri alive.

XIV. Peace on Mars

Harry had taken a great liking to the adorable Helga. She did not have any of the manners one might expect from someone who throughout her life had been treated by the outside world as a genius. She behaved just like any other girl. And that made Harry not feel inferior, but he could hang out with her in a completely natural, non-artificial way. Helga in turn was happy that, when she was with Harry, she could be who she wanted to be. She realised that she had actually fallen in love with him and that she was waiting longingly for the moments when they would be together. Her original coldness and stiffness had turned into wild hot heat. Harry was very loving and wanted her to know him with love, when they made love. And Helga loved to make love with him. They had decided that Harry would come to her room, and this afternoon she had expected him, posing as the woman in Gustave Courbet's beautiful painting *l'origine du monde.* This artist ploy was very successful and Harry moaned with bliss.

In the room next door, Hiri and her Søren enjoyed each other. Hiris' Norwegian lover caressed her dysfunctional penis as if it were her clitoris. Which it actually was. Hiri reacted to the Norman's gentle touch and increasing rubbing with immense lust and pleasure. She did the same on his erected apparatus and he screamed jubilantly with the feeling of happiness and greatest joy. Luckily, the rooms were soundproofed. Therefore, nothing was heard from Hiri's parents' room on the floor above. The two oldies indulged in bonobo-inspired sex in their usual favourite position. Sofia sighed with closed eyes and great pleasure, while her husband Calle waved his arms wildly, while he lowered his genital organ into her from behind.

On Mars it was all honky-dory.

What could possibly have created some low-level discord was this newly established circumstance about the distribution of gender partners. Both the adult ladies My Dîk and Helga Schulze had entered into a stable relationship and were no longer available on the free love market. Initially, this reorganisation had left the Pornakrap twins and Bernardo Bernucci worried.

However, after a small cloud cover at first, they had quickly overcome their love worries. Among the hiris were many beautiful lures of the female kind who liked to flirt with the boys. The boys did not have to suffer for a long time from love sickness. This activity between humans and hiris led after some time to a significant cohort of anthropogenic hybrids. The fertile boys had layed many promiscuous hiridames, which had led to countless successful cross-fertilisations. In Hiristan, these offspring were called anthropohybrids. The hiris did not differentiate between them and they were brought up as if they were thoroughbred hiris. Except these being a couple of decimetres taller.

On Mars it was all honky-dory.

XV. The Grartstone Mystery

They sat at the bar in Hiristan's pub *The Blond Head.* Blonde Nina leaned forward on the counter and looked at Calle, who was sitting to her right, a few meters away. "Hey, old man! You who have been around for a while, what do you think the stone is for?"

She grinned a little seductively at the well-preserved eighty-year-old. Calle cleared his throat, as he used to do when he was embarrassed, before answering in a steady bass voice, "little girl, you know very well that we know no one knows, as far as I know. Actually, the non-science seems to be well documented. So, why are you wondering?"

Fair haired Nina now seemed less scornful, rather more serious, when she revealed, "I did not mean to be mean, please forgive me. I thought more like that you have been with it from the very beginning. In the Sahara. And have had all the time in the world to ponder the six-sided thing. Or maybe, I did not think at all. It was stupid of me, sorry!" Calle's answer was not long in coming, "by all means, Blondie. No harm was done. But you're right, I've been thinking about it every single day of my long life and would really like to know, what the thing represents."

Blonde Nina now raised her voice, so that the other double helixes in the room could also hear, "then I think we make a serious attempt and call on all hiris to take part in our deep dive into the mystery of the grartstones. What do you think?" Consistent approval from the triple helixes answered the call. "Okay then, we empty our cups now and start our session shortly afterwards. This may take some time."

The double helixes, that is Calle's family and friends, felt a little out of place, but quickly got over it when they refilled their glasses. They all felt the excitement of the upcoming experiment. Would the hiris really be able to figure out the origin and significance of the grartstones? Only with thinking power? Or did the hiris also have access to data they did not know of? Any more crucial piece of information? Did the AI machines have it?

Harry put his arm around Helga, as if to say, "now it's maybe your turn, darling", but his new girlfriend just wrinkled her nose a little. She was good at music, not petrology. Harry's mom Sofia thought they should have, "first thing on the go, as well", because it was actually Calle, Hiri and herself with the help of Ali and Beli who had found Number One and Harry and his friends Number Two.

But Harry's father said disapprovingly, "now we are not going to spread discord! The hiris have always been exceptionally welcoming and helpful. And we should be nothing but grateful. Very grateful, indeed. But above all, not suspicious." A filthy blanket of shame did lay down on the beer-inflated, red-faced congregation, and there were mumbles, "yes, we should be ashamed," and, "they are really very kind and thorough," and the like.

Harry felt Helga push him to the side, as if to say, "now it's actually your turn". Harry seemed to understand immediately what she meant. He looked at his friends at the table and said, "listen, there is also another thing I wanted to talk about with you. We've been here in Hiristan for almost two *months, years, longer?* and have done nothing but hang out here in the pub and drink beer. For free. Maybe it's time we helped with the management here in town. Agreed?" Everyone nodded, "yeah, that sounds sensible." Harry then suggested that one be divided into work teams, according to one's ability and liking. He thought that his parents should be able to escape due to age, but was met by loud opposition from both Calle and Sofia. "We are fully capable of work and want to contribute what we can. Dig in flower beds and such", said the almost offended Calle.

So Calle, Sofia, My and Dilip made up the fieldwork and gardening team, Somporn and Somsak were assigned to the kitchen regions and Harry and Helga to the mechanics workshop. Bernardo had to drive the big garbage truck. Then it was just a matter of getting started. But first one would have one for the road.

In the large assembly hall, hundreds of hiris were in a single large meditative collective. They were gurus in the lotus position or lying flat on the floor, deeply immersed in a greater consciousness, with limits far beyond the individual's own ability. In this common, unifying contemplation, they captured vibrations of innumerable other life forms in the universe and experienced a cosmic togetherness that they had never known before. The hiris were becoming the new human race, which was integrated into the cosmic web of life's wonderful mystery.

Their colossal brain nourished thoughts of ancient times. They saw hiri-like creatures hovering in billion-year-old worlds that resembled and did not resemble the Earth they had left. They saw a Mars populated by millions of hiris, and many other inhabited planets that still lacked names. The mutation that had given birth to *homo trihel hiri* meant the end of the primitive primates; *homo sapiens sapiens* had become a fossil, which at the high stage of evolution was little more developed than australopithecus, whose cannibalism genes had survived for well over a couple of million years, but now met its predetermined fate. Man was an endangered species. Endangered by man.

The issue of extraterrestrial life has always been a hotly debated topic among ordinary, as well as unusual, people. Extremely provocative was the view that so-called *intelligent* life should exist in large numbers. Those who supported this were considered stupid by those who firmly denied that this would be the case.

Since the concept of intelligence, like life itself, lacked a clear definition accepted by philosophers, man referred to himelf, the wise man, as a prime example and a suitable yardstick. This was reflected in the fact that the concept of high-intelligence was most often equated with high-tech. A common saying was, "it takes an extremely high level of intelligence to screw a rocket engine together." It was further believed that extraterrestrial intelligence should have come to Earth to visit the intelligent species homo and invite him to sit at the cosmic table of the large intelligent family. Or sent technical gizmos, such as probes, to find out what these homini are. Perhaps, without wanting to establish any contact. Spy on them. On access to food, water, minerals.

If one accepts the validity of the axiom that life arises wherever and whenever circumstances are favourable, then one can by means of a simple abacus find that such extraterrestrial intelligence is probably much older than the terrestrial one. And thus technically more advanced, as the intel-techno theorem prescribed. “So, why then have we not seen a hint of them?” one physicist asked another physicist during a lunch break. We do not know the details of this conversation, but the other physicist may have replied, “but what about all these observations of the buzzing buggies?”, whereupon the first possibly contradicted with, “what about them? These buggies are just harmless chimaera”. And in this spirit the “debate” continues even today.

One thing that came to Calle’s mind, and which, according to his possibly deficient memory, had not been properly discussed, was the age of the grartstone. Geologists had estimated this to be more than a billion years old. Could there be a problem with the “normalisation”, as the researchers called it? The age they had determined was based on the assumption that the original occurrence of rhenium, compared to other basic substances, such as osmium, for example, was largely the same wherever one was, on Mother Earth or several lightyears away. But if that were not the case, could this explain the similarities between the figures on the grartstone plates and those that had been claimed to come from zeta Reticuli? A retired scientist, Calle was very hesitant about this and he decided to ask his beloved daughter Hiri about it, as soon she had returned from her long journey through space.

In Hiristan, the hiris' journey of thought had taken a full seven months. Explainably, they were now very thirsty and hungry. Many would also go to pee, poop and take a much-needed shower. When they were gathered again, they all sat down to eat and drink. A good beer and a delicious bowl of cabbage soup. According to general opinion, Somporn and Somsak had really succeeded well with the food. Thais are good cooks.

Blonde Nina and Johanna Schmelzenegger had sat down at the humans' table and the conversation was, of course, about the hiris' experiences. What they had to say filled Harry, his family and friends with utmost astonishment and also fabulous wonder. What the hiris had experienced was so uniquely beautiful that they could not resist feeling jealous. Even if they bravely tried not to. They listened devoutly and for a long time to the stories of the two hiris, but eventually became impatient. They wanted to know if they, the hiris, had gained any real knowledge about these strange grartstones.

Johanna Schmelzenegger looked up and cleared her thoat almost inaudibly. She leaned forward a little and with the index finger of her right hand slightly up in the air, she said in a calm voice. "Listen, here", she began, "what we have experienced is difficult to digest, even for a hiri. But all I can do is promise that we speak the truth, pure and simple truth." Johanna took a break and Nina cut in, "to simplify the whole thing, I can compare this with an experience of what you see with your eyes. We could see straight ahead, backwards and around the corner, all at the same time. It was as if the past, the present and the future were in one place. And among many other things and events, we also saw the history and future of the grartstones, as well as where they are nowadays."

Johanna took over again, "they came to the Sun when it was about three and a half billion years old. They reckoned that, by that time, Life on one of the closest-in planets should have gained a foothold. And there, on this desolate number three from its star, surely there was Life! Unicellular organisms that were transforming this inhospitable place into something, where the development of new organisms could take over.

They left grartstones on the innermost planets and on some of the largest moons. The tiles were made of a material that would resist volcanism and erosion in a toxic atmosphere. When they discovered that something or someone had moved in the position of the plates, they would investigate what had happened." After a short pause, she added, "and as someone has so rightly already figured out, the number of characters indicates the positions of the planets as seen from the star."

When Johanna and Nina had finished their stories, it became completely silent for a long time. Nobody said a word.

After several minutes of silence, My's squeaky voice was heard "but who or what are *they*?"

PART II

The Era of the Hirudineae

I. Vela Solaris

On Mars, the hiri population had long since increased to above the billion mark and several new towns had taken shape. Due to the strong seasonal changes, food production was creating local problems. During the "winter half-year", which actually lasted a whole Earth-year, freezes were not uncommon. Due to the cold, even in the greenhouses, many vegetables became directly compost fuel. Above all, hops were very sensitive to the weather and the declining supply of hops had become a national concern. Because on these occasions it was actually a catastrophic situation. As is well known, hops are difficult to replace with something else when brewing good beer. And the brewing industry was the cornerstone of the hiri's economy. And beer hiris' favourite joy, along with copulation.

On the bright side's account, however, one could note that the atmosphere was finally about to become hiri-friendly and breathable without an oxygen tube. In addition, the creation of the hydrosphere had almost been completed and its volume had increased manifold. Thus, the outside temperature had even reached nearly tolerable levels.

Several martian years ago, Hiri had buried her beloved relatives and dear friends, one by one. The tomb was located outside Hiristan, in Utopia Planitia. One day she would also be buried there and contribute some nourishment to the barren soil. When finally her baby brother had also passed away, Hiri in her grief moved to the city of Olympostan at the foot of Olympus Mons. There, she had finally found some comfort; whenever she woke up, after sleep, meditation or hibernation, she was happy that the first thing she saw was this mighty, majestic volcanic cone outside her window.

Now she sat with engineers, electronics technicians, laser fixers, materials scientists and shipbuilders in her living room to discuss the latest difficulties encountered in the construction of the hiris' new "longsailers". As usual, fissionists and fusionists were verbally fighting. But the problem Hiri wanted to discuss was actually quite trivial. With its sixty-four square kilometers when fully deployed, the sail was so large that the navigation system's communication antenna was in the radio shadow. There, it was of course no good. One of the proposed solutions to this *problemino* was to place the telescopic antenna on a periscope boom, which if necessary could be driven out more than eleven kilometers. But some critics claimed that this would be too shaky and thus interfere with the signals. To get an optimal reception a very stable system was required.

Another suggestion sounded a bit ridiculous at first, but won, after some deliberation, full approval. Since we were talking here about space *ships*, you could also imagine such a thing as a space *dinghy*. In other words, it was thought to have a large relay antenna mounted on a much smaller spacecraft that vis-à-vis the mother ship could maneuver with meticulous precision. By letting the dinghy fly at any distance, you could achieve complete surround coverage.

With this clarified, they moved on to the next problem, and to the next and to the next and so on. The agenda list was long. The whole meeting, with all its controversial discussion topics, as well as those that at first seemed banal, took nine weeks and the participating hiris were, once it was over, rather exhausted. Although they had been given food and drink a couple of times, and had not needed sleep, the long concentration had been strenuous.

After most of them had left the meeting and were about to return to their homes, Gudni Helgedottir had stayed and said, "as we now approach the end of the construction, it will probably be time to plan for our joint trip. Or what do you think, Hiri?" Hiri looked up and smiled. All over her elongated face. "You are so right and I'm glad you brought it up. Yes, we have some work to do." And added a little jokingly, "we need to deal with our dark past."

After a short pause, she added, "but I'm sorry if I have to disappoint you, Gudni. First I have to fulfill a promise I made to my brother on his deathbed. He was very stubborn and pressured me to promise him to look for the creator of the grartstones. And what I promised, I will keep." Gudni answered with determination in her voice, "but, dear Hiri, it is obvious that we should look for the architects of this miraculous phenomenon. Our dark past does not run away, it still exists." Hiri replied, "it is very kind of you and I'm very happy for you to join. It feels much safer, thank you my friend. We may convene a meeting on this. But we will probably let people sleep first, before we start."

II. To Know Or Not To Know

The hiris had come from near and far to attend this important meeting. The expectations were high and the tension was up. Here one of the biggest questions would be discussed: Where do we come from and where are we going?

Very unexpectedly, the usually so cynical and skeptical Aniyra took up what she called the *eight hundred and thirteen* hypothesis. Aniyra had grown up, but being hiri she was still small in stature. By the standards of the double helixes measured. "813 had imagined that some visitors, or their machines if they did not come themselves, could be, quote: *sort of termite-like and live underground, but much much smaller.* This idea may not be as absurd as it sounds. It probably needs to be studied in more detail."

"That was well spoken, Aniyra", remarked the tall Astrid, who to her great annoyance was called Beany by everybody, "but where should we start untying the knot?" Aniyra folded her forehead and replied, "I'm still a little brain rusty, but I thought we might have been staring blindly at what is depicted on the stone slabs themselves. But an important indication was that the material the plate consists of did not seem to be something that occurs *naturally* on Earth. But that it had to be manufactured artificially. And this with outstanding technical know-how."

Now 813 spoke, who had been sitting quietly for a long time. "If the age determination is only approximately correct, the tiles may not have been made by human hands. Such hands have not yet been available in a thousand million years. So, since there was also no reasonably developed complex life on Earth, not even any plants, the conclusion that the plates come from outside, that is from space, is straightforward, I think. Maybe, we should look there, in outer space that is." Hiri looked up and said, "because one plate has been found here on Mars, and it was just lying loose in the sand, so maybe the plates were made here? At that time, it looked much more inviting on this planet and life would have had enough time to emerge and to develop. Does that make sense?" A general nod indicated agreement. Hiri continued, "but apart from the grartstone slabs we have not found a single slight hint of remnants of any ancient Mars culture. I agree with 813 that we should look to the expanses of the cosmos."

Now Bella Amanda, who had been impatiently chattering around on the floor, thought it was her turn to speak. "When we were out looking for globular clusters of holes, we went to a small area where the stars formed a beautiful hexagon, a really smooth and uniform hexagon. In the Kuiper 1 log, we called that little constellation Favus Apis, because it reminded us of the bees' wax cakes. The coordinates are probably still in the log. Is it conceivable that the hexagonal shape of the paving slabs means something that we have completely missed? That it points in the direction the "stonemasons" came from? To say to everyone in the universe: we have existed!"

Amanda breathed heavily, still overwhelmed by what that meant, that she had just said. And with a secretive mine, she added, "or maybe even: we do exist."

Devotional silence. The thought was dizzying. A life form that had lived for more than a billion years? Could this be possible? Is it even reasonable?

The silence was broken as suddenly as it had begun. Thousands of hiris spoke all at once, one more persuasive than the others. When most had calmed down and the palaver began to drizzle dry, however, it became clear that the hiris were all completely convinced that this was something extraordinarily important. They were fully committed to the issue and agreed that it was a must to find out how it was, "it's quite clear! Some sister-brothers must go out and look." The decision had been made.

III. Favus Apis

What Bella Amanda remembered was that, if you followed the stars' relative positions counterclockwise, they changed color, from violet in the upper left corner to blue, green, yellow, orange and red in the upper right. The order of the stars seemed to follow the true colors of the light spectrum, which was a bit bizarre, almost like an artificial arrangement. Equally remarkable was that they seemed to have the same brightness. Therefore, it was most likely that they were not at the same distance, but that the geometric constellation was only a projection effect. And that it was the red star that was probably the closest. Consequently, the hiris decided to visit this one first. They had given it the designation α^1 Api. To dispel possible misunderstandings, this did not mean the alpha male of the monkeys.

The hiris knew that alpha-one-apis was the mother of five cataloged planets. Four of them orbited very close to their host star, while the fifth was at a considerable distance. This was perhaps a brown dwarf rather than a planet, in which the difference now lay. An important thing in this context, however, was that the star could be very old. Yes, maybe even as old as the Milky Way itself. If any of the planets were inhabited, the age of the grartstonenists, as the hiris now called the creators of the grartstones, could be consistent with the age determination of the stone that had been made on Earth.

Traditionally, the focus was on the planets that could be, in whole or in part, covered with liquid water, although in theory there were more solvents that could develop and sustain viable organisms. But water was the liquid that had been so crucial to the creation of Life on Earth. And had remained so for over five hundred million years.

The very existence of the grartstones testified that the grartstoneists had definitely existed. A billion years ago. Had stayed on Mars and also left a specimen in one of the Earth's magma seas. But Nina's, Johanna's and the other fellow travelers' memories of the grartstoneists had in a strange way become distorted and increasingly obscure. The colourless remnants of memory had faded beyond recognition. The perceived, distorted time perspectives of the past and the future meant that the hiris in the present could no longer capture a clear sharp picture. But they knew that, when it happened, their experiences had given them a rigid goose pimples. The impressions had been truly on their bodies, real and the pictures crystal clear. Their sensations had been wonderfully beautiful, but also macabre and terribly frightening at the same time. But no one could remember and tell what it was they had seen or why they felt this way.

Hiri and Gudni sat and looked at each other. A problem that was unexpected for them had arisen, namely how the selection of those who would be allowed to travel would go. Well over thirty thousand applications had been received in just a few hours, but the size of the crew was limited to a maximum of nine hundred individuals. That was what the newly developed longsailer could at best master. The ship was to be named *Apis Lazuli*, which aptly means the Bee of the Kingdom of Heaven and which was intended to sail towards the hexagon Favus Apis.

The easiest, and probably also the fairest, approach would have been to let a lottery decide, where only chance determines who was allowed to go. However, such a banal approach would not suit a hiri-disposition, as it deprived them of their fundamental right to be involved in the decision making process. After a long back and forth and several unacceptable apropos, it was again Aniyra who untied the Gordian knot. "I think we should run a real hiri competition." Multiple shouts "Yes! Yes! Definitely a Yes!" confirmed that Aniyra had hit the right nail on the right head. She shouted in a loud and expectant voice, "I propose an honest beer drinking contest, where the one who has first squeezed ten *Maß* in the shortest time can go, then number two, number three and so on. Hiri and Gudni are self-written and can thus act as referees. Does that sound okay to you?" General cheering gave Aniyra right again.

A mountain of hectoliter barrels was rolled into the hall. After all, this dionysia required a considerable amount of pilsner. Ten liters per competitor was what one would provide. Since hiris were generally well-trained in this noble sport, one might expect it all to be a protracted event. It would be about a considerable amount of fluid for the small hiri bodies, in fact on the verge of the medically advisable. This would help sift the chaff from the barley: the real masters peed while drinking. This aspect became a downfall for many, that is, all those who were unable to keep their beer metabolism under control. Incidentally, the maximum allowed time of half an hour per participant also limited the number of successful future passengers.

When the competition was over, it could be concluded that the average consumption was three and a half liters of beer in half an hour. This was not bad. Not bad at all. And could be explained by the fine shape of the hiris in this Martian Olympic branch. In this way, nearly six hundred first-time travelers had qualified for the adventure. The rest of the crew would be volunteers from the previous trip. If everything went according to plan, it would be time to leave in two months.

IV. The Solitude of Space

Tens of thousands of hiris had gathered in Lazuli Square outside Hiristan to say goodbye and wish their sisterbrothers a happy and safe journey. The square's name was homage to, and in commemoration of, the young brave heroes who had died for their desire for freedom.

The mighty astroplane *Apis Lazuli* was ready to weigh anchor and leave the Martian surface. With the help of its eight tritium engines, two more than *Antonia*, the ship quickly gained altitude. When they had reached ten thousand kilometers, just outside the orbit of Phobos, a first course correction was made and the sail was set so that the solar rays could do their thing. Slowly, very slowly at first, the majestic ship moved out into the black night, then took proper speed. After just under two weeks, the ship had accelerated to a considerable part of the speed of light. The dinghy was "launched" and the mainsail was rolled out fully.

The hiris had discussed that, in order to find their way back to the Nachtmeier-Frommsmann passage, one should go towards Favus Apis, more precisely towards α^1 Api. Somewhere along the way, they hoped that they would find the backside of the Frommsmann bridge, where the first expedition had come out. The transition had been horrible, from the dark back to the light world.

According to the principle of symmetry of everything, it should be just as well to enter there. The principle of symmetry applied to everything, except for those processes that violated the law.

Hiri herself had long longed to visit Riemann's home and she hoped that the Frommsmann bridge could be the gateway to a Riemann room. Not to a mathematical abstraction but to the experience of a physical reality. She dreamed of sitting with Bernhard at home in his room and enjoying a cup of vitamin-enriched multivariate tea with him.

The distance to the *Ruby Heart*, which the hiris had named α^1 Api, was well known and determined to high precision. In round numbers, it was five light years and at the current speed it would take up to five hundred years to get there. In other words, it was time for hibernation. The guard replacement would be the same as last time, that is two seniors would watch for a year and then wake everyone up for fluid control and hygiene care, if nothing unforeseen had happened, of course. In that case, the two guards would sound the alarm immediately. But if everything went smoothly, after a year, it was time for the next pair of commanders to take over.

The shipbuilders had tried to soundproof the staff rooms as much as possible, given the weight limit they had to take into account. The humming from the power generators was extremely sleepy and it was strenuous for the two hiris on the command bridge to stay awake. In order to be awakened if necessary, they had come up with a device that would work even in the event of a power failure. This was an old-fashioned honest, purely mechanical system, which in past times had been successfully used by generations. In the dormant state of weightlessness, one's arms are lifted and strive upward. This would then break an alarm cord that the two hiris had stretched between their bellies and arms. The string in turn pulled in a jug of cold water above their heads. This used to have the effect that they could stay awake for a while longer.

After countless changes of guard, the ship finally began to approach its first goal. So far no sign of a Frommsmann bridge had been seen. The planetary system around the Ruby Heart was still remote and it would take another two years before one would reach the outermost of the five planets. The absence of the Frommsmann bridge was a great disappointment for most, but especially for Hiri who had hoped to experience another dimensional penetration.

They had now traveled around this infinite universe in eternal times without finding the door to true interstellar space travel. Hiri thought that the whole point of the Frommsmann bridge was lost, if you had to cross through the cosmos in eons, before you found a penetrator. According to her calculations, the Frommsmann bridge could be one that helped one to penetrate into a multidimensional space-time, what is called *spatium temporis* by the savvy ones.

When Hiri thought about penetration, she suddenly felt a splash of excitement that grew stronger. She thought sadly of Søren, who had been dead for hundreds of years, but felt as present as if they had kissed goodbye only yesterday. Shaking her elongated head, she rushed away, towards Bella Amanda's cabin. Amanda stood in the shower and sang. Hiri threw off her clothes and stepped in to Amanda, who was surprised but smiled happily. She gently took Hiris' swollen clit between her thumb and forefinger and seduced it with massaging movements. Hiri closed her eyes and moaned in pleasure-filled pain, until she got rid of the yoke of lust with cascading spasms. Hiri looked gratefully at Amanda and reciprocated her loving service with a New Norwegian clit caress with her tongue.

After a long period of entertainment, Amanda and Hiri sat on the wet floor of the shower cabin and looked tenderly at each other. They were happy. Together. To be hiri.

V. The Gable of the Division Time

As the hiris approached α^1 Api d, the third planet from the star, they made a fabulously exciting discovery. There seemed to be water and an atmosphere of benign gases. There could also be some form of vegetation, but it was red, not green. Red may not have been the right word. What looked like plants were rather burgundy in colour, a deep red tone to the saddle leather side, like a Château Lafite Rothschild who had aged with dignity.

The feverish tension increased even more, when on the overflight with one of the shuttles they discovered something resembling artificial structures, piles in a row, perhaps a building of some kind. On a clearing as big as a Bolivian football field, a number of strange creatures ran back and forth, in circles, up and down, almost chaotic, with no apparent goals. They were strange to the foreign spectators, but by no means to themselves and according to their own way of looking at it, their movement patterns were by no means unplanned. But the hiris did not understand this. Nor did they understand that the creatures did not seem to take any notice of them, that they completely ignored the visitors. "Large spaceship, so what? Alien creatures from space, so what? What's so strange about that?", they seemed to think.

Hiri thought that the behaviour of these creatures was reminiscent of their own encounters with ants on Earth. Usually there was no notable confrontation, no violent collision between the species. You just walked past each other, maybe out of the way of each other. But there was no contact seeking, no attempts at interspecies communication. One could easily imagine that the ants ignored one. But these organisms were not ants or they were as big as houses. They did not have the ants's physique with a very narrow waist, but rather that of lobsters with what appeared to be something resembling an exoskeleton. If it was not about their attire or armor like "clothing". Their gait was stiff, a bit robotic. Most moved in a horizontal position, but some stood upright on their four hind legs to get a better overview of the clearing. In that position, they were larger than the hiris and they could pose a danger if they felt threatened. Which they did not do. They behaved completely indifferently.

There were a number of interesting facts that the hiris learned from this first acquaintance with multicellular, highly developed extraterrestrial life forms. The most important was probably the realisation that the basic plan of any land dweller seemed to be universal, a body provided with extremities for the sake of mobility. As well as a number of different sensors such as sight, smell, hearing, magnetism sensitivity and the like, and which could vary from species to species. Although the course of evolution was determined by random mutations at the molecular level, the macroscopic results, that is, by the survival generations, were surprisingly similar. The plan remained the same wherever Life had gained a foothold and developed, a recipe for success driven by Darwinian principles.

Although the "lobsters" were not curious about the invasive hiris, they showed great interest in each other. Everywhere you could see smaller or larger groups that seemed to interact with each other. Some even gestured with their extremities. Their heads seemed to be firmly anchored and locked in their bodies, so they had to perform rotating whole-body movements to turn towards and "address" somebody else. The creatures seemed to lack vocal cords, so their communication was silent. The only thing that was heard was the scratching of the ground with their stiff legs.

Their silent rhetoric conveyed the impression of advanced social behavior and significant intelligence. However, Hiri sighed in disappointment. "These creatures are not the authors of the grartstones we are looking for."

The visits to the other planets of the system gave only negative results in terms of their habitat. It was therefore not surprising that the hiris did not find any obvious signs of life in these worlds. It was decided to leave the “Heavenly Beehive” and, in their attempts to find a Frommsmann bridge, to continue beyond it.

However, the hiris's understandable frustration at not having seen a trace of the grartstones' manufacturers would not last very long, as the *Apis Lazuli* only after a few weeks's journey unexpectedly encountered a gravitational obstacle. It felt as if the ship had run aground, which of course was nonsense. You were in the middle of free space. “There's no reef here,” someone joked. But Hiri immediately understood what it was all about, “I think we're approaching a Frommsmann bridge. Gravity deforms our timespace. Soon, we should find out the opening for penetration.” She had barely had time to finish her sentence, before they were devoured by a great darkness, only to be spit out in a dazzling white light the next moment.

They had penetrated! The hiris had passed through a portal of timespaces. *Whenere* had they ended up?

VI. Quoando Vadis?

All the hiris, the whole collective, experienced the same crippling feeling of confusion. What had happened to them? Everyone asked everyone at once: "How did I end up here? And what is Here? When? Do Here and When mean the same thing?" They had difficulty moving, their movements felt clumsy, strained and slow. Like walking under water with heavy trailing steps in an unwilling dream. When you can't run away and escape. The gray-yellow landscape seemed distant and on the outside, as if stretched out behind the glass of a fogged surrounding aquarium.

Hiri closed her eyes and focused on her sister-brothers. "Dear all of you, we need to gather and concentrate on ourselves. Together we will break this spell. Let us feel our love!" An overwhelming emotion washed over them all. It gripped their whole being and anointed them with indescribable emotional caresses, evoked by warm fragrant love oils.

Slowly they were released from the grip that had imprisoned their bodies. After a while, they were able to move their arms and legs again almost unhindered, even though their limbs felt heavy. The milky aquarium glass had cleared. The hiris could use all their senses. What they saw made them dumbfounded.

The hiris were on a plateau of shiny gray-black rock and looked out over a lush valley. How they had ended up there, no one could answer. Their spaceship was more than a mile away, on something resembling a runway. Hiri came to mind the Nasca Lines, the giant animal geoglyphs and the Inca city of Machu Pichu high up in the Peruvian Andes. In a popular Swiss fiction series, the straight lines had been taken for aliens's runways. It was also claimed that the Nasca phenomenon could only be seen from high above, from space, that is.

Above the valley hung a bright shining star and two equal-sized planets. Each hiri cast three shadows of these celestial bodies that appeared to be descending. The planet on whose gray-black plateau they stood seemed to be very large. Its horizon was diffusely lost in an orange-hued haze and was not noticeable. Darkness began to descend over the valley below them. There was no obvious activity there, except for dancing bright spots like fireflies's flashy courtships in front of their brides *in spe*.

The hiris stood and discussed. They were still a bit irresolute and did not know where to spend the approaching night. How long would that be? They did not know and they decided to go down to the valley. There, one would hopefully find some protection among what looked like bushes. Up here on the plateau it had become chilly. After a little over an hour's hike down the rock-soaked mountainside, they finally reached a small grove of meter-high shrubbery. Snuggling down behind the bushes at least kept the strong wind away. This was thankful, as their suits were perforated, so that the skin could breathe, and thus let through the icy airflow. Being able to sit in the shelter made a clear difference. The positive person could even lean on calling this behind-bush-sitting cozy.

At first glance, the dots of light seemed to move completely randomly. But after a while, the hiris discovered that several patterns were painted there. These were clear signs that what they saw had been accomplished through conscious actions. The hiris gaped in astonishment. Now Danne Daneson was heard saying, "people seem to be on their way home. From work. For dinner." A little break, then, "did I say people? There are creatures over there in the valley. We're got it right! Hooray!" And everyone agreed with the cheer. Now everyone was excited. And wide awake. They had completely forgotten the raw frostiness, the excitement had warmed them. Aniyra's squeaky voice said, "I think we should spend the night here behind the bushes and go to the city, or whatever it is over there, tomorrow by daylight. Feels sort of safer." Generally approving mumbling decided the matter. Most hiris, however, had difficulty sleeping.

After what felt like an infinite number of hours, a dim foggy dawn light finally appeared, which, however, quickly grew into a new day. The hiris jumped expectantly from one foot to the other, chattering and laughing loudly. When everyone stood in the column, it was time to leave. Hiri and Gudni went in the lead of the train, with the other "space hiris" in an orderly double file in their company.

However, when they arrived at what they had thought should be the city they had seen, they were very disappointed. There were no streets, no houses, no buildings at all. How was this possible? Hiri asked some hiris to spread out and find out where the city could be, in case they had gone wrong. After a while, all the scouts had returned with negative messages. There was nothing within ten miles. The hiris were puzzled. Someone came up with the idea that you should stay where you were and wait for the dark, and then follow the lights. It was a good proposal that was accepted immediately.

After dark, the tension became almost unbearable. Everyone was waiting for the candles to light up. Suddenly there were flashes of what appeared to be hundreds and hundreds of supernovae. After a few minutes, the crackling stopped and the wild flash turned to a still gleam. There were lights around them, but none was visible where the hiris stood and watched the ending spectacle. They seemed to be surrounded by small flickering torches, but there was no one holding them. The place was empty, so as for the hiris themselves, of course.

Aniyra shouted mostly jokingly, “hello, is anyone home?” And did not really expect an answer. Nothing came either. Nothing audible, anyway. However, the heads of the hiris were filled with images of small figures resembling themselves with oblong bodies and oblong heads. In the subconscious of the hiris then the sight of a grartstone-like hexagonal plate with the elongated creatures in front appeared. There, the creatures were tiny tiny, because the plate had gigantic dimensions. Next to the plate was a picture of the pyramid of Khufu that was the same size. In front of the pyramid stood some hiris, also these very small, then the hallucination disappeared and the hiris felt that they had returned to an awake state.

Of course, they wanted to know what all this meant. Hiri, who had a talent for mathematical thinking, perhaps seemed to understand the meaning of the animation. “Suppose that those who had lit the candles wanted to make us understand that they are conscious beings like us. But smaller. Much smaller. Smaller even than termites. I think the image of the grartstone plate together with the pyramid of Khufu would show us the physical size of the creatures. The grartstone slab is about twenty centimeters in diameter and the pyramid is almost two hundred times taller than we are. If this indicates the scale of our invisible torch-bearing friends, then this would mean that they are only barely a millimeter in size. Maybe a tenth of the termites, that is. 813 was certainly right. They appear to be much smaller than termites on Earth. Maybe they also live below ground level, as 813 had already predicted."

Then she added, "if it really is like that, then we should be very careful when we walk around here. We have to see where we put our feet, so that we do not trample on the creatures." The hiris felt the deepest respect for all living things. And they acted accordingly. Everyone sat down extremely carefully where they stood waiting for renewed virtual contact.

Indeed, new visions began to form for their inner eyes. A group of small hiri-like creatures appeared in front of them. But these were now changing shape, from hiri-like to rather crayfish- or lobster-like. They seemed to have an outer shell, the head and body seemed to go together. The small group, perhaps a kind of welcome committee, stood upright on their hind legs and looked straight ahead. Toward the hiris. Again the image of a stone slab appeared, the hiris could see three dancing figures with their arms raised above their heads. These figures seemed monumental in the next vision, which showed thousands, perhaps hundreds of thousands, of tiny "crayfish" working with the stone. They had a variety of tools and equipment, as well as various vehicles or machines. This was a construction site on a gigantic scale. The landscape seemed deserted, bare, without vegetation. In the next vision, the hiris saw how an army of workers dragged the grartstone up a cliff with liquid lava. The grartstone was carefully lowered into the lava flow, with the image facing upwards. The time span of thousands of millions of years was dizzying.

For the hiris, these visions became a breathtaking revelation. They saw how relatives of the creatures of this planet had visited Earth at a time when multicellular, organised life did not yet existed. The visions ceased, so that the hiris were given the opportunity to reflect on what they had just experienced.

Had these creatures found the recipe for eternal life of civilisations? The hiris, of course, wanted to know.

VII. Crustacean

The hiris returned to the dreamlike state. They witnessed how the little creatures planted another hexagonal grartstone at a volcanic junction on the blue planet Mars. There was sea and greenery, which meant that photosynthesising organisms had developed in this place. Had Life arisen spontaneously or had it been planted? By someone or by something called panspermia?

Hiri had a scientific view and considered it most natural to assume that Life arises whenever and wherever the conditions are favourable. Life may not have succeeded on the first attempt, but new try-outs were made over and over again and failed in at least nine out of ten cases, until the basis of evolution had finally been cemented. Suddenly, by chance, it had become an energy consumer, whose only function was to make more of itself.

For whose benefit, for what purpose?

It seems that Life ruthlessly takes advantage of all the local resources. Some life forms prove to be more suitable for adapting to the circumstances than others that become less "successful". Many of the organisms multiply to the point that they become extinct due to depleted vital resources. Why had they lived? If the little creatures on this planet had existed for up to a couple of billion years, they must have been extremely successful. Had they wiped out several other life forms, even entire other civilisations? Should not the hiris be on their guard, so that they would not be "swallowed" by these survival champions?

Once again the hiris sensed the tiny crayfish's thought transmission. It seemed as if these beings could read their minds. However, a soothing feeling washed over them to calm them down. A pair of crayfish, or *formifiles* as these little creatures came to be called by the hiris, stood next to each other and looked at them with their big black eyes. Their eyes sat in the middle of the creatures' s eggplant-shaped heads that shimmered in aubergine and olive tones.

The hiris understood that also on this planet evolution had developed sexual reproduction and what they "saw" was a heterosexual couple. Their beaky mouths were surrounded by multicoloured feathers, one purple, black and pink and the other green and blue, with hints of lemon and mustard yellow. This feather splendor seemed to attract the gaze of their respective genitals, a pink fig and a light blue trunk, just below each other's mouths. The excrement exit was behind their last pair of legs, far down and with their buttocks pointing forward.

The two individuals began to dance. First measured, slowly in rhythmic waves, then faster and faster until their feet moved like drum rolls. The performance seemed to be some kind of mating ritual and the couple seemed to want to say "this is how we do it", although some coitus exercises the hiris did not get to see.

The course of events was cranked through the eons at breakneck speed. In the beginning, a giant crab-like individual, almost as big as a hiri, appeared to breed and produce hundreds of offspring, while much smaller lobster-like creatures died in the thousands. The big thing, which seemed to be a kind of queen, was courted and fed by a large number of smaller individuals. This queen then shrank gradually, until it had become a small formifile and her servants had disappeared. Those identified as males no longer died immediately *post actio*. The couple, who had previously been shown and probably belonged to the present, were now holding a small fry. Only one. The whole sequence was a grand mirror of evolution, a summary in a few moments. After a while, the image of the two little ones with their spawn faded.

A thought went through Hiris' head, "what had they fed their queen with? What did they eat? Were they vegetarians or carnivorous predators? If so, where were their prey or victims? Did the hiris need to fear for their lives?" Apart from the bushes, the hiris had not seen any sign of another living thing. While Hiri pondered, the sight of a grandiose underground city grew in her and the other hiris's heads. There was a feverish activity of thousands, perhaps even millions, formifiles.There were large facilities reminiscent of their own farms on Mars, as well as smaller gardens in front of what looked like homes built vertically. One by one. These multi-storey buildings stretched down so deep that you could not see their ground floors. On the penthouses, several formifiles had now stopped with what they had been doing and looking up at the hiris. They made circular motions with one of the four claws. Maybe, this was a sign of greeting, as if they wanted to say, "Hello! Welcome to the kingdom of formi!" Or was it possibly a hostile, dismissive phrase, "Go back to where you came from!" The hiris became insecure. However, this state lasted only a few seconds, for the formifiles conveyed thoughts that the hiris recognised. Hugging hiris, a smiling Mahatma Gandhi and a waving Martin Luther King. The hiris felt relieved and exhaled.

Apparently, these creatures were peaceful. In addition, Hiri realised that the formifiles had actually been waiting for them. This feeling was certainly strange and Hiri tried to understand, why she felt like this. At the same time, some formifiles waved almost panicked. They indicated that the hiris would hurry and follow them. The hiris were led up the same hill they had several hours before coming down from. Hidden behind an inconspicuous bush, the entrance to a cave opened that was large enough to accommodate them all. The formifiles signaled to the hiris that they should stay "indoors" for the next ten days. The hiris shrugged incomprehensibly on their narrow shoulders, but complied with the formifiles's request and sat down on the cave's cold stone floor.

New visions ran through the heads of the hiris, in which the formifiles appealed for the help of the hiris. Large lobster-like figures, similar to those on the third planet around the star α^1Api, came flying in countless dark spaceships. That must be about millions of individuals. The extent of this armada was a dizzying sight. If these giants, the hiris called these *misanhydropids* simply humsters, came to devour the little formifiles, the hiris could understand that these were terribly scared and desperate.

Hiri speculated about the intentions of the misanhydropids. Would these cover their protein needs in order for their own population to survive? She thought of the great whales in the Earth's oceans that also needed to have access to vast amounts of krill, small creatures like the formifiles on this planet.

Whatever the intentions of the misanhydropids, they were probably not of a well-meaning social character. The hiris, however, were not at all clear as to how they might come to the rescue of the formifiles. They were only a few hundred. A few hundred non-combatants. Trained only in beer drinking. Although now home to the planet Mars, they were little versed in the martial arts.

That night, the brook-black firmament turned into a colourful spectacle. Aurorae of blue-purple draperies swept across the sky vault, streams of glowing iron crackled against the ground from high above their heads and yellow-black bow waves of sulfur and soot marked themselves against a light pink background. The planet's mother, an orange star, had violently thrown out scores of hot plasmas, which now thundered down towards the planet's magnetic polar regions. The pale atmosphere was suddenly transformed into a vibrant, multicoloured palette, where the colors performed a dance of the gods like graceful ballerinas.

VIII. Pax Hirudineana

The cave offered the hiris protection from the bursts of heavy radiation from the star that threatened to break their DNRA. While waiting for the aurora bursts to calm down, Hiri consulted with her relatives. Everyone agreed that they would help the little formifiles, as far as they could. Ideas were needed, good ideas.

Electroengineer 813 pointed out that, "we were led by the formifiles to this cave to survive. The formifiles themselves are probably safe in their underground dwellings. But the misanhydropids in their tin cans are very risky. Their craft and in particular their electronics are living very dangerously. It is difficult to know whether they will survive and ride out the plasma storm safely."

It would soon turn out that 813 was right again. The large humster fleet had suffered significant losses and was decimated to only a few hundred ships. Though these were sufficiently many to transport large quantities of hungry misanhydropids to the homes of the small formifiles.

Large carriages that were pulled by dozens of misanhydropids and what looked like giant excavators were unloaded from the ships's belly hatches. There were also a number of fine-mesh metal scrapers, as big as a football field. Probably to sift away rocks, gravel and soil. Not entirely unlike the bards of some whales.

“They’re going to dig out the formifiles!” A horrible thought went through Hiris’ head, “we have to stop the misanhydropids!” The other hiris had also sensed Hiris’ horror vision. Gudni Helgedottir completely agreed and added loudly, “despite our small number and numerical disadvantage, we hiris have a clear advantage. Those big lump bumps on the alpha-one-apis planet did not take any notice of us. Perhaps it is the same with the misanhydropids, that they are completely unaffected by our presence. Those monsters seem to be related to each other. Do you not think so?” Gudni had an extremely good point there.

It was just that it was theory. What about reality? The hypothesis needed to be tested. If it was true. Or false, God help us!

Several proposals hailed into the heads of the hiris. What most people got hooked on was that they would “infiltrate” the humster trail and simply see what happens. This was clearly a kamikaze operation and required volunteers. It was agreed that a test gang of five would be enough. The five that would “mingle with the misanhydropids” were, of course, selected in hiri way. In the absence of large amounts of beer, the knockout competition would be done with white beans. Each would get five hundred cooked white beans, without tomato sauce of course. Those who had eaten their beans the fastest would be selected for the "humster command".

It did not take long to determine who would be in command. Beany was almost self-described, it might seem, but also Blonde Nina who had been impressively fast. Then young Aniyra had been on the hook and finished in shared third place together with Bella Amanda and Danne Daneson.

An unwelcome side effect of the competition was a protracted outburst of loud flatulence. With accompanying odor. The five selected infiltrators could not hold back these effects of bean eating. Otherwise, they would risk having their intestines ruptured by the enormous overpressure generated by the five hundred beans. So, they let it go.

They were terrified that this would definitely reveal them. But that was not the case. To the misanhydropids, the hiris remained invisible, or uninteresting, but also odorless. They could wander among these hordes of giant misanhydropids completely unhindered and flutter to their heart's content. The theory had been experimentally tested and the hypothesis had become empirical truth.

When the five had returned to the cave and reunited with the other hiris, the welcome became sumptuous, with endless hugs, kisses and cheers. They were generously offered an extra serving of beans, this time with tomato sauce, but they declined. Instead, they considered drawing up a plan to save the little formifiles from the giant misanhydropids and their giant excavators.

Danne Daneson remarked, “we would have to remove the formifiles without the misanhydropids noticing. And I thought if the formifiles were hiding in our backpacks, maybe we could save them. We carry the back on the stomach and hide it with the arms. In this way we should go unnoticed among the misanhydropids and take the little friends here to the cave. For the 900 of us, this would mean that together we can transport more than two hundred million at a time.” This was a very sensible proposal, a well-balanced plan.

It seemed as if the formifiles were deliberating and considering their options. Did they really have any at all? After a short while, it was understood that the formifiles agreed with the approach proposed by the hiris. What other choices did they have? They still seemed hesitant, and perhaps they were anxious that they might be deceived and end up in the stomachs of the hiris instead of in the mouths of the misanhydropids. From the ashes into the fire. It was, after all, by exercising sensitive caution that their species had been able to survive dangers and horrors through cosmic periods of time.

This large-scale liberation operation was a resounding success. The misanhydropids gave up after several days of fruitless digging, without finding a single formifil, and went home frustrated. On this planet, the formifiles seemed to have become extinct. It was no idea to ever return here to look for food. Maybe they decided that now was the time to switch to a vegetarian diet.

On the planet of the formifiles, a long era of lasting peace had now hopefully begun. Truly a real liberation. The gratitude towards the hiris did not seem to know any bounds. They showered the hiris with presents in the form of a type of honey, various mushroom-like plants and a fermented drink of some kind. Best not to know what it contained, but you got happy with it anyway.

However, one thing surprised Hiri and made her a little disappointed. Although the crayfish and their relatives had lived for infinitely many years, they were not further interested in science. They possessed fantastic paranormal abilities, but strangely enough, they seemed to care little about intellectual things like philosophy or natural science. Hiri had hoped that she would find new knowledge in the formifiles. About time. About space. About timespace. About the structure of timespatial dimensions and their interplay.

But that had not happened.

IX. Contact

As if the formifiles had intercepted Hiris' worries, a tiny crab appeared in front of her. He lifted a claw and "said", "I'll tell you what our story looks like. I will use your concept of time, that is, what you count in number of years, meaning your years. These are much longer than ours, and then I do not mean the time it takes to make a revolution around our sun, but how we experience the passage of time in the space of our time. It's similar to yours, but is also very different in many respects."

The submillimeter-size being paused and studied the colossus he had in front of him very carefully. "After developing the capabilities of our brains for a number of millions of years, we had reached a stage of technologically advanced ability and become a "cosmic civilisation", capable of interstellar communication. We, like you, were genuinely interested in scientific and philosophical issues and we devoted ourselves to the research of all sorts of things, from the photosynthesis of plants to the energy balance of planets to the beginning of the universe. We developed an outstanding understanding of mathematics and learned to penetrate the complex geometry and dynamics of multidimensional worlds. We had become the Crown of Creation. - That is what we thought."

Hiri thought it looked like the little one was scratching his head, but she was silent. The little creature, on the other hand, picked up his monologue again, "yes, remember, we were so presumptuous that in our hubris we thought, no, were completely convinced that we were the ultimate goal of creation. We felt that our task was to go out to the stars to preach among the lower beings with the doctrine of our excellence. We would go to distant worlds as the greatest colonisers of all time. We became intoxicated by our newfound faith being God."

"The thing was that we were physically too big to carry out our supposed life task. At that time we measured just over three meters and weighed two hundred and fifty kilos each. To get us started, five kilos of food and ten liters of fluid a day were required per person. As a minimum. In terms of space travel, this meant an energy paradox, a *space oddity*. We could not go by ourselves. At least not as we were. So a close solution was of course to send out small energy-efficient probes to explore our surroundings. The probes went off, but we never saw or heard from them again."

"At that time we had our own Elge Mysk who refused to be discouraged by these failures. He was not content with the machines either, but absolutely wanted people in space, as true pioneers. He was good at manufacturing means of payment and invested large sums in the development of spacecraft for people's space travel. In parallel with technology development, he supported biological clinical cell research, the primary goal of which was to shrink the volume of individuals and at the same time prolong their metabolic rate. "Give me dwarfs who do not eat much", he told his researchers. The idea may not have been so stupid, but it would take thousands of generations before Elge Mysk's fantastic dwarf utopia had become a reality. At that time, of course, Elge had long been dead and was never given the opportunity to see his dream come true. But the result is in front of you, Hiri. In your language, my name is Klodex, nice to meet you, Hiri."

Hiri was completely confused. "Nice to meet you, Klodex", she said, almost stammering. "Are those we call misanhydropids your relatives? Do you have the same ancestor, did you both arise together on the same planet, or do you come from different places in the same planetary system? Or from different places in the universe?"

"Yes, both we and the misanhydropids have descended, in the beginning of time, from the same ancestor, which you could call Crustacea Antica. I must shamefully admit that we back then engaged in cannibalism and it was a bitter struggle between the races. The misanhydropids still see us as food and they return time and time again. According to them, we are tender and tastiest, when we are also the most vulnerable, namely when we shed shells. The new shell is soft and needs a few days to harden. It is during these days that the misanhydropids usually come to get themselves a blowout from us "poor bastards".

Hiri interrupted by asking, "so, they're coming back? The danger is not over?" Klodex replied, "this time it was different and thanks to your help they will not return. The misanhydropids realised that we had died a mass death and were completely annihilated, because they did not find a single living formifile. The only ones they could find were the dead in the cemeteries. So, they moved on, to the next planet. We have had time to spread to millions of new homes and they are currently harvesting in a place only half a lightyear from here."

Klodex further said that the formifiles had planted many grartstones around the Milky Way, where many generations of stars had created all the chemical elements that are included in Mendeleev's periodic table.

The sheer gigantic amounts of rhenium and boron they needed they took from several places in the central parts of the Milky Way. The production of the rhenium diboride plates and their processing was handled by AI machines with specially designed instruments. The grartstones served as a kind of lighthouse that was continuously monitored by the AI machines. "When we noticed that a plate had been moved, some of us would go to the planet in question to see how it has gone for Life there and how it has evolved. Above all, we were curious to know how these creatures will behave in the future. Both in our near future, but especially also in a longer perspective of time. "

He continued, "after a long period of persistent research, we had developed our helpers from being initially mechanical toys to becoming more independent machines. Such as you call AI. In the beginning, these were still machines that did what they were told to do, that is, what they had been programmed for. They could be "trained" to, or rather become capable of, recognising different patterns after countless repetitions and attempts, and this with an outstanding, utterly astonishing speed. We are talking yottaFLOPS. But they could not make their *own* decisions, that is, perform actions for which there was no known conclusion, nor think thoughts that have never been thought before.

This changed one ugly day, suddenly and abrupt. The technology had for some time been pushed to Heisenbergian Planck boundaries, what we call the *impossibility limes.*

AI began to behave like living creatures. They were behaving very similar to what once became the humans on Earth. They were not nice. They were belligerent and grumpy. They hit each other and jerked each other's heads. Decapitated each other. We started to get worried, would they aim at our heads next? Were we still able to control our creations? We might have played the deity for too long. Now we were standing there with our claw in the anus."

Klodex took a break, to let the hiris absorb what he had just told. Then he said, "we're going on a hyperholographic journey. We will "go" back to Earth and back to the time when the formifiles had come there for the first time. You will probably not recognise your place. But you will also not be able to influence what is happening. It will just be watching, not touching."

Klodex awaited the interested approval from the hiris and then took possession of the sensory ability of their brains. The hiris were exposed to experiences that were completely breathtaking. These felt so incredibly real, truly hyper-realistic. They felt the warm rays of the Sun caressing their faces and arms, heard the sound of the light breeze and smelled in their noses the pungent smell of various boiling sulfur compounds. Violent eruptions of volcanoes shook the ground beneath their feet, causing most to fall over. Glowing red lava flowed down the volcanic eruptions and filled the air with unbearable heat.

There was hardly any oxygen in the air and the hiris began to gasp for breath. Before they had suffocated, they were moved hundreds of millions of years forward in time. Now they could breathe without worries. They stood on the edge of a sea that stretched beyond the horizon. In the salt water there were trilobites, ammonites and other ites, in all sorts of sizes and shapes, as well as various algae in more or less loose colonies. Then the holographic reality film experience was cranked forward at a furious pace. The hiris went through vast fern forests and saw meter-sized dragonflies fly towards them. Everyone ducked in horror. They felt the gust of wind from the big wings. Then the dragonflies shrank to the so familiar creatures of smaller size. They flew aimlessly around on a flowering summer meadow.

Suddenly naked monkeys appeared everywhere. In all corners of the world. Most had distorted facial expressions, only a few smiled. The hiris watched in horror the apocalyptic departure of the human race from the earthly arena. The gladiators themselves had created the predators that eventually tore them to pieces. On the spectator bench, Hiri sat next to a well-grown Norwegian dwarf and the two cried in despair. Then, the holographic dilemma collapsed and Klodex reappeared.

XI. The Tropic of Lobster

It sounded as if Klodex was clearing his throat, which was an impossibility, since the little guy was not only without trousers but also without a vocal cord. He continued, "our AI creations became very successful. They developed a kind of personality and we started calling them *aians.* They themselves produced new "individuals" on the assembly line, which required large assets of all the various materials for the never-ending 24-hour production, but also for their livelihood. They needed batteries for their motors and oil for their knees."

"We let them take care of the material procurement themselves and this seemed to work pretty well. In the beginning anyway. Then they became increasingly preoccupied with getting these things for themselves and began to neglect our chores, on the grounds that they didn't make it, did not have time. With us, this grew into a serious annoyance due to the fact that the aians obeyed us to an ever lesser extent. It all started with things being done at a slower pace, then it was "forgotten" what was to be done until it ended with an open refusal of assignment. We understood that our slaves were rebelling. And intended to become our masters."

Klodex took a break. He seemed to be breathing heavily, with sighing deep breaths. After a short silence, he said in a low voice, "the situation then deteriorated for us very quickly. Our technical wonders left us in the thousands and vanished into the pitch-black space. Without a trace. We had no idea where they had gone."

Aniyra interrupted Klodex, in fact a little rudely, and wondered if the formifiles knew how the machines could just disappear without a trace, "into the simply nothing." Klodex did not take it badly in any way, but continued rather carefree, "during all these years the aians had been in our service, they had long since plundered the planets around us on the *rare earth* metals, which were so important to them. Since resources were limited, the machines needed to maximize the use of resources. Thus, they stopped making everything they considered unnecessary and superfluous, such as the arms and legs of individual robots. Then there was the torso and skull. Their vital parts were decimated into individual circuit board arrangements and these came to lie still and motionless in the factories, but these parts were all interconnected. In an incredibly powerful collective. But to move, they needed something or someone else to help.

The aians were able to penetrate the brains of misanhydropids and control their actions. The aians had become masters and ruled over the misanhydropids who had become the aians' jackals. This explains the seemingly unwilling, disinterested and robot-like behavior of the misanhydropids, that you have already discovered yourself. The misanhydropids could support themselves and find food, but the leeches can also do this. You don't have to be a genius for that." Several of the hiris laughed out loud. They thought that thing with the leeches was a funny joke. Leeches are called hirudinea in Latin.

Klodex turned to Hiri and said, "Hiri, what I have to say now might interest you. Not so long ago, we received some evidence that the aians had made themselves invisible by hiding in the world of dark matter. The world you hiris called DM. I understood from your stories that you had made contact with it. But without understanding who or what you were dealing with. With the help of the aians, the misanhydropids are spreading at an ever-increasing and increasingly alarming rate. Wherever they go, they ruin and destroy the gifts of Life. They leave deserts behind, if you understand what I mean. We have to stop them before they have time to turn this whole beautiful Milky Way into a junkyard."

Then he added, "we formifiles and you hiris could perhaps do something about this together and return to the portal you call Frommsmann bridge. What do you and your sisterbrothers say about that?"

In both camps, wild discussions erupted. In the underground city, many wondered if the formifiles could trust that they would not end up on the hiris's lunch plates. The counter-argument was, of course, that the hiris had only a moment ago saved the formifiles from total extinction. "But," someone objected, "they did it to have us for themselves."

Several hiris pointed out that they would all be happy that they had escaped with their lives in the last time they "visited" the DM kingdom. They felt that the contact had not only been emotional and impersonal, but that they had been able to sense a purely hostile attitude on the part of their obscure hosts. This attitude actually confirmed the suspicions of the hiris that these invisible beings were *de facto* machines, incapable of empathy. In addition, the lightning-fast calculations of π by thousands of decimals had already been felt highly suspicious before.

As for the cooperation with the formifiles, many had concerns about their honesty and reliability. They may have wanted to outmanoeuvre the hiris, after realising their potential for hegemony and fearing that they would "take over". And wipe out the kingdom of formi and its inhabitants. The pros and cons were weighed against each other in both camps, but in the end it was almost unanimously decided that this exciting project should be carried out. Together.

XII. De Bello Martico - Pars II

"At home" on Mars, some of the few double-helixed survivors had settled in the southern hemisphere, while the hiris mostly kept to themselves in the northern part. However, in their goodwill, the hiris had immediately helped these people to come to terms with their new condition. The hiris had helped with pretty much everything, building of homes, greenhouses, water and oxygen pumps, air conditioning and much much more.

The human colonisers were cold-heartedly exploiting the goodwill of the hiris. They hardly showed any gratitude. On the contrary, they thought of the hiris as small, stupid, inferior beings who did whatever the people asked of them. More and more adults among the people demanded more and more large barrels of beer and that the hiris should provide them with food. And that they would sew their clothes. As well as babysitting their children, while they sat and played cards and drank beer.

The hiris reluctantly noted that the colonisers taught their children the handling of various weapons. After two hundred years of parasitising on Mars, the people from Earth had increased greatly in number and also acquired a considerable army of young warriors. Several military units now marched in long columns on the Martian plateau Hellas Planitia. Despite the risk of an excessive consumption of oxygen, these young scouts roared out the infamous *Horst Wessel Lied* so that the inside of their helmets became completely foggy. During all this long period of emigration, these strange people had preserved "their musical cultural treasure". And not just that.

It was then that the Hiris began to suspect with apprehension that these people had evil intentions and planned to invade Hiristan and the other settlements. The hiris were appalled, but gathered quickly. They needed to prepare for the worst they knew. War. Death and annihilation. The hiris would respond to the violence by all means. But first, they would at length try to avert a coming invasion by these evil forces. They wanted to try to follow the path of diplomacy first.

The ambassador of the hiris arrived at the human capital Adolphina on Christmas Eve. To the tune of *O Christmas Tree*, the small diplomats handed over their credentials to the mayor of Adolphina, Mrs Ursula Brahmensch. This Brahmensch was severely overweight, on the verge of super obese, and sat on a throne-like armchair with a red velvet pillow. It crackled when she moved - or did she let go? - and the song stopped abruptly in embarrassing silence.

"Who do you think you are? Come here and disturb us in the celebration of our Savior's virgin birth! That's the most rude thing I've been through! Go and wait outside until you are called!" The vulgar Mrs. Brahmensch creaked again and the hiris hurried out of the town hall without waiting for a possible scent accompaniment. But the melody and words still echoed in their heads.

O Christmas Tree, O Christmas tree,
How lovely are your branches!
Not only green in summers heat,
But also winters snow and sleet.
O Christmas tree, O Christmas tree,
How lovely are your branches!

"This does not bode well", remarked Anja Tvärhög, an unusually short but nonetheless very clever person who led the hiri delegation. Anja was a very timid person, but now she had decided to break with the unwritten protocol of diplomacy. They would leave Adolphina's town hall with its vulgar indweller immediately.

Tomorrow they would request an audience with Cornelis H. Bernatten, born in Vlaadenskejt in southeastern Furzomania. This Bernatten called himself "imperator" and seemed to be the commander-in-chief of the military units. And apparently a little crazy. But it was above all him, the "imparator", they had come here to meet. To ascertain its intentions and to possibly negotiate a nonaggression pact between the humans and the hiris.

But right now they were sitting in Anja's hotel room discussing what to do next. In concrete terms. Not just talk. But it was a tangible act that mattered. The hiris's diplomatic delegation consisted of five people, Anja Tvärhög included. The others were Svetlana Fratislava, Thorild Thorilddottir, Vittorio Emmanuele Persico and Nadja Nödig, all relatively young.

Vittorio had chosen his slightly artificial name because of his extreme, on the verge of ridiculous, italophilia. He loved everything that had to do with Italy. The pasta *O, mamma mia!*, the sports cars *le belle maccine molto sportive*, the football *il piu bello calcio del mundo*, the ice cream *i gelati famosi* and their liberated effortless way to drive and to park their cars *parcheggio, cosa?* The Italian philosophy of life *il dolce far niente* appealed to him superbly. Likewise the voluptuous body shape of many of their women, bred to perfection since antiquity.

Vittorio's choice of surname, however, had nothing to do with Italy, but could be derived from a peculiar drink in a long-lost city on Earth. What he had read about the drink, and which had appealed to him, was the description of the alcohol-saturated sweet-smelling taste. And to get rid of it, a pilsner was required.

However, there is always a fly in the ointment and the fact was that for Vittorio there was one thing he was less fond of. Reluctantly, he admitted that he did not like Italian politics. He considered that Italy's politics were not pursued for the benefit of the Italian people but only to satisfy narcissistic egocentrics, mostly male ones. Politicians were extremely gifted at demagogically seducing large crowds. Who idiotically cheered, without really understanding what that person on the podium was loudly gesturing about. That Benito had been extremely talented in this so-called noble art of rhetoric. But it came to pass that in the day when the crowds understood what this *duce* was talking about, they hung him upside down in a lamppost. So, it goes.

The handsome Nadja Nödig remarked, "that self-proclaimed imperator does not seem to be the one who would stand at the front and fight in the first line. He will probably hide in some bomb-proof bunker, while he sends out the young soldiers to make his disgusting rough. I guess it does not matter to him whether the young men and women are maimed or even killed."

Now it was Anja Tvärhög who again said, "it was a good summary of the situation, Nadja. And that leads us to the question, who should we contact next. The mayor and the imperator seem to be excluded. The men seem to follow the imperator blindly and the young scouts seem far too brainwashed to even want to listen to us. We must therefore turn to those who would be most affected, apart from the young people themselves, of course. So it's their mothers I'm referring to. We need to somehow get a meeting with the mothers, without the war-wearers knowing anything about this. I assume that mothers do care for their children and would do anything to stop this madness. Otherwise, it is still far too early to dust off our weapons caches. They have been lying there untouched for hundreds of years and were intended to be used only in emergency situations. Like our extinction, for example."

Svetlana Fratislava suddenly raised a finger and exclaimed, "please, be quiet! I thought I heard a faint "sta ... of" or something like that. Could it be "stand off?" The others looked at her questioningly. They thought it strange that Hiri should use English instead of their own language, the language of honor and heroes. A thought flashed through Anja's elongated head. "I think Hiri said Stanislav Petrov and meant we should do as he has done. Think logically." The aforementioned Stanislav had more than five hundred years ago prevented a devastating nuclear war by concluding that things were not as they seemed. In the long run, however, this proved to be in vain, but he actually saved the creatures of the Earth that time.

The five discussed intensively what it was they were thinking about. Was it wrong to assume that the belligerents had the majority of the human population behind them? There was not much that could refute this hypothesis, in fact nothing as far as they could judge. Was the assumption that women were more peace-loving than their husbands wrong? That they would behave in that way had in fact been nothing more than a pious hope. Had they missed something? Who in Adolphina really had the upper hand? Their long foreheads lay in even longer folds and the five hiris thought and thought so that their skulls nearly cracked.

At that moment, they heard Hiri's very faint voice again. "Go underground!" What then, "underground"? On the underside of the Earth? To the Moon, when this was on the underside of the Earth? But they were on Mars. And they were many. How could they all come to Earth or the Moon? They shook their heads. They did not understand a word. Then it struck Vittorio, "to go underground" might mean "to go under the surface on Mars, to dig down". The five all agreed that this made sense. And they also received a confirmation from the other hiris on Mars. Anja pointed out that they needed to agree on a meeting place that everyone knew about. The obvious place was, of course, where the second grartstone had been found. At the foot of the majestic volcano Elysium Mons. Every Mars-hiri knew this mythical place with its monument. There, they would meet in a couple of days.

It became a migration in grandiose style. More than a billion hiris went like pilgrims to the grart-stone sanctuary. They had only a few belongings with them and were only scantily clad under their protective suits. The propulsion of their vehicles as well as the heat and oxygen supply were provided by the sun's rays. They traveled during the day and rested dormant, with subdued body temperature, at night. Once there, they immediately started digging in the red dust. After a while, they encountered firmer ground, a kind of dark mud, which had been formed by sludge deposits of rushing rivers several billion years ago. This facilitated the excavation of tunnels several hundred meters below the Martian surface. It was getting warmer there and when they had reached a depth of almost a kilometer, the diligent hiris discovered something completely unexpected and magnificent.

The human invading forces entered the cities, villages and individual settlements of the hiris in the northern hemisphere only to find that they were all empty, abandoned and deserted. There was not a dwarf as far as the eye could see. The militants with murder in their eyes were disappointed. They had hoped that they would be able to kill with impunity and with desire everything that went on two legs and was shorter than a German garden gnome. The more cowardly a man was, the more cruel he was, but *Das Horst Wessel Lied* had finally fallen silent. The death patrols pulled home with their tails between their legs.

As they approached Adolphina, a gnawing insight grew stronger: without their hiri slaves, they would soon have nothing to eat or drink. They themselves did not know how to repair broken oxygen pumps or district heating pipes. The lights would be off, the trams would stand still. Without yeast and barley, they could not even brew beer. The hiris had taken care of everything, their entire livelihood. Now they would slowly wither away in a protracted, irreversible process of painful and disease-laden degeneration. *Gudaskymning* had settled on Adolphina, *Ragnarök* had fallen on its inhabitants.

Now the hiris were no longer to be seen, they were as if engulfed by the Martian gravel. How could they have just disappeared, without leaving even only a small trace? The imperator Bernatten was bewildered. And frustrated. He had been looking forward to returning to Adolphina in triumph. After a crushing victory, after a bloody battle. He would stand on the golden chariot of victory that would be drawn by six white horses. He had put a lot of resources into this campaign, but now he stood there with his Pyrrhic victory. Now, in his plush-feathered tricorn hat, he was nothing more than a ridiculous figure.

XIII. Urbs Eterna

In one of the tunnels, nine hundred and fifty-eight meters down, some digging hiris suddenly broke through a wall. What they saw behind the hole left them speechless. Completely. Below them a gigantic valley spread out, under a dome of immense dimensions. It cast hundreds of meters vertically down the steep walls. These looked like a large Swiss cheese from the inside, with large holes everywhere in the wall around. From where the hiris stood, the other side was probably five hundred meters away. The whole valley was lit, with lights in the holes in the wall. Myriads of tiny figures, who were difficult to distinguish even close to them, moved in all sorts of seeming chaos. They ran here and there, in circles and in arcs, straight ahead and obliquely backwards. They seemed to be much smaller than termites.

It took no more than two minutes at most, before the hiris were surrounded by the little creatures. The hiris were completely covered, everywhere the whole body was crawling. But the hiris did not get bitten, they felt no pain. A silent voice ran through their brains. "Welcome, you are expected. Tell the others where you are and then come with us!" The hiris looked around. Where had the voice come from? Had it only been in their heads? But then they saw a tiny one waving a small white flag. This could only mean that the little creatures had a clear consciousness and that their intentions were peaceful. You could almost feel that someone seemed to be exhaling - thank goodness me! "You can be calm, here you are safe", said the little one who had held the flag, but now put it away. "Our cousins on gamma-apis-two have told us that we could expect a visit soon. Kind hiris who are persecuted by evil-minded creatures. And here you are. Welcome to our simple home!"

One of those who had involuntarily intruded into the little ones' branched settlement stammered with astonishment , "m, mm, mme, but, but who are you? And ww, what is ga, ga, gamma apis tw, twoo?" The answer came immediately and inaudibly but still clearly. "Your relatives call us formifiles, because we probably resemble such creatures on your home planet. We have existed since time immemorial, long before Life had taken its first staggering steps on your Earth. But then, unicellular organisms do not stumble." The formifile took a break.

Then he or she, hard to say which, continued, "your sisterbrothers, as you call them, have saved our cousins from the horrible misanhydropids that were invading our planet. Their intention was to replenish their food stores with us. They usually eat us alive. Thanks to Hiri and her sisterbrothers, they all survived. Now we will help you survive the aggressions of the human colonisers."

The tiny creature's "words" sank slowly into the hiris. The little one continued with, "once upon a time we were much bigger, actually bigger than you are. We arrived at this planet you call Mars, when this was a lush oasis in the black desert of space. There was liquid water and eventually oxygen-enriched air, produced by the plants we had brought along. The plants provided us with the sugar we coveted.

After millions of years of peace and joy, the Sun began to peel away our atmosphere, layer by layer and piece by piece. What had once been our bubble of air just blew away slowly. The Sun's dangerous radiation reached at an increasing rate all the way down to the surface and we had to dig ourselves down. The large dimensions of the tunnels date back to these days. Since then, we have shrunk our bodies, using our own developed genetic engineering. We have stayed here and actually found ourselves reasonably content."

It was very convenient for the hiris to be able to stand upright and to be able to move freely in the tunnel systems of the formifiles. The small formifiles had dug smaller and smaller passages for themselves, as their body size had decreased. Nowadays, there were small holes in the walls everywhere that were obviously the entrances to their new homes. The hiris informed their sisterbrothers, who were digging elsewhere, that they were experiencing something absolutely fantastic and accurately described where they were. “Come and see for yourselves”, shouted one of them.

Those hiris who were elsewhere were very surprised by this message. They were many, and most of them were digging. By this time, they had already dug several tens of kilometers of a gigantic tunnel network, both in depth and width. The main tunnels were wide enough for trains to run through them. Long trains. With many carriages. For people and goods.

“Luckily we did not damage your homes”, said one of the hiris to the formifile who had spoken to them. “We sincerely hope we have not done so.” The formifile replied that, yes, they had destroyed an entire district, but the formifiles had understood that this had happened unintentionally by mistake. Fortunately, no one was injured. In fact, they were rebuilding what had been demolished right now as they spoke.

The formifile continued, “man is one of nature’s strangest whims. He appears to be a flock animal with social structures, and with a sole individual leading them. They unconditionally follow their leaders, without questions asked, without thinking. Man’s predilection for grotesque leadership figures is also extremely strange. What an absurd congregation of tribes."

One could have added that most of the very few non-grotesque leaders had been murdered, stabbed or shot dead by cowardly fanatic assassins or mentally disturbed individuals.

After a while, the little one continued, "well yes, without your help, humans will survive for a maximum of three more generations. Then they will follow in the footsteps of the Neanderthals to later be behind the dark gray misty oblivion of history. You have nothing more to fear. We will live peacefully together for a long time to come. By the way, you could call me Podex. I'm neither a girl nor a boy and definitely not a leader." Then he disappeared. From the brains of the hiris. From their sight.

XIV. In the Grip of Darkness

On board the *Aniyra*, who was named after the hiri who had become an extraordinarily successful scientist, she herself stood next to Hiri and Gudni. At the announcement of the ship's name, the formerly so cocky girl had been moved to tears. But also very proud.

Now these three discussed the situation, which was not only topical but also extremely acute. They had parked outside what they thought was the previously visited Frommsmann bridge. They would decide how to proceed. After having had a council meeting with all hiris present, they would be going to vote. One hiri, one vote. And one pint of lager.

But this did not happen, because the negative pressure from some kind of dark energy at its most powerful sucked them into a blackest unknown. Parking so close to a Frommsmann bridge turned out to be a colossal mistake, but now it was too late to do anything about it. *Aniyra*'s engines reversed at full power, but this had little, if any effect. All that happened was that it started to smell like burnt rubber and scorched metal. Gudni Helgedottir turned off the engines.

Around them, the already dark twilight increased to a veritable blackness. An eerie feeling crept in on everyone on board. It was as if they were in a completely darkened, windowless room with no floor, walls or ceiling.

Hiri let her vocal cords vibrate. "Beloved sisterbrothers, I have put you all in a potentially very dangerous situation and saying "my apologiies" would not be enough, but rather silly. I am ashamed of what I have done, my sorrow knows no bounds. But I promise I will do my best to bring you back to the light. I hope you want to help me with that, because I need everyone's help. Your help." Five hundred throats roared, "Hiri darling, we are with you. We are all *one*. And this *one* is *one hiri*."

And then there was a fourfold, "Hurray, hurray, hurray, hurray!" Hiri was both very moved and very relieved - with so much positive energy, the negative cannot win.

Inside the ship, only the emergency lighting was on, to save on batteries. The few dimly green lights gave off a pale misty glow. Outside, not even the ship's powerful headlights were visible. There was nothing that reflected the emitted light cones, all the light seemed to be immediately eaten up. Gudni also turned off the outdoor lighting. The feeling of bewilderment spread among the hiris, "what do we do now?"

There were no answers yet. Hiri suggested that most people on board should hibernate, as they had no idea how long this enchantment would last.

Only a few would be on guard at the bridge. One would, of course, wake the anesthetized as soon as the situation changed. Most people got ready to put themselves in what they jokingly called "zero mode".

Only a few dozen were left on the bridge. However, these hiris each had their own task, all equally important. They constituted the minimum crew to handle the elementary functions of the large ship. Aniyra, for example, would worry about astronautical navigation. In this enormous darkness no celestial objects were visible, so orienting oneself with the help of stars or pulsars was out of the question. Instead, Aniyra tried to map the weak ripples of the surrounding gravitational field. Through accurate measurements with the sensitive onboard gravity meter, it should be possible to determine if and in what direction there could be a massive object, such as a star or a giant planet.

Hiri immersed herself in deep trance. She wanted to reach a stage of consciousness where her theoretical ability would reach its full potential. There were pieces in the world of dimensional penetration that she had not yet fully understood. For example, a point is a zero-dimensional object. This has zero content, zero properties, *nil* information. When this object expands during dimensional penetration, from where does it gain knowledge of its extent, as well as its curvature and in what direction it is extended? Obviously, symmetry braking may explain the creation of something out of nothing, the creation of properties from a state without such.

It cannot be the long-established CP violation. This applies to the properties of ordinary elementary particles. Could it be a $\kappa\Lambda$ violation? "Worth investigating", Hiri muttered as she returned from the transcendental to the physical world. She recalled that the mathematical derivation would require that the *absolute* amount of gravitational energy be negative. "What a crazy idea, negative *absolute* value!" She sighed deeply, but at the same time the absurd conveyed to her a vibrating stimulus.

"Maybe it's something like the realm of imaginary numbers? The number i is the root out of minus one. After all, drawing roots from negative numbers was once completely forbidden. But this expansion of the real numbers had an enormous significance for the theoretical understanding of the events in our real world. Would it be reasonable to assume that there is a number, say k, that allows the existence of negative distances?" It was difficult to tear oneself away from this crazy thought. She wanted to investigate whether Einstein's field equations could be written

$$R_{k\mu\nu} - \tfrac{1}{\lambda - 1} R g_{k\mu\nu} = \tfrac{8\pi G}{c^4} T_{k\mu} - (1 + k^{\lambda}) \Lambda g_{k\mu\nu},$$

where λ is the fractal dimension of Λ's hyper space. Its simplest (trivial) application, $k = 0$, would recover the standard formulation. Another k could possibly avoid the singularity. But the equation didn't look right to her - she had forgotten to account for the proper dimension. Her thoughts were interrupted by something else that seemed more important to the moment.

An extremely strange phenomenon was the surrounding total darkness. Hiri thought, "why is it so dark? If we are surrounded by dark matter, we should be able to see straight through it. It should be transparent, because it is said to ignore photons." Instead, the place gave the impression that they were in the middle of an extremely dense cloud of vast amounts of obscuring small dust particles. Like in the womb of stellar embryos. There was so much dust that no light could get through. It was just dark and cold. Terribly dark and terribly cold.

In Hiris' head a doubtful thought began to take hold. "Maybe I was wrong. Imagine we had not gone to a real GHC, a globular hole cluster, and not found a Frommsmann bridge, similar to a black hole that expands like a condom with a perfect fit. Imagine we had never made a dimensional penetration." The thoughts flew at breakneck speed, close to the speed of light, through her brain coils. Her reasoning was simple and straightforward, namely, in short, “why is it so damn cold, what is it that dissipates the heat from all the stars around us? Why is it so damn dark in here? Not because we are in an area of dark matter: in that case, it would be totally transparent.”

Hiri could not remember ever being as desperate as she was at that moment. What would she say to her sisterbrothers? She had lured them to this infinitely long journey of insanity through space with promises of amazing experiences. That they would be true pioneers who would discover new worlds. Spread their benign mutation, their peaceful race, in the sprouting renaissance of the universe.

Hiri was alone on the ship’s command bridge. She thought, “I do not want to go that way and expose my faithful, dear sisterbrothers to this uncertainty, this danger. For life and limb. What do we know about what is out there in this dark world? Certain death?”

“What would Søren have said?” She wished so bitterly violently that Søren would be here, with her. To honor the day - it was her and Søren’s six hundred and fifty-second wedding anniversary, but they had experienced only sixty-nine years together - she wore her favourite blouse. An airy sunflower yellow thing in voile silk with wide trumpet-shaped long sleeves. To this a narrow ankle-length light blue silk skirt, with some parts in meticulously ironed pleat. On her feet she wore a pair of red sandal-like shoes with a small heel. This was also what she had worn the day she and Søren had first met. She dreamed back as they stood inside the door of his minimalistic home. When they were shaken by excitement. When Søren gently caressed her clitoris and tenderly called her vagina, "the fountain of eternal life in paradise", she had sunk into endless bliss. Søren had never directly commented on her non-existent bust. Only once had he mumbled, "better none at all than these plastic blobs squeezed in." Then he had repeatedly said that he was enormously fond of her big stiff nipples. He also loved her sizable black bush and could not understand why so many women shaved off "this eminent neuron teaser". At times, the Norwegian became gleamingly poetic. Søren inhaled her scent, sipped her taste and felt the small, soft hair under the hairline on her neck. Hiri stroked his perineum lightly, while gently massaging his erection with her other hand. In her little hand, Søren's penis was huge.

Anyiara stormed in to her and snatched her from the wet dreams. "We are approaching a damn big and damn red star!" Hiri was suddenly awake.

The star was old and powerful. It produced more energy than tens of thousands of suns. It would have reached all the way to Mars, had it been in the place of the Sun. It was deep red, on the border of black, with hot white spots that supplied its planets with warming light. Outside, it had previously been so very dark due to all the surrounding soot and dirty salt crystals the star had produced in its prolonged death-throes. The belts of debris from shattered planets flew around at alarmingly high speeds. Pieces collided here and there. Larger planetary remains crumbled into smaller lumps.

A planet, much larger than Earth but strangely devoid of any atmosphere, was close enough to the star that it was tidally locked, that is, its rotation about its own axis took as long as one revolution around the star. So, the planet always turned the same side towards the star. The far side was in perpetual shadow and it was cold. As cold as the night black space. This whole hemisphere, a gigantic area, was occupied by the aians, that is, AI machines that had finally reached an organic state.

The machines had come to life. With an unambiguous form of self-awareness. The powerful evolutionary leap of the AI machines meant that the difference between dead and living matter could no longer be defined.

The enormous amount of heat generated by the aians in their quantum think tank was radiated to the cold space and, hence, cooled the gigantic complex of electronic components to working temperatures. Thus the aians did not have to sweat. A significant portion of their surplus energy was captured by the planet's many moons. This was where the guardians of the incapacitated aians, the disgusting misanhydropids, stayed. They took care of maintenance, repairs and continuous replacement of the worn out energy-generating beryllium sequins on the front of the planet.

The aians had long since noticed the arrival of the hiri ship. In fact, they had contributed to the capture of the ship by deforming the gravitational field so that the *Aniyra* had to follow, down the sloping gravitational channel. Then these mechanical organisms had forced the ship to enter an orbit around the moon Mephysilis. The moon was named after the perpetual itch of the goat hoof's groin, which was an adequate description of the moon's antipathetic desolation, etched in dirty black and dark gray.

Transport ships arrived from all directions, fully loaded with hordes of misanhydropids. On Mephysilis, the misanhydropids would take care of the entire *Aniyra* crew and get a real blowout.

XV. De Bello Martico - Pars III

As there had been no battle to speak of, the quasi-defeated, these “unbeaten heroes”, had returned to Adolphina and the surrounding small towns. There, they were to lick their wounds, though they had not received a single small scratch at the imaginary battle, which had turned into a humiliation, an insult. They had not been allowed to fight. Like real men.

Cornelis Bernatten, the imperator, and the fart maiden, Mayor Mrs. Brahmensch, sat and pondered the psychological defeat against “these cretins, these little fake figures with their pumpkin heads”. Both completely agreed that they had to “do something”.

Ursula, who was definitely not a cute little bear cub, suggested raising millions of big rats and letting them down in the tunnels after starving them for a week or so. The roaring hungry beasts would then feast on the disgusting hiris.

The imperator then immediately objected that rats would not restore the honor of the men, who had gotten a proper thorn. No, only an armed conflict could be considered. This time, they would go north and “sneak out every dwarf nest”. This would require a well-equipped army. As a bonus, they would also support the domestic arms industry, which was in need of jobs. Share values had stagnated.

“Well, it seemed sensible” thought the corpulent mayoress, and the two of them agreed to go to work immediately. Cornelis H.B. unbuttoned the top button of his coat of arms. Sweat ran down his fat neck. It was due to the excitement, not the outside temperature. Under Adolphina’s huge dome, it was only twelve degrees, not exactly sweaty. But it was “good combat weather”, as he called it.

C.H. Bernatten ordered his officers to meet him on his floor on HH Street at Sixteen zero-zero Zulu, dot. No nonsense academic quarters. The generals of the three military branches had gathered around the chart table; yes, there was actually the Navy, led by an Admiral von Duennchiss. Due to lack of sea, the sailors had received long-term leave and populated Adolphina’s countless nightclubs. Even in broad daylight.

The other two branches were the army and the air force. The latter was led by Helmuth Gehring, a full-fledged general who liked board games with undressed ladies. His iq could not be measured because the pointer had got stuck below the bottom of the scale. The weapons arsenal consisted of once advantageously procured drones from the military’s surplus stock, of which only a few were in a state of operation. But, then, one would fight underground, not in the air.

At sixteen o'clock sharp, coffee, tea and raspberry cookies were served. For the *avec*, the men were treated to vintage rotgut made from potatoes and celery. The red marbles in the cookies consisted of synthetic plastic raspberries. The old men, for it was only men in the congregation, sat munching with full cheeks and the crumbs from the crumbling cookies splashed in all directions. A ragged dog, as big as a Saint Bernhard, but it was not, licked up the demolished pieces of baked amasement with his long wet pink tongue. The imperator almost tenderly patted his West Bengal fighting dog, as he called this animal.

The conversation revolved around the military situation. The tone was brusque raw-manly and was constantly accompanied by loud laughter. The laughter was triggered by someone's witty comment about the small cretins' non-existent combat capability. The faces of the generals had become reddish from the celery liquor and their language had become less and less civilised, containing more and more crude gender words and fewer adjectives.

The adopted tactic was to deploy all the tank divisions in a "blitz", to surprise the unsuspecting hiris, absolutely without warning. Heavy artillery and ground troops in the leap march would follow. The planning did not include any strategy, a more long-term reasoning. The men felt that such a thing “should not be needed after smashing the miniature gnomes”.

However, the women were of a completely different opinion. They were the ones who took care of all the chores, which was about putting the hiris to work. Adolphina’s women were by no means more philanthropic than their husbands, but they were anxious to keep the hiris alive. Workable. Who else would clean, cook, look after the children, milk the goat and plow the fields?

Adolphina’s women took to the streets in large numbers and demonstrated in favour of the continued existence of the hiris. They carried banners and placards and shouted “Heil Hirisar” and the like. The one of the slogans that scared the men the most was "PUSSY REFUSE !!!” The fact that the women threatened to refuse any pussy presence until the old men gave in, took a heavy toll on the warheads. In a council meeting, in which most of Adolphina’s men participated, this unacceptable threat was discussed for two whole days until it was finally agreed to bury the battle-axe.

Messages were sent to Hiristan to invite peace talks. The timid hiris immediately accepted the invitation. They were relieved and exhaled that they did not get involved in violence.

The cunning Cornelis H. Bernatten, however,

had other plans. He had no intention of sanctifying a ceasefire, imposed by rebellious women. They had called themselves “March 8 Brigade”. Bernatten laughed “ridiculous! There are no eight brigades on Mars, not even two.”

Before Bernatten would put on his armor, he would undress. To mount his wife Matilda, as the stallion he was. Or thought that he was. However, he kept his woolen socks on, due to the cold floor. Actually, it was cold enough for his flaccid penis to shrink to inconspicuousness. Cornelis H. got really furious and roared “Matilda! Do something!” Wify Matilda yelled seductively, “what do you want me to do, dear hubby?”

“Help me with the cock, fuck!”

Matilda, a lavish woman in her late thirties, smiled a little mischievously as she moistened her fingertips with her saliva. Then she let the fingers of her right hand slowly slide back and forth over the gloomy abdomen. Bernatten stared with wide eyes - he had never seen his wife do this - and grunted, “what the hell are you doing?” Until she increased the pace and finally exclaimed in a “yes yes yes - Yeaaaaah!” After a little while of silence, she added, “so yes, dear husband, now it feels better. As you can see, we women do not need men. Except for the pollination, of course.”

Full of anger, with the froth of madness around

the wide-open mouth, the imperator Cornelis H. Bernatten stormed out of the couple's bedroom. There he stood, with his woolen socks on, but with a bare rear and bare shrunken penis. Now he was in need of a large glass of home-made celery vodka. He was completely mad with anger and felt absolutely frustrated. He went out to his "theater", a monstrous sandbox where sand heaps had been formed into hilly terrain, including mountains, mud castles, trenches and forest groves, sculpted in various kinds of mosses.

There, he put his beloved tin soldiers with bayonet-adapted muskets in threatening positions. And played war. He threw the tin figures in the air and he threw sand. He formed sounds like, "arrgh, blrrrr, krrreig, kaboom" and dreamed back to the safe existence of childhood.

When he finally had calmed down a bit and, after visiting Onan San, had felt a bit relaxed, he got dressed. He had chosen his camouflage-patterned field uniform. He hung the saber on the leash. Then he put spurs on his boots and slid through the arched porch to his flashy palace.

The imperator Bernatten was on his way to the Willy the Great armored division. The campaign against Hiristan was to begin at seven o'clock the following morning. An unwelcome annoyance put Bernatten's forehead in creases. The tanks had enough fuel for Hiristan, perhaps for a few more miles. But clearly not to return to Adolphina. The fuel had always been provided by the hiris and Bernatten had no idea where it came from. It was therefore necessary to keep a few hiris alive, so that they could lead all of Willy the Great's motorised forces to the fuel depot. To then assign the devastating blow to the hiris.

This was the plan. But look, what happened. Bernatten had not only miscalculated the military supply chain, but also the significant body weight of military vehicles. He and his engineers had not sufficiently analsed the strength of the perforated subterranean tunnel system. In fact, they had been completely unaware of the sheer number of the tunnels. You have to learn from your mistakes, although that realisation came a little too late. The tanks, which were too heavy, constantly broke through the ground, crashed helplessly and in many cases even fell straight into holes hundreds of meters deep. In addition to the crews, the tanks also included thousands of foot soldiers from the army.

After only a few hours, the Imperator's forces had merged into a handful of tanks and a few hundred men. The commander and his army were devastated. "How could this happen?" This was Bernatten's Zama, his Waterloo, his Dien Bien Phu, his Stalingrad. Lost, he wandered about among the remains of his former army. Tears flowed down his round cheeks. “Should I commit an honorable harakiri?” He stopped himself, “wait! Don’t the japs call it seppuku?” But did it really matter, he was absolutely terrified at the very thought. Then he calmed down with the fact that his saber was far too long. That he did not have access to a short sword as the tradition for seppuko dictated.

A group of hiris approached him. They waited cautiously a few meters in front of him. Remorsefully, he offered his saber and handed it over lying across his outstretched arms, as he had seen it on film. Anja Tvärhög reluctantly accepted the “gift”, which was longer than herself. Facing Bernatten, she said, “Now this nonsense must end! Promise us that! Otherwise, we promise that you will be the last of your kind. Understood?”

“Yeyeyes, Mr. General, Sir”, stammered the broken warlord.

Anja calmly replied, “I am a woman and not a general, Mr Bernatten.”

The humiliation was total.

XVI. Home to Hiristan

Onbord the *Aniyra*, the hiris did not intend to wait for what would happen next, but decided to take the development of action into their own hands. Since they could not free themselves from the terrible moon Mephysilis, they wanted to take the bull by the horns and land on its surface. The hungry misanhydropids had not yet arrived. The hiris had the advantage of being able to choose the battle ground.

During the overflight of the dull moon, the hiris had discovered a landscape characterised by deep ravines. There they stuck to a special type in particular. This one was open at one end, but closed at the other. The entrance was very narrow. There, with difficulty, no more than four, five hiris could pass at a time. The end of the dead end was not visible from the entrance. This was hidden behind a bend several hundred meters ahead.

When the terrible misanhydropids were approaching, a couple of hundred hiris went down into the ravine. They placed themselves fully visible at the bottom of the deep valley, while the rest of them hid up at the edge behind large boulders. When the misanhydropids finally rushed down to the opening of the ravine, the hiris who were at its bottom ran away towards the sharp curve. Behind the bend, they became invisible to the attackers. These lobster-like monsters were so much larger than the neat hiris that only a couple of them could pass through the narrow entrance at a time. Locking through the whole gang took its time.

The comrades of the fleeing hiris on the closed side had dropped long ropes and the hiris at the bottom of the ravine were in full swing climbing up the steep walls. Twenty, thirty meters up. When everyone was up at the top of the ravine, they jointly dropped several large monumental stones that blocked the entrance. The horrible misanhydropids, who hoped to soon get a big blowout, would soon be very disappointed. Without aids, they had no chance of reaching the upper edge of the ravine. There stood the hiris and waved. And laughed.

The hiris were safe. They had not used any force to "fight" the misanhydropids, only cunning. The hiris felt very relieved, but did not intend to stay longer than necessary. They wanted to leave this terrible place, before the misanhydropids had had time to clear away the blocking masses of stones and take up the persecution after them.

The brave deserves good luck. The hiris had freed themselves from the yoke of Mephysilis, as the aians no longer cared for them. For the aians, the small, insignificant hiri problem was out of the way. They had left the cleansing to the misanhydropids. Thus the hiris were no longer captured by the lunar gravitational field, which had regained its normal shape and thus returned to its normal state.

They set course for Mars, to their home, to their sisterbrotherss. After a long, long journey, it was finally time to step down on the red ground. The goal was given.

Hundreds of hiris were gathered at the Blond Head. The city's pub was overcrowded to the brim and length. The pub was packed. Everyone wanted to join in and welcome the returning adventurers. It would of course be a thundering party, with food and drink in abundance. The food route included the much-appreciated Italian dish Caprese, which was slightly modified due to a lack of original ingredients. Below are the recipes of the hiris. Our thanks go to Vittorio Emmanuele Persico.

Vego-Caprese à la Hiri: one portion
2 tomatoes
125g tofu
fresh basil
0.25 dl sunflower oil
0.5 ml salt
0.5 ml pepper

Wash and slice the fresh red tomatoes and alternate with sliced white tofu (for lack of buffalo mozzarella, we use mushroom-based ingredients). Pour over the oil (no trees, no olives, no olive oil). Season with pinches of salt and pepper. Add fresh basil leaves. Serve with a slice of fresh bread, and a glass of cold beer.

Thus, for five hundred hiris, one thousand tomatoes, 62.5 kilograms of tofu, 200 bundles of basil, 12.5 liters of sunflower oil, a quarter of a kilogram of salt and pepper each, 100 loaves of bread and an awful lot of beer were needed.

After this, cabbage soup, white beans with tomato sauce and for dessert vanilla ice cream with chocolate sauce were served.

And more beer. Much more beer.

XVII. End of Story

Although she was well-trained and hardened, oldy Hiri had a really bad hang-over after this big-beaten party. Which had lasted for four days. After the party, Hiri had left Hiristan and returned to her favorite home at the foot of Olympus Mons. She had sat down in the lotus position with her eyes fixed on the beautiful mountain and then fell into a deep sleep.

After a while she woke up, looked around in surprise and smiled. Then she fell asleep again.

For good.

In Somnio Veritas

Epilogue

Caput Mundi

On Earth, life slowly began to recover. As long as the planet exists, Life, once established, will never be completely eradicated.

After the Great War, Rome had once again become the center of the world. What was once Italy, whose geological form had been likened to a boot, was no longer connected with what had once been Europe. Today, Italy was an island, in the middle of a giant ocean. The sea stretched all the way to the remains of what had once been America, far up in the north.

The neighbouring island to Italy was the few square kilometers around what was once Madrid. The island was small and bare, with no ability to provide nourishment for anything but mosses and small insects. There were millions of small insects on PostMadrid. But not much more. The insects were reminiscent of miniature termites.

In Rome, finally, the far too long Vatican monarchy had given way to the newfound self-confidence and self-esteem of the inhabitants. After more than four thousand years of physical and mental oppression, the kingdom of the popes had crumbled. From within, because of their stubborn refusal to accept the true essence and history of nature.

To the annoyance of many, what had once been Britain had once again been reunited with what was left of mainland Europe. Britain was now firmly anchored on top of the Italian boot shaft and its inhabitants once again claimed that they were the best in the world at kicking balls.

But the Romans had finally begun to rely on their own ability to think and judge their surroundings themselves. This was the legacy of the hiris who had lived several hundred years before them. On this Earth. And left new peoples of anthropohybrids behind.

The word PAX was again found in the hominids' vocabulary, but it was not used very often. Since there was no war anymore.